When Jesus Wept

BODIE & BROCK
THOENE

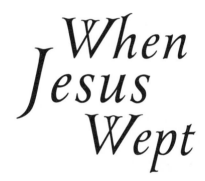

When Jesus Wept

Jerusalem Chronicles, Book One

ZONDERVAN.com/
AUTHORTRACKER
follow your favorite authors

ZONDERVAN

When Jesus Wept

Copyright © 2013 by Bodie Thoene and Brock Thoene

This title is also available as a Zondervan ebook.
Visit www.zondervan.com/ebooks.

This title is also available in a Zondervan audio edition.
Visit www.zondervan.fm.

Requests for information should be addressed to:

Zondervan, *Grand Rapids, Michigan* 49530

Library of Congress Cataloging-in-Publication Data

Thoene, Bodie, 1951-
    When Jesus wept / Bodie and Brock Thoene.
        p.   cm. — (Jerusalem chronicles ; bk 1)
        ISBN 978-0-310-33593-1 (softcover)
        1. Jesus Christ—Fiction. 2. Lazarus, of Bethany, Saint—Fiction. 3. Bible. N.T.—
    History of Biblical events—Fiction. I. Thoene, Brock, 1952- II. Title.
    PS3570.H46W53 2013
    813'.54—dc23   2012030905

Cover design: Kirk Douponce
Cover artwork: Robin Hanley
Interior illustration: Ruth Pettis
Interior design: Katherine Lloyd, The DESK
Editing: Ramona Cramer Tucker, Sue Brower, Bob Hudson, Anna Craft

Printed in the United States of America

13 14 15 16 17 18 /DCI/ 23 22 21 20 19 18 17 16 15 14 13 12 11 10 9 8 7 6 5 4 3 2 1

For all the Thoene grandchildren:

Tommi Jane, Wilke Lynn, Turner, Connor,
Titan, Ian, Jessie, and Chance.

Much love from Bubbe and Potsy.
All the promises of Psalm 91 are yours.

Authors' Note

Jesus clearly believed in the power of stories. He told parables—stories—to stretch the minds and transform the hearts of his listeners. We too believe in the life-changing power of stories, and that's why we're passionate about writing fiction.

In every work of our fiction, there is truth, based on research, and there is imagination, based on our minds and perspectives. We weren't here, on this earth, as Jesus walked among the people, but through the verses of Scripture and our imagination, we have portrayed to the best of our ability what he might have said and the way in which he might have said it. *When Jesus Wept* is how we imagine the events might have happened for Mary, for Lazarus, and for all the other characters in this story.

Can lives, bodies, and hearts truly be transformed? With Jesus, anything is possible! Through *When Jesus Wept*, may the Messiah come alive to you ... in more brilliance than ever before.

Bodie & Brock Thoene

When Jesus Wept

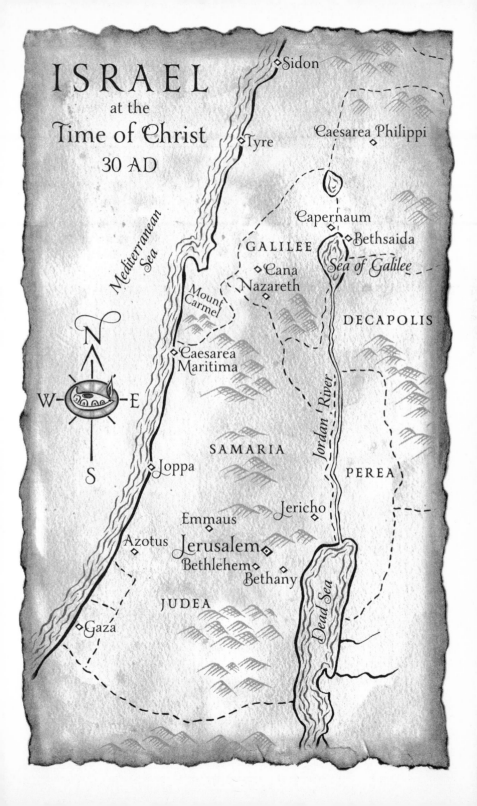

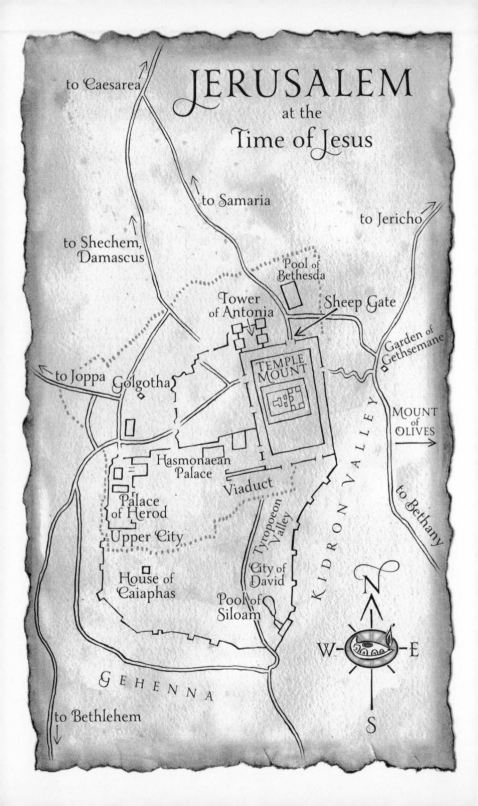

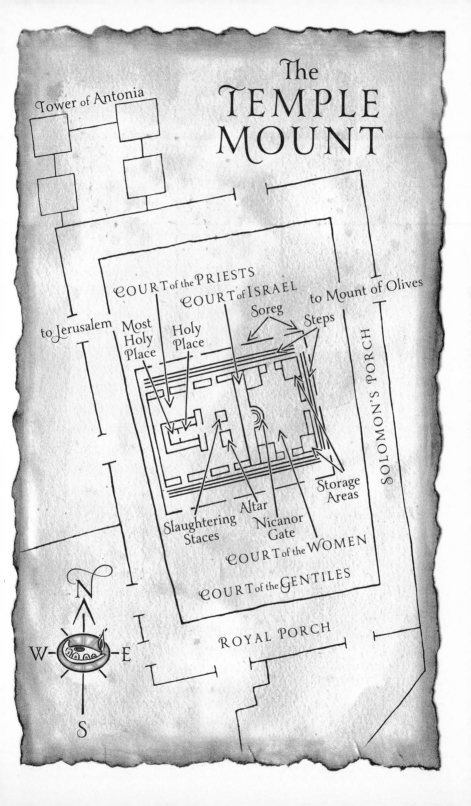

Prologue

Before he called me forth from the grave, Jesus wept. His was not the loud, frantic keening of the women who mourned outside my tomb. His was a sigh and a groan and a single salty tear. It was, at first, almost imperceptible, even to those standing closest to him.

But his sigh shook the universe, and the place where I was quaked. I stood in the midst of those who watched and waited for all things to be set right.

Jesus groaned, and the heads of angels and saints turned to look down upon the earth in wonder.

His tear trickled down his cheek, and a spring burst forth at my feet. Pure, clear water spilled from its banks and flowed down a mountainside, leaving a myriad of new stars, like flowers, blooming and rising in its wake.

I remember thinking, *On a clear night, constellations above the earth reflect on the still surface of the sea. But here? Only one of Jesus' tears contains a galaxy.*

My eternal companions and I listened. We heard his voice echo from Bethany across the universe! He commanded, "Roll away the stone!"

We all waited in anticipation for the next word from his lips. Then Jesus spoke my name: "Lazarus!"

Surely he could not mean me, I thought. But all the same, I whispered, "Here I am, Lord."

Centuries have come and gone since his holy sob ripped me loose from timeless conversation with the ageless ones. Ten thousand, thousand scholars and saints have asked, "Why? What made the King of Heaven bow his head and cover his eyes and spill holy tears onto the earth? Why? Why did Jesus weep?"

Part One

When the LORD your God brings you into the
land he swore to your fathers, to Abraham, Isaac
and Jacob to give you … wells you did not dig,
and vineyards and olive groves you did not plant
… be careful that you do not forget the LORD,
who brought you out of Egypt, out of the land
of slavery.

DEUTERONOMY 6:10 – 12

Chapter 1

The sun rose over the garden where my wife and newborn son lay in a newly cut tomb. Thirty days had passed since my Eliza had died in childbirth, taking with her all my hopes and joy. Spring had come to Judea. The vineyards were all in bud, bursting with the promise of new life, but in my heart, death reigned. My life had been pruned as savagely as the most severely clipped and seemingly barren vines in the depth of winter. Ironically, today was my thirtieth birthday.

By rote I spoke the final words of *Kaddish* and placed two stones of remembrance before the grave. The official days of mourning were at an end, but as I walked to the Bethany synagogue *mikvah* to wash away the ashes of my sorrow, I still carried the weight of my grief with me.

Near the ark containing the Torah scrolls, a minyan of ten village leaders prayed the morning prayers. They did not look my way or speak to me of Eliza and the baby. There was nothing left to say. Custom declared that this morning was officially the moment for me to get on with living.

I accepted their seeming indifference as I stepped into the cool bath and immersed myself, sinking my curly, unkempt hair into the water's tomblike embrace. When I emerged, I still found my thoughts returning to the beautiful woman I had loved with all my heart, and to the baby boy who had lived only three short days.

If only …

Did my persistent sorrow show in my face? Did resentment for the brevity of grief permitted me reflect in my eyes?

Judah ben Perez, my friend since childhood, greeted me when I had dressed in clean clothes and emerged into the late spring sunlight. Now we were both widowers—he for many years—but I resented and rejected any comparison between his stoic acceptance and my too fresh, too painful sense of loss.

"The peace of HaShem is with you, David ben Lazarus, my brother!" His tone was too bright, as if he had forgotten Eliza was gone. His words hurt me like light hurts the eyes when one looks directly into the sun.

"And with you, Judah."

"Welcome back." He took my arm as though I had been gone on a long journey. "Have you heard the news from Jerusalem?"

Being a rich merchant in the nation's capital, Judah was much better positioned than most to receive the news from the wider world. His trading caravans regularly made journeys to and from Petra, Ecbatana, and Alexandria. Amphorae of oil or wine or dates or wheat, each bearing the clay seal of the House of Perez, were frequently seen on the docks of Caesarea Maritima. From there they were soon en route to Antioch, Athens, and even Rome itself.

The Roman province called Coele-Syria that stretched from Damascus to the Nile included the Jewish homeland and was rightly called the Breadbasket of the Empire. Pomegranates and sycamore figs grown on my land took their places in the straw-lined baskets of commerce conveyed by Judah's export company.

Sometimes it amused me to think that grapes from my

Bethany estate, raised under my care, picked at my direction, crushed under my supervision, and transformed into wine of my vintage, made much longer voyages than ever I had done or dreamed of doing.

I never cared to visit Rome, but the fortunes of my house were increased every time a Roman senator's wife praised the product of my labor. Therefore, I had always looked forward to Judah's reports.

He was counting on that interest now. As transparent as was the device, I was still grateful for his concern.

Though the politics of Rome and Jerusalem were unfolding a mere two miles from where we stood, I shook my head. I had heard nothing of the outside world for the past month. "What now?"

"The new Roman governor, Pontius Pilate, is staying at old Herod's palace. He has held meetings with Caiaphas and Annas. The high priesthood is well and truly in the complete control of Rome. Sacrifices are offered daily by Caiaphas in the Temple for Rome and Emperor Tiberius. Every synagogue is commanded to pray for Tiberius."

"May HaShem bless and keep Tiberius ... far away from the land of Eretz-Israel." I smiled slightly as I uttered the rabbinic blessing for our oppressors.

"Tetrarch Herod Antipas has taken Herodias to his bed."

"The wife of his brother."

"And here's the big news ... Caiaphas himself performed the marriage ceremony. The sect of Pharisees is in an uproar. A very quiet and fearful uproar, but even so ..."

I pondered this news. "It's sure to lead to unrest in the countryside, where people still have a conscience. What will Pilate say about such an unholy union?"

"Pilate could care less about his morals. I mean—" he glanced over his shoulder before continuing—"was there ever a more wicked ruler than Tiberius Caesar? As long as our people do not fall into open rebellion, and we hold our tongues and pay our taxes and—"

"Pay and pay and pay. Was there ever such a time as this? Come, Messiah! Deliver us!"

"Herod Antipas has gathered up his entire court and gone off to his palace in Galilee for the season. Out of sight of the people and Pilate."

I walked with him toward the road that led to my home. "That's better for all of us. May HaShem bless and keep Herod Antipas ..."

"Far away from us ..." Judah paused.

The departure of Antipas from Jerusalem was a good thing. His oppressive rule was far worse than that of his father, Herod the Great. Antipas was fully controlled by Rome, while possessing the same vices as his "Butcher King" father.

Judah's strong jaw stiffened as he waited until a group of village women carrying laundry baskets passed us on the road. When he was certain no one could hear, he resumed. "Well now, my friend, let me tell you. There is unrest in the air. There has come a man ... a prophet or a lunatic, depending on who you ask. His name is John. Some say he is Elijah the prophet returned, as holy prophecy teaches. He appeared in the wilderness east of the Jordan, preaching against Rome and Herod Antipas. He calls the common folk to prepare for the coming of the Kingdom of God. He warns of HaShem's judgment: fire and destruction raining down upon the House of Herod."

I stopped in my tracks and studied my companion's excited face. Was this ripple of rebellion the same feeling that had caused the Maccabees to rise against the Greek oppressors some two hundred years before?

"Either a fool or a true prophet of the Lord. What do you think?" I asked.

"I've been waiting to go see for myself."

"Waiting?"

"For you to return to the land of the living." He raised his eyes toward the gates of my home, where my sister Martha waited for me. "Would you like to come with me? To see this fellow yourself? To hear what treason he speaks?"

I did not answer at first but considered all I had heard. Such a man was not only a danger to himself, but dangerous for everyone who stopped to listen to him. "Work in my vineyard is what I need to focus on."

Martha raised her hand in greeting. "*Shalom*, Judah! Good morning, my brother! I have a meal prepared. Enough for you too, Judah."

Judah laughed. "As always, Martha. Enough for me and ten others."

"Will you stay and sup with us?" she asked.

"I will. So much to discuss with your brother."

"David ... welcome back from your long journey." Martha kissed me. "It is a new day, my brother. Was all well at the synagogue?"

We would not speak again of Eliza and the baby. "It seems prayers for rebellion against Herod Antipas have been heard," I replied, touching the mezuzah on the doorpost and reciting the blessing.

"Beautiful day, then." Martha led Judah and me to the dining table, laden with the finest foods. A feast to bring me back to an enjoyment of life. It occurred to me that Judah had planned all along to walk me home. We did not speak openly about the present state of corruption among our leaders but discussed Scriptures and the history of our fathers, who had managed to survive corrupt and apostate kings in generations before us. In this way we explored the world we lived in, by remembering what had gone on before.

Had there ever been a time like this in all the history of Israel?

The answer was yes.

Was the God of Abraham, Isaac, and Jacob faithful to those who remained faithful? The answer, of course, was yes. But that did not mean good men would not suffer for the sake of our holy commands.

Judah and I ate slowly, chewing on God's Word as the true feast of our minds and hearts. Hours passed and my pain lessened. I was surprised by my ability to smile at my friend and my sister again. Only the night before I had doubted I would ever smile again.

The last prayer of thanks was given, ending our meal marking my return to life from the House of Mourning.

My sister Martha concentrated on the matters of the house and servants. Her work for me and my estate was perfunctory and effective. But the house seemed bland and flavorless without the great love and joy of my wife to season it.

My heart lived in the dungeon of despair. At night, in the time when darkness exaggerates everything, my thoughts were without the hope that morning would ever break.

Chapter 2

*I*n spite of my sorrow, I welcomed the sun each day. Work was my one consolation. The vines of the House of Lazarus were lush and beautiful. My winemaker was a thin, sun-parched raisin of a fellow named Samson. He had spent his life in the vineyards and risen through the ranks as a laborer to become one of the finest vintners in the land. Under his supervision my vineyards flourished, and the Lazarus estate wines were praised in the halls of the great.

Very early one morning I mounted the white mare to survey my property. Samson preferred to ride a donkey, which allowed the little man to be closer to the ground. Three of Samson's pet goats followed after us.

"You see, sir, I bring my own 'cheesemakers' with us. Very good with wine and dried apricots." Samson whistled to the goats, whose pleasant faces seemed to smile in agreement.

We rode through the vines planted on the rocky limestone of the south-facing vineyard. The fruit on these vines was smaller and the foliage less exuberant than the opposite side of the hill.

When I commented on this, Samson slid off his obedient mount, patted his goats, and leaned in to examine a tight cluster of grapes. He plucked two berries, giving me one and holding the other in his open palm. "Inhale the aroma, sir."

I obeyed. The fragrance was rich and sweet. "Ahhhh," I breathed.

Samson was pleased with my response. He gestured, and together we popped the berries into our mouths at the same moment. The flavor burst on my tongue. I let the juice linger.

"Good," I said.

"An understatement, sir, if I may be so bold."

"Intense," I corrected.

He plucked a bunch and handed it up to me. "Breakfast. It's good to be alive on such a morning as this, if I may say so, sir."

"Good. Yes. But still not easy."

Samson joined me in our impromptu meal. With a wave he embraced the struggling vines. "These are your most faithful vines, sir. They struggle for water every season. Set their roots deep in search of every drop. Pull flavor from the limestone and thin soil. And their clusters are filled with passion for life."

I agreed. "This south field will make our finest wine this year."

"Every year, sir. I do admire the heart in these vines." He held a deep purple grape up to the light. "Not like their brother vines, who have an easy existence growing on the opposite side of this same hill. Not so much flavor in the fruit. Grown from the same cuttings. Planted the same year. But an abundance of water and less harsh growing conditions in the northwest field has made the grapes ... hmmm. If I may say, sir ... the vines on the north produce more fruit but with much less character."

I held another grape to my lips and sucked the juice. "I once heard my father say he would pull out these vines and plant something else."

"Your father was a fig grower at heart. Not a winemaker, begging your pardon," Samson suggested.

"You talked him out of that, if I recall."

"I had to prove him wrong, sir, if I may say so."

"And so you have done."

Samson glanced toward the fading pastels as the sun rose above the horizon. "Vineyards. The only crop I know where a hardship in the maturing makes the end result exquisite." He turned his face toward me. Behind his drooping eyelids I saw that he understood my hardship.

"What about a righteous man like my grandfather?" I challenged. "When Herod the Great took his vineyards?"

The old man leapt upon his donkey, then hesitated, considering his response. "There are hardships, some injustices, which only God can address. I am not a scholar of Torah as you are, sir, but I know the Scriptures pertaining to vineyards. If I may say, the case of what happened to your grandfather and the ancient vineyards of your family—is this not what the evil king Ahab did in stealing the vineyards of Naboth? In the time of the prophet Elijah, when Elijah preached against Ahab and Jezebel. And she had Naboth slandered and murdered in order to steal his vineyard."

"I remember well the story. And its conclusion. Such an act brought God's judgment on Ahab and his queen."

Samson waited for me to ride on. "Do you recall all of it, sir?"

I recounted the tale. "Ahab and Jezebel killed Naboth, the good vintner, and ripped out the ancient vines in order to plant a vegetable garden."

"And for murder and the theft and destruction of the vines, God's justice was fierce against those two."

"No bringing back the life of Naboth. Or replanting the vineyard."

"Heaven, they say, is a very big place with many beautiful vineyards. The Lord once showed my heart that Naboth lives. Naboth is in heaven ... alive and happy now. Naboth and his family tend ancient vines for the Ancient of Days. That heavenly vineyard produces wine we only dream of. But we who follow the words of the Lord will one day taste the heavenly wine."

"*Omaine.* And I will look forward to that day." I agreed with my lips, but my heart questioned that evil men like Herod could rip out my ancestors' vines.

We rode west toward the village of Bethphage, the House of Unripe Figs, which stood between Bethany and Jerusalem. As we approached the western boundary of my property, I saw a familiar hill. The beautiful vineyard and fig orchard before us had once belonged to my mother's father. Through injustice and treachery, it had been confiscated by old Herod the Butcher King forty years earlier and was now part of the royal estate of Herod Antipas. I knew what had provoked Samson to discuss ancient history, modern politics, and divine justice.

"Bikri," I murmured. The vision of my grandfather's betrayer, now a wizened, pitiful old cripple, rose in my mind.

"Bikri, indeed, if I may say so, sir. Falsely denouncing your grandfather, of blessed memory. Never was a finer man, nor a kinder, nor a more generous, than your mother's father, whose name you bear." Samson spat noisily and messily before wiping his chin on his sleeve. "Thrown in prison by old Herod on the word of a scoundrel like Bikri."

"They say Bikri was afraid for his own life."

Samson bristled. "Even so! He was supposed to be your grandfather's friend! And it wasn't just fear. It was greed! Now Herod Antipas holds title to what should have come to you."

"Never mind," I urged, despite dark thoughts of my own.

Evil, it seemed, was never completely vanquished. The demons merely disappeared for a time and then claimed another host willing to do their bidding. Just as King Ahab of old had located false witnesses against Naboth, Herod had carried out a similar plot against my grandfather, except that my grandfather died in prison before his trial.

Shaking off the grim recollections, I added, "People say old Herod went through many horrors before he died. And we all know what became of Bikri. Father took me to gaze down on Bikri twice a year as I was growing up. Passover and the Day of Atonement. We always stood on the parapet above the portico where Bikri lays. Father said to me, 'Remember, son. Bikri is an example of God's justice.' I go there still when I am tempted to doubt God is a just and righteous judge."

"Struck down in his prime before he spent half of the bribe money he received and now lives as a friendless cripple most of forty years," Samson agreed. "God is just ... at least in the case of Bikri. Still, I miss your grandfather. No bringing him back. And what he missed. The joy of watching his grandchildren grow up. I'm of an age now, dreams of grandchildren for me and Delilah. That's my goal." He patted the donkey and mused awhile as we rode. "It was wrong to steal his vineyard, wasn't it, sir?"

We passed the time in silence, each of us trying to reconcile what we believed of a just and merciful God with the injustice and evil all around us. I saw Samson give me several sideways glances, as if regretting bringing up painful memories.

Finally, deciding to change the subject, Samson passed the remainder of his grapes to me. "Sir, have you considered what you will name this year's vintage? In light of all that these vines have struggled with? All the hardship they have so faithfully endured to present you with such a gift as this harvest will bring?"

Until that moment, I had not considered what I would have stamped on the clay amphora that would hold this wine. "I will name it *Eliza*. There will never be another like her."

"Excellent choice, sir. Most appropriate. This will be the finest wine ever made in the winery of the House of David ben Lazarus."

※

As the grapes ripened and neared harvest, John the Baptizer preached about a spiritual harvest. He became more strident in his message. He called Herod and his wife *adulterers* and compared them rightly to Jezebel and King Ahab. As for the politically appointed religious leaders, the Baptizer told them to their faces that they were vipers and false shepherds who had betrayed God and his beloved people. Just like the prophet Elijah, John made enemies of many dangerous men that summer.

※

Judah again came to supper. John the Baptizer was on his mind.

Judah washed his broad hands and patted his muscled stomach. "I am full and happy," he said to Martha. Then he turned to me. "So. When will you be ready to journey to the Jordan to see this prophet for yourself? Can we leave tomorrow, David?"

I trusted my sister and my steward with managing the vineyards and the fields in my absence. Martha was a woman of strength and good sense.

"All right, then. I am curious about this prophet ... curious, if nothing else. A few days' journey. Always best to see for myself."

"It's settled, then," Judah concluded, acting as if I could not see the wink he gave my sister, acknowledging the success of their plot. "I'll bring the horses round in the morning."

Chapter 3

Martha prepared provisions enough for Judah and me to travel for five days. Dried figs and apricots, flat bread, and goat cheese were packed into a rucksack. I carried a wineskin so we could add wine to improve the water we found along the way.

As if afraid I might still back out of the pilgrimage, Judah rode up to my gates just after dawn. Seated on his splendid bay, he was leading a gentle, white mare for me.

I could not manage more than a perfunctory nod in reply to Martha's cheerful *"Shalom!"* as we set out to join the stream of pilgrims moving eastward.

I turned my head slightly as we rode toward the narrow path that led to the garden and Eliza's tomb. A pang of longing surged through me, but I set my face forward and squared my shoulders. I was certain that by the time I returned from my pilgrimage, Martha would have packed up Eliza's personal belongings, removing all trace of her from the house, and distributed her clothing to the poor. Though they did not speak of it, I knew Judah and Martha had planned my journey to remove me from this final act of letting go.

By noon the broad way had narrowed. Judah and I were far from alone on the dusty road leading down from Jerusalem to the wilderness of the Jordan. Word about John, who was called "the Baptizer," had spread far and wide. The hungry hearts of my oppressed people were stirred by the rumor and the hope. Bands of common folk flocked to hear his preaching. Those moving down from the mountains were met by returning pilgrims. An excited murmur passed from one group to another. Was John the long-awaited Messiah of Israel?

The first night of our journey, campfires dotted the rugged hillsides. I gathered sage and made a small fire. We spread our cloaks and settled in. After our meal, Judah closed his eyes and fell asleep. I lay on my back and studied the vast, star-studded canopy above me. Countless jewels glistened in the moonless night. I remembered the Lord's promise to Abraham — that his descendants would be as many as the stars in the sky and the sands of the seashore. How could this ancient promise be true?

In recent years under Tiberius, there had been a slaughter of thousands of observant Jews. Thirty years before tonight, this very road had been lined with crucified Jewish leaders who had refused to worship the Roman emperor. Thirty years before tonight's tranquil sky, a slaughter of innocent children in the vicinity of Bethlehem had occurred when a rumor surfaced that an infant king had been born there. Shortly after that, the dynasty of Maccabee priests had been killed off. Now Rome had replaced righteous leaders in the Temple with corrupt puppets like Caiaphas and Annas. History proved that from the beginning, the great political powers of earth were determined to destroy our identity as Jews. Two hundred years earlier, the wars of the Maccabees had been waged against the Greek Empire for the sake of our religious freedom to worship and live as Jews. Jews had won our right to worship the God of Abraham at a great price.

Under the rule of the first generation of Maccabees, we

remained a free and holy people, dedicated to the One True God. Then, year by year as our elders passed away, the sacrifices of our freedom fighters were forgotten. For the sake of convenience, new Jewish leaders made alliances with Rome. For the sake of Rome's protection, we had given up our freedom and our identity. We were now in exactly the same situation as we had been when Judah Maccabee fought against the Greeks who required our people to offer polluted sacrifices to pagan gods.

Who would stand up to Rome? Where was the savior of our people? How could we now withstand the persecutions of Rome and remain a people who worshiped the One True God?

I whispered my evening prayers and then spoke in my heart to heaven: *If ever there was a moment when we need the Messiah, now is the time.*

❦

The shuffling footsteps of a multitude awakened me the next morning. As the road narrowed, the flood of pilgrims overflowed as they surged away from Jerusalem and toward the Jordan, trampling the wildflowers on the hillside. The crowd increased at each byway and crossroad.

My fellow travelers were made up mostly of young, strong men. Unlike the joyful families who normally choked the highways during religious holidays, these fellows were of military age and had the lean look of rebellion fixed on their faces. As they passed us, they glanced askance at Judah's mounts staked out and placidly grazing. The *am ha aretz*—the people of the land—had no resources to keep animals as costly as horses. It made us suspect to them as well.

Judah inclined his head toward a heap of boulders that

formed a sort of gate above the pass. Roman soldiers in uniform stood watch above us.

Judah remarked under his breath, "Look at them. Stationed there under the guise of protecting travelers from bandits."

I replied, "Hoping for a reason to slaughter Jews."

"Then they truly are afraid of this fellow, John the Baptizer."

"Can Rome think there is danger in one man who lives in the wilderness?"

A grim-faced peasant overheard us and said, "We pass through the stone gate as sheep, but perhaps there will come a day when John will send us forth as lions."

His friend rested a hand on the hilt of a rusty sword. "I long for that day, brothers! When the courage of the Maccabees is revived and we take back our nation!" His accent was thick with the dust of Galilee.

Judah nudged me, then urged the peasant, "Be careful what you say, Galilean. You don't need to draw a sword to have your tongue cut out as a rebel."

The peasant challenged me. "Some say the Baptizer will rally us to fight when he calls all of Israel to overthrow Herod Antipas and Rome. What do you say, brother?"

I paused long before I answered, knowing that both Rome and the Herodians had planted spies among us. A careless word could bring a charge of treason and lead to crucifixion. "I'm curious about this wild man, this John. Why he stays out of Herod Antipas's territory."

"He's more afraid of Herodias, the wife of Herod Antipas, than he is the Romans," the peasant interjected. "The Baptizer has taken a great dislike to her and Antipas. He preaches openly about the sin of their illegal marriage."

His friend added, "That witch would have John killed the

minute he dares step foot in the territory of Antipas. What we need is a combination of a prophet like Elijah and a general like Joshua."

The peasant smiled, revealing two missing front teeth. He put a finger to the space. "This from a Roman foot soldier and his friends, who beat me in the marketplace for entertainment. A tooth for a tooth, the Scripture says. Perhaps John is sent from God … the fellow to help us pull a few Roman teeth." He gestured toward a group of Sadducees, who stepped to the side of the road to pray. "The prayers of religious leaders who do not believe in God are no use to us, brothers."

Judah pared an apple and offered a slice to the travelers. "Prophets seldom make good generals."

The peasant spit through his gap as we passed beneath the gaze of the sentries. "I ask only for the Baptizer to call down fire from heaven first, and then I'll wade in and finish the job."

I surmised these coarse Galileans were neither spies of Rome nor of Herod, nor any real threat to anyone but themselves.

Past midday we came to a place opposite where Elijah the prophet had been taken up in a fiery chariot hundreds of years before.

I heard the Baptizer's stern, rasping voice even before I saw him: "Who warned you to flee from the coming wrath? Produce fruit in keeping with repentance."[1]

The crowd was intense and silent, listening. Judah and I made our way along the west side of the Jordan. John was preaching on the riverbank. He was square built and sturdy like a laborer in a stone quarry. Sun-coarsened face was framed by a beard, which was long, parted, and braided. Black hair was tied back. Dressed in camel skin and wearing a wide leather belt, he matched my childhood mental image of Elijah.

The prophet directed his ire at the Pharisees and the Sadducees I had seen praying by the road.

"And do not begin to say to yourselves, 'We have Abraham as our father.' For I tell you that out of these stones God can raise up children for Abraham."[2]

Heads snapped up, and the skeptical expressions of the religious rulers hardened into anger. They had lived their lives in hypocrisy, counting on their genealogy to save them.

The Baptizer had offended the authorities in Jerusalem from the beginning. Although they themselves had no authority from God, they greedily accepted their positions from Herod, who was granted his authority directly by Rome. Under their tables, religious money changers at the Temple paid bribes to the Herodian officials for concessions granted to them. Any threat to Herod was, in fact, an indictment of their hypocrisy as well.

Even at such a distance as the Jordan was from Jerusalem, John's denouncement of Herod was dangerous to the status quo.

Judah and I spotted priests and Levites sent by the Temple magistrates. Arms crossed and chins upturned in fury and defiance of John's message, they waited among the throngs for their opportunity to discredit the prophet.

A family of three brothers emerged dripping wet and joyful after their baptism. A trio of Pharisees stepped up to the riverbank.

With a broad smile, John called to them: "Have you too come all this way to repent and be baptized?"

The youngest of the brotherhood of pious Pharisees, a fair-skinned fellow who appeared as though he had never spent a day working, raised a bejeweled hand and mocked, "Then who are you? Are you Elijah?"

John replied, "I am not."

The second Pharisee, darker and older, roared, "Are you the Prophet?" by which he meant the enigmatic figure promised by Moses the Lawgiver.

John shook his shaggy head. "No."

Then the three religious rulers were joined by others who pushed their way through the crowd to stand and challenge John's preaching.

"Who are you?"

"Give us an answer to take back to those who sent us."

"What do you say about yourself?"[3]

"What right do you have to preach as you do and demand repentance?"

The ordinary folk stirred and began to shout back at the religious rulers: "Let him alone!"

"He speaks to us the truth about Torah!"

"Why do you come here to threaten and trouble a man who teaches us the truth?"

"Go back to Jerusalem and leave us in peace."

The possibility of violence grew. I leaned closer to Judah when he grasped my arm. "We should go," I urged. "Now. Or be caught in the middle of something ..."

Judah nodded but hung back. "A moment more. I want to hear the Baptizer's answer."

I was certain if anyone tried to harm John there would be a riot. Then I spotted the bodyguards behind the Temple officials. Disguised soldiers moved forward through the throng. They covered their military clothes with civilian cloaks. But their coarse features and cold eyes identified them for what they were: cousins and relatives of Herod on the family payroll!

I turned to go.

Then, suddenly, alone in the gently flowing water of the Jordan, John raised his arms to quiet the crowd. He replied in the words of Isaiah the prophet. "I am the voice of one calling in the desert, 'Make straight the way for the Lord!'"

Again the eldest Pharisee questioned him, "Why then do you baptize if you are not the Christ, nor Elijah, nor the Prophet?"

John declared, "I baptize with water, but among you stands one you do not know. He is the one who comes after me, the thongs of whose sandals I am not worthy to untie."[4]

I stopped midstride and turned, searching the crowd. Had I heard correctly? The one we had been waiting for was here? The Lion of Judah! Among us? And yet we did not know him? Did not recognize him?

A mixture of amazement and confusion surged through the onlookers. The Pharisees regarded one another in astonishment. Soldiers, hands on the hilts of concealed daggers, glared at those who surrounded them.

Who did John recognize that we did not? I thought of Samuel the prophet who searched the fine strapping sons of Jesse until he at last anointed the youngest … a shepherd boy … who was to become King David. Jesse himself had doubted the prophet's judgment when David was selected, but the Spirit of the Lord knew the identity of the future ruler of Israel.

Judah caught up with me as I turned. His eyes were wide. He was breathless. "Did you hear that?"

I nodded, scanning the multitude for the one to whom John referred. There was no hint on the expression of anyone that he might be the Messiah in disguise.

Judah held tightly to my sleeve. "Did you hear?" he repeated. "The Baptizer says the Righteous One is present! Surely we can't turn back now! What if he is revealed and we might have met him? If the Lion of Judah is about to roar, we must stay!"

I recognized the jackals of Herod's guards and the pet dogs of the hired priests. No one I saw appeared to be the Lion of Judah, and yet John the Baptizer had guaranteed that none of us would turn back until the identity of the long-awaited Messiah, the promised Son of David, was revealed.

❦

Judah and I camped out under the stars that night.

Cook fires dotted the hillsides like the bivouac of a vast army. In truth, however, we were a divided camp. The Pharisees, eager to carry back news about a new rebel messiah, joined the soldiers on the top of the ridges.

I gazed beyond the ridgeline at the stars in wonder that the Anointed One was alive and might be viewing the same night sky. Perhaps even at that very moment, Messiah broke bread by the glow of a nearby bonfire.

"Do you suppose we'll get to speak with him?" my friend asked.

"I hope for it," I replied. "But I also pray we are not deluded by our hope."

Pilgrims, inspired by John's words, began to sing the old song my namesake, the shepherd David, had sung as he tended the flocks. The words, meant for the ears of the Messiah, must have irritated the soldiers and the hypocrites. They set a watch and lay down with drawn swords in fear we would rise up in rebellion.

Beneath the encircling bonds of their watchfires, we eagerly waited for dawn and the coming of our Messiah.

A deep baritone voice started the song, and we all joined in as one great choir:

"Why do the nations rage
   and the people plot a vain thing?
The kings of the earth set themselves,
   and the rulers take counsel together
      against the LORD and against his Anointed One."[5]

I imagined myself among the ancient Hebrews as they left Egypt and camped in the wilderness. What song had my forefathers sung as they set their faces toward freedom and their masters pursued them from behind? How the cavalry of Pharaoh must have mocked the Jews!

"They say, 'Let us break their bands asunder
   and cast their cords of control from us.'
He who sits in the heavens laughs;
   the Lord holds them in derision.
He speaks to them in his deep anger and troubles them
   in his displeasure and deep fury, saying,
'Yet I have anointed my King
   firmly on my Holy hill of Zion.'
I will declare the decree of the Lord:
   he said to me, 'You are my Son;
      this day I declare I have begotten you!
Ask of me, and I will give you the nations
   as your inheritance, and the uttermost parts
      of the earth as your possession.
You shall break them with a rod of iron;
   you shall dash them in pieces like potters ware.' "[6]

Judah and I sang out with all our strength.

I imagined that the Temple spies and soldiers on the crests of the hill were frightened by the warning in the lyrics just as we who chanted were made still more bold.

"Now, therefore, O you kings,
    act wisely; be instructed and warned,
      O you rulers of the earth!
Serve the Lord with reverent awe
    and worshipful fear!
Rejoice and be in high spirits with trembling.
Kiss the Son, lest he be angry
    and you perish in the way,
      for soon shall his wrath be kindled.
Oh blessed are all those who seek refuge
    and put their trust in him."[7]

As our song resounded against the rocky slopes, I thought I heard the voices of many angels joining in.

I slept with the melody ringing in my ears.

Chapter 4

*I*f I imagined the psalm would serve as warning to bring the religious imposters to their knees, I was mistaken. By the time morning dawned, the number of mockers and soldiers in the camp of the Pharisees had doubled. And still more were marching toward the Jordan in hopes of killing the Lion before he could roar.

Even before we knew who Messiah was, our world was divided by John the Baptizer's announcement that the Son was now among us.

We had awakened just before sunrise as bakers and fruit sellers moved among us with heaping baskets. Word that John had said the Messiah was present and about to be revealed had reached the tiny villages and farms in the surrounding countryside. Weavers had abandoned looms, and elder shepherds had left flocks to the hirelings to come.

With these newcomers, the presence of skeptics and armed soldiers had increased. Like locusts threatening my vineyards when the leaves were still new, the scoffers attempted to devour joy and expectation of what was to come.

We washed and hurried through the morning prayers as the spaces beside the riverbank began to fill. I purchased bread, cheese, dates, and nuts, and drank deeply from the sweet wine we had brought from home.

Judah wiped his mouth with the back of his hand. "I told you this was quite a circus."

I gestured across the river toward a troop of uniformed Herodian foot soldiers who had arrived while we slept. They remained on the east side of the Jordan River, in the Perean territory belonging to their master, Herod Antipas.

We knew they would not cross over into the west where John the Baptizer stayed. The west was governed by Rome, which, so far at least, tolerated John's preaching. The troops of Antipas could only wait like hungry jackals in hopes that the Baptizer would foolishly cross the watery border.

But John the Baptizer was no fool.

Judah nudged me hard as yet another disguised gang of armed watchers arrived on the west bank. "If there's going to be violence, neither side is safe. Shall we stand in the middle of the river?" He leaned close. "I wonder where *he* is?"

I knew without further explanation to whom Judah's query referred.

Judah pointed to distant rain clouds. "It's going to rain. If he's coming, he'd better get here soon."

I surveyed the common folk, searching faces and expressions in hopes of spotting someone extraordinary. Children splashed in the shallow water. Women chatted. Young men carried themselves with a swagger, as though they were prepared now for the Son of David to lead them into battle. Old men frowned and remembered other wars and earlier messiahs who had come, which had instead led to disaster and defeat.

No more than a day's journey from this place, the prophet Elijah had called down fire from heaven to destroy the enemies of righteousness. He had slaughtered pagan priests and turned back the troops of evil King Ahab and wicked Queen Jezebel in terror.

The Messiah would certainly wield that kind of power against the mockers and the tyrants who ruled our lives. All of us hoped, that morning, that if Messiah was among us, he would call down heavenly fire upon the forces who gathered on the west bank and lead us home in freedom.

Judah and I scrambled onto a boulder and observed as John the Baptizer, surrounded by disciples, arrived. The crowds parted and applauded.

A woman shouted, "Will Messiah come today?"

Others called out, "Where is he?"

"Who is he, John?"

"Show us who he is!"

Higher up the bank the mockers cried, "Yes, John! Herod Antipas wants to know where Messiah is hiding!"

"And why he is hiding!"

"Is the Messiah afraid of Herod Antipas?"

"Does he fear Rome?"

"Show us your deliverer!"

John bowed his head and prayed silently as the two camps hurled insults at each other.

"Traitors!"

"Rebels!"

"Hypocrites!"

"Ignorant, impious peasants!"

Dark storm clouds moved toward us. A gust of fresh wind touched my face, and I smelled approaching rain. I saw a flash of lightning and heard the low growl of thunder. The sky broke loose with a downpour, and suddenly hundreds scattered and ran for shelter.

Judah grabbed my arm as I turned to go. "Wait! Not fire this time, but rain. Look!" Judah pointed at the shaggy Baptizer who stood, fearless, in the water.

The Baptizer raised his hands and let the pelting rain wash his face.

I nodded and did not bother to cover my head with my cloak.

We watched as Herodian soldiers, Pharisees, and Temple lackeys scurried away like packs of drenched dogs to find shelter in the nearest villages. The clouds rolled after them, as if in pursuit of those who fled. Only a few hundred of us remained by the time the storm broke.

And there was John, undaunted, in the midst of the stream. His disciples, following his lead, remained with him, waiting.

The sun broke through, and a brilliant double rainbow sprouted and grew like a vine across the sky. Its unbroken arch spanned east and west.

John smiled behind his beard and looked past the remaining crowd. His words rang clear. "Behold, the Lamb of God, who takes away the sin of the world!"[1]

All eyes followed the wild man's gaze. And then I saw the one John was talking about. He was an ordinary-looking young man about my age, I guessed. Brown hair parted in the middle. Strongly built. Dressed like a laborer who had just completed a long journey. He was wet, drenched to the skin, like all of us. He walked straight toward John and the river.

John proclaimed, "This is the one I meant when I said, 'A man who comes after me has surpassed me because he was before me.' I myself did not know him, but the reason I came baptizing with water was that he might be revealed to Israel."[2]

Judah and I moved nearer as the stranger waded into the water and stood before John. He put his hand on John's shoulder and spoke in a quiet voice. John nodded once, sank to his knees in the water until the man blessed John, then helped him stand. The two men stood face-to-face for a long moment. Then, to my amazement, John baptized him, immersing him fully in the exact manner he had baptized the common folk of Israel.

Again the thunder rumbled, just above our heads. I imagined I heard, or rather felt, a deep voice in my chest.

" ... *beloved Son ... I am well pleased ...*"[3]

Had heaven spoken? Or was it only thunder and my imagination? I could not say for sure. Glancing at Judah, I asked, "Did you hear that?"

He nodded. "Thunderbolt. Too close. Danger here in the open."

I waited a moment longer, then left Judah as the man emerged from the water and strode back toward the hills. It began to rain again as I hurried to the knot of men gathered around the Baptizer.

"Master! Is he truly the one?"

"What's his name?"

"Did he tell you who he is?"

"His name is Jesus. He comes from Nazareth," John explained.

They questioned, "But ... Nazareth?"

"Can Messiah be a Nazarene?"

John said, "I saw the Spirit come down from heaven as a dove and remain on him. And I myself did not know him, but the one who sent me to baptize with water told me, 'The man on whom you see the Spirit come down and remain is he who will baptize with the Holy Spirit.' I have seen and I testify that this is God's Chosen One."[4]

It occurred to me that perhaps John was nothing more than a religious fanatic. Such fellows surfaced from time to time, then faded away. Still, I was curious.

What if ...

Judah and I made our way back to the village in the pouring rain. All the rooms at the caravansary were filled, but I paid a poor man to vacate his place so we had shelter for the night.

Judah was disappointed when I told him that the Baptizer had said Jesus was from Nazareth. He shrugged. "So, it was just a thunderstorm after all. It will pass. Everyone knows Messiah can't come from Galilee. If he was David's son, he would be born in Bethlehem. That's what the prophets say."

I did not argue but thanked Judah for coming with me on the journey.

Judah clasped my hands in friendship. He told me he understood what I must be feeling and that this had been an amusement if nothing else. "I hoped you would find comfort by spending a few days among the rabble. Camping beneath the stars. Perhaps when you come home again you'll be ready to find a new wife. I will pray for you."

Judah's comment stung me. *Find a new wife?* My grief was too deep to consider such a thing, even though I knew what he was hinting. It was as if my friend did not know my heart or understand the depth of my sorrow at all. I had lost my wife and my son. Every hope I had for the future had been wiped away. It was not so easy to shrug and decide to begin again.

I said, "You are a great comfort to me, my friend."

But at that moment he was not.

As I spread my cloak on the fresh straw, I thought of the only woman I had ever loved. I wondered if I would ever find joy or hope or love again. The fire of sorrow burning in my heart had not been quenched by the rain. And Jesus, the ordinary-looking man whom John called "the Lamb of God," did not match my vision of the Messiah. A lamb? Jesus had not roared like a lion, driving out our political oppressors as the people expected.

Nor had he delivered me from the tyranny of my loneliness. I was not ready to pick up the pieces of my shattered life just yet. I told myself with a wry smile that perhaps I would be a witness if Jesus of Nazareth baptized the world with fire from heaven. Now that would be a story! Something to help me forget what had happened. In truth, I intended this journey as a diversion to keep me from my empty house ... my empty life.

I returned home just as sorrowful as when I had left it.

Chapter 5

When I received Judah's message bidding me to come to supper at his Jerusalem home, I had mixed emotions: eagerness and some anxiety. Judah was my best friend, and more than that, we were partners in business ventures. There was much I wanted to discuss with him.

Whatever was spoken of in the halls of power in the City of David or elsewhere within Rome's Imperial arms, Judah knew. What I wanted to hear most from him was: what does Rome think of another rumored Jewish messiah? What does Rome think of Jesus of Nazareth?

With so much to discuss, why did I hesitate to take the first steps of an hour's pleasant stroll toward Jerusalem?

Because Judah had a younger sister named Jemima.

Our families had been close for generations. We were even related—Judah and Jemima being cousins to me through my mother's line. There had once been a time when my father and Judah's had plotted and schemed to weld us even more closely together through marriage.

When I was fifteen and Jemima eleven, the idea had seemed absurd to me. After all, did I not have two annoying sisters of my own? Why would I want to marry one such?

By the time I was seventeen and she a vivacious and marriageable thirteen, I had already fallen in love elsewhere, and the notion was shelved. Jemima had never married, and Judah had hinted to me more than once that I had broken her heart.

While I now felt ready to turn from my oppressive grief and take an interest in the world again, still I had vowed to never remarry. But if I ever did, I told myself, it would be someone like Jemima I would seek.

That was a troubling and not a comforting thought.

※

Anticipation and trepidation dogged my steps from Bethany to the outskirts of Jerusalem. The sun was high and beat upon my back as I moved with the throng. The wide road, built by conscripted labor in the time of Herod the Great, was packed with caravans, commerce, and pilgrims. Righteous and unrighteous rubbed shoulders in the ascent. The sounds of psalms mingled with bawling camels and shouts of drovers urging their livestock forward.

I peered up at the watchmen on the walls above the gate. Sunlight glinted on the armor of a Roman soldier.

A poor farmer, with his wife and children gathered around him, sang a psalm of treason against the oppressors who scowled down at us from the parapet. His voice was a rich baritone so beautiful that it rivaled any in the Temple chorus:

"For your servant David's sake,
    do not turn away the face of your Anointed.
The Lord has sworn in truth to David;
    he will not turn from it;
of the fruit of your body will I set upon your throne
    if your children will keep my covenant."[1]

A current of humanity from around the world surged upward toward towers and walls that enclosed the great Temple first built eight hundred years before by King Solomon to honor the Most High God of Israel. Along with other pilgrims entering the Holy City, I joined him in the psalm:

"For the Lord has chosen Zion;
he has desired it as his habitation.
This is my resting place for ever;
here I will dwell, for I have desired it.
I will abundantly bless her provision;
I will satisfy her poor with bread.
I will also clothe her priests with salvation:
and her saints shall shout aloud for joy."[2]

We all knew the Presence of the Lord had long since departed from the Temple. The priests were corrupt and in league with our oppressors. The poor who came to Zion to worship were cheated in the Temple courts. Though they prayed for Messiah to come, their prayers for deliverance seemed to go unheard. Beggars camped along the road and held their cups out to passersby.

Still, we sang in defiance of reality. We fixed our hopes on the promise of what would come to Zion some day.

"Behold, how good and how pleasant it is
for brethren to dwell together in unity!
It is like precious oil upon the head,
the beard of Aaron,
running down on the edge of his garments."[3]

The brute soldiers played a game: spitting on our heads as we approached the pedestrian entrance. I saw them grin at one another when an old man glanced up in thanks to God and was splattered in the face.

I chose to enter the broad commerce gate instead. I walked beside a camel for safety as we entered the tunnel that opened into a teeming marketplace inside the city walls. Tax collectors, merchants, and thieves occupied that place. All were of the same mind: to prey on the weary travelers.

"Wine to drink!" A child, barely taller than the clay jug he stood beside, and much the same shade of earthy brown in skin and clothing, offered a cup dipped from the amphora to a burly traveler.

The pilgrim was dressed like a Greek. He paid his penny and drank deeply. In a flash a cutpurse moved in and stole the man's money pouch, dashing into the throng. A cry of surprise and fury rang out. The victim threw down the cup, and I joined him as we pursued the young thief through the booths and livestock.

"Stop! Thief!" I cried, as the young man purposely knocked down a cascade of wicker baskets, blocking our way.

The stranger I had tried to help stumbled and fell. Our pursuit ended when the thief vanished in the mob.

Winded and drenched with sweat, the pilgrim let me help him to his feet. "I'm sorry," I said as I brushed him off. "He's gone."

The fellow's lips pursed in disappointment. "He did not get everything. But he took enough. I am Porthos of Athens. Traveled far to worship the Lord in Zion. Now I must pray that I will be able to pay my fare and return home again. I thank you, friend."

"My estate is not far from the city. Bethany. I am David ben Lazarus. Ask for me in the village if you need a place to stay." Glancing toward the sun, I knew that I was late. Judah and Jemima would be waiting the noon meal for my arrival. I parted from Porthos. Clamping one hand tightly over my moneybelt, I hurried toward Judah's house.

It was hot. I covered my nose against the stink of animal dung that littered the paving stones leading from the souk.

The streets were steep and narrow beyond the clamor. Feeling a sense of relief as I left the confusion behind, I turned to the right and climbed a series of steps, rising from the hovels of the poor toward the mansions of Jerusalem's wealthiest citizens.

Judah's mansion was high on the western hill, with a clear view of the Temple Mount and the palaces belonging to the Roman governor, Tetrarch Herod Antipas, and the high priest. The blocky bulk of the Antonia Fortress, barracks of Roman soldiers, glowered down on the Temple courts to stifle dissent. *Worship your Jewish god if you choose*, it seemed to say, *but know that Caesar is lord.*

For High Priest Caiaphas, over whom the Antonia's shadow daily fell, this dichotomy of deities was no struggle at all. He, like his father-in-law, the high priest Annas before him, had long since compromised their piety in exchange for wealth and power.

Our Roman oppressors and their henchmen passed by the walls of Judah's house many times through the day, coming and going to their own grand mansions. As I emerged from the winding alleyway onto the broad avenue, trumpets proclaimed the procession of Roman cavalry accompanying a nobleman on horseback. I guessed they were on their way to see Governor Pilate.

Pausing in the shadows, I watched them approach. Pedestrians scrambled out of the way of prancing horses and the hobnailed boots of the foot soldiers.

The celebrity, a middle-aged man dressed in gold-trimmed

robes, rode a dappled gray horse. The animal was barely under control. Eyes wide with fright at the noise and nostrils flared, the creature danced sideways up the road. Iron-shod hooves sparked on the flagstones. In a glance I knew the horse was not safe to ride. No doubt the man on its back had chosen his mount for pride and the aura of strength and not for manners.

A fitting metaphor for many things about Rome, I thought.

I looked toward Judah's house and spotted movement outside the entry. Was that Judah and Jemima in the street? My friend and his sister were standing beside a cart loaded with oil jugs. I was late. Perhaps they were there watching for my arrival. I waved, catching Judah's attention.

As he spotted me, he jumped up on the cart, waving to return my greeting. The rear latch of the cart failed, and five precariously balanced amphorae tumbled out just as the Roman nobleman neared the spot. The containers of oily fluid crashed onto the pavement right in front of the skittish horse. The animal whinnied and reared. Its master tried to control the panic, but iron shoes slipped on oiled stone, and the horse crashed down, throwing the rider against Judah's wall.

There was no time to think. I ran toward the injured man. Bodyguards with shields and swords pushed me back, as if I had intended to harm the bloodied rider.

"They tried to assassinate the ambassador!"

"Go! Quickly! Arrest them!"

"Sedition! The house of Judah ben Perez! A rebel!"

As Judah's gates crashed open, I tried to explain what had happened, what I had witnessed. "An accident! It was an accident! I'm their guest. They were looking for me. The jugs broke loose! It was not meant to harm."

I was beaten into silence by an apelike sergeant who lunged

from the ranks. He knocked me to the ground with the handle of his javelin, striking me hard on shoulders and head. He continued to hammer me long after I stopped resisting.

The last thing I remember was the screams of the women inside the gate and the command from the decurion: "Arrest them! A nest of rebels, this House of Perez! Take them all away!" I tried to shield my head as blows continued. And then I passed out.

Chapter 6

*D*avid?" Martha's calm voice was like still waters in my roaring ears. "David? Are you awake, my darling brother?"

I squinted into the light as my sister smiled down at me. Pain stabbed through my head. My body ached everywhere.

"What ... happened?" I stammered. The light streaming from the window was too bright, even though my eyes would barely open. "An accident?"

"A Greek Jew named Porthos brought you home," she explained.

"Home? From where?" I struggled to sit up, but she pushed me back on my bed with one finger.

"From Jerusalem."

"From Jerusalem? Why was I in Jerusalem?"

"You went to visit Judah. And his sister. Do you remember now?"

"No." I searched my memory and could not recollect anything past breakfast with Martha.

"When? After breakfast?"

"It was two days ago, David." She stroked my forehead with a cool cloth. My head felt three times its normal size, and one side of my mouth would not work properly.

"An accident?" My body hurt too much for this to be a small matter.

Behind Martha, a burly Greek in a turban spoke from the corner of the room. "You were beaten by the Roman soldiers, my friend."

I blinked at him. "I don't know you," I said bluntly.

"I am Porthos, whom you helped in pursuit of a cutpurse when we entered Jerusalem. I chanced upon you unconscious in the street outside the home of your friend Judah ben Perez."

Some glimmer returned. "I went to visit Judah. Yes?"

Martha nodded. She gently touched my cheek. "Yes. David, do you remember what happened?"

"No. I ... something about ... a thief ... and this fellow Porthos. And then ... climbing the Street of the Stairs to Judah's house. But then ... nothing."

Martha glanced toward Porthos, imploring him to explain.

He moved nearer, pulling up a stool. "As a Roman contingent passed the house of your friend, a cart spilled its load and the ambassador's horse threw him. He will live, but Judah and his family were arrested."

"But that cannot be ... Judah?" A row of spiny stitches stretching from the corner of my mouth toward my ear prickled my cautious fingers.

"Yes. I regret that when you tried to give testimony, you were beaten nearly to death." Porthos patted my arm.

"And you. Helped me. Saved my life."

The big man leaned back as though my comment was a wasp to be avoided. "No. Not me. I am not so courageous as you. I did not interfere with your beating. I saw the villains drag away your friend Judah and lead his family away. He fought like a lion. The women went meekly. And then, only after everyone dangerous had gone, I gathered you up and brought you home here to Bethany."

Martha said, "I barely recognized you. Your face is badly swollen."

I touched my cheek and winced. I managed to sit up. "What's to be done?"

Martha and Porthos exchanged a glance.

"You must get well, brother," Martha said in a matter-of-fact tone.

I argued, "I mean, what's to be done for Judah? Innocent! For Jemima and their mother. Arrested unjustly!"

Porthos furrowed his brow. "Many on the street witnessed the accident. And it truly was … an accident. A few tried to speak up for Judah, but you see … look at yourself. Clubbed into silence. An example for others who may wish to set the record straight. Truth makes no difference to tyrants."

"But surely I can go to the high priest. Give testimony to the Sanhedrin."

Porthos shook his shaggy head. "It was not a matter for the Jewish council to deliberate and judge. It is a Roman matter. Your friend was tried and condemned the very same day. That's all I know."

🥀

I recovered quickly from my injuries and returned to my work.

Samson and his winery goats were a small legend in the world of the Roman Empire. My estate also sold enormous wheels of cheese produced from goat herds that grazed on the pastures. Samson's pets had nothing to do with dairy production, yet, from the time I inherited the property, I devised a seal showing three goats on a wine vat. This was pressed into the wax that protected the cheese.

This seal and Samson's goats were destined to safeguard more than the cheese.

Samson and I were in the barn where new barrels for the harvest were being made by my cooper, a young man of about twenty-five. My barrelmaker was a British slave named Patrick. From his youth he had been trained as a blacksmith and barrelmaker, tasked with building containers to hold provisions for the Roman army. His foot was crushed when a stack of barrels shifted during a rough sea voyage. To save his life the gangrenous leg had been amputated below the knee. Unable to march or work, Patrick was of no further use to Rome.

He had come to my vineyard five years earlier when old Samson recognized value in Patrick's skill. Upon Samson's advice I purchased Patrick for a few denarii at the slave auction in Caesarea Maritima. We brought him home in a wagon. Though Patrick knew few words in our language, Samson showed him an enormous stack of cured wood, the blacksmith forge, and tools for barrelmaking. The young cripple seemed pleased. Leaning on one crutch, he hobbled about the shed. He nodded and grinned his approval. He selected one lightweight, straight-grained piece of palm wood, hefted it in one arm, and said, "Not good. This not for wine." And he tossed the palm plank toward his cot.

The morning after his arrival, I heard the blows of hammer on metal and smelled smoke from the forge. When Samson and his goats came to fetch me, we hurried to the workshop.

Patrick was already at work and walking.

Samson declared, "Sir, you got a bargain in this one. In the night the lad fashioned himself a wooden leg. Lined it with fleece for his stump and fastened it to his body by leather straps attached to his belt. I have the feeling he'll be an asset to our winemaking, if you don't mind my saying so, sir."

Years had passed, and Patrick's cleverness and skill were

indeed assets. The quality of the wine depended much on the quality of the barrels. Patrick's work was admirable. Our cooperage now had three apprentices under Patrick's supervision.

He stood as tall as any strong man and worked as hard as two. He had modified and perfected his wooden leg until he walked with an almost imperceptible limp.

Patrick now spoke our language with almost no accent. He addressed me with the same affectation he had learned from Samson. "If you don't mind me saying so, sir, it's got to be all oak. Away with the palm. Though I prefer palm for my false leg, it plays the grapes false in the fermenting."

Samson agreed. "Bitter, in my opinion, sir."

"And also acacia wood. Acacia. No good, if you don't mind my saying so," Patrick added. "I say oak is the wood. Harvest in the winter … less sap. And—"

The clatter of shod horse hooves interrupted our discussion.

Samson moved toward the door of the barn and stood framed in the light. "Romans." Samson's goats gathered round his legs. He turned his face toward me. "Two soldiers, sir."

At that news, Patrick retreated to the lean-to that was his living quarters. He drew the curtain across the door. I knew he feared his former masters with good reason. His apprentices left off their labor.

Moments passed and a Roman sergeant in leather body armor walked toward the shop. He demanded of Samson, "Where's your master, old man? The woman at the house says he's here."

I stepped forward. "I am David ben Lazarus, master of this estate."

The brute-faced Roman slapped his fist against his chest. "Hail, Caesar."

"Shalom," I replied, unwilling to respond in like manner.

"You are a friend of Judah ben Perez," he demanded.

"I am."

"You have been making inquiries, so we hear. Saying around Jerusalem things such as, 'Where is Judah? What have they done with his mother and sister' … and such as that."

"And do you have news of my friend?"

I noticed that Samson and the goats had stepped into the shadows, where a stack of barrels leaned against the wall.

"News? Ha! Of a man accused of sedition? There will be no news … The tribune sent me to give you this warning."

"And what is that?"

The sergeant's eyes narrowed. "He sent me to tell you to shut up and quit asking the questions. For your own safety. A favor to you."

I could not help but ask, "Why would a Roman tribune wish to warn a Judean grape grower?"

At this, the sergeant cracked a wide grin. "For the sake of them three milk goats." He jerked his thumb toward Samson and the trio of animals around his legs.

"I'm afraid I don't follow …"

"Tribune's been a great lover of them cheeses of yours. He wants a wheel in return for his favor."

I nodded at Samson. "Fetch the sergeant a wheel of the Three Goats, if you please."

Samson hurried from the shop.

The sergeant was not finished. "Tribune says he never tasted better cheese as from them three milk goats there. Wondrous, he says. Dreams of it on campaign. Then he hears the very goats are not more than a few miles from where he is stationed. A miracle, he says. One wheel provided on every new moon will satisfy his appetite. But you are to quit asking the question about your friend. Consider them all dead and shut up about it, or there won't be anything he can do to help you."

Samson returned with the heavy, wax-sealed round of goat cheese. He placed it into the sergeant's arms. The soldier examined the seal, then peered at the three goats nudging Samson's legs.

"Aye. That's it. These are the very milk goats, then? Best cheese in the empire." He slapped his fist against the cheese. "Hail, Caesar!" The sergeant turned on his heel, mounted his horse, and rode away.

We were all silent, except the goats, who laughed and gently butted Samson's knees.

"Well, then," Samson said at last. "That's that."

Patrick emerged from behind his curtain. He was on crutches, and his half leg dangled. He shrugged and explained, "They would not want to take a lame man back into service."

Patrick's apprentices eyed him with surprise and returned to work.

I clapped Samson on the back. "We must never let on, eh? The three goats who grace the seal of our cheeses are neutered males you raised from kids and could not bear to slaughter."

"Aye, sir. Wethers, every one. My dear boys never gave a drop of milk for cheese, sir. Nor will they. It would indeed be wondrous and a miracle of biblical proportion. That's why they smile so." He scratched their heads affectionately. "Our secret, eh, boys?"

Chapter 7

*P*orthos continued as our house guest. My sister and I welcomed him and gave no thought to how long he might remain with us. He was a middle-class merchant who sold copper cooking pots in the agora of Athens. He was a gentle bear of a man. Quiet and wearing a crooked smile on his broad face, his father was a Greek, but his Jewish mother had raised Porthos in the faith of Yahweh.

He grew up learning Torah while living in the Greek culture. He told us he often sat near Mars Hill to listen to the philosophers.

"At last I saved enough to make pilgrimage to Jerusalem where the God of Abraham, Isaac, and Jacob made his dwelling place. I made this journey so I could return to Athens and argue with intelligence about the true identity of the Unknown God. And the moment my feet crossed the threshold, I was robbed. Ah. Men are the same everywhere, are they not?"

My household found Porthos pleasant and entertaining company, well spoken and educated in philosophy in the manner of the Greeks.

I invited Samson and Patrick to join Porthos and me on my patio in the cool of the evening. As the stars winked above us, we four men sipped fine wine and spoke of Jews and Gentiles, of things of God and Torah, and of the rumors of Jesus of Nazareth in Galilee.

Porthos told us of the philosophers on Mars Hill. "They seem so high above us, rich and robed, as we merchants sell to the common folks in the marketplace below." Porthos swept his hand across the horizon. "How many temples to how many gods surround the common folk of Athens? And yet there is one small temple built to the Unknown God, for fear they may have left one out and he become angry. Ha! The Unknown God is the one and only God in heaven and earth ... the God I know and worship ... the God of Israel."

Patrick, who was not a Jew, asked, "I hear about the God of Israel every hour of every day as I work. Samson won't let me forget that the Only True God is Israel's God. Finally I believe it, though I don't know why. So, can't you just go up there and tell those fellows?"

Porthos raised his bushy eyebrows, "Once I tried to join in their discussion. They spoke of politics, gladiators, world government, and the fierce gods of Rome. Roman gods, they deduce, must be more powerful than any others."

Samson laughed. "How could a kettle-seller possibly convince anyone?"

"I spoke of Torah—that through the Prophets and the Psalms, the Unknown God is revealed. I told them of the soul, of right and wrong, and of heaven ... the abode of the righteous."

Samson leaned forward. "You told the Greek philosophers these things? You're a man of courage!"

Porthos shook his head. "Not so. They laughed at me. And when they did, I blushed and hurried away. Even so, in my market stall, when common folk spoke about the cruelty of the gods of Rome, I told them about the Lord, the One God who is named Merciful. One day Messiah will come and heal and forgive our sins. And the lion will lay down with the lamb. Now here's the miracle. The poor and humble, even among the Greeks, are eager to hear more of our God of mercy." Porthos held up a thick finger. "That is where we must begin to share the truth … with those who have nothing. Like John the Baptizer has done."

I had remained silent as I considered the injustice of our oppressors. I wondered quietly what had become of Judah and his dear mother and gentle sister. What had become of all the nations and kings throughout time who had chosen to rule their people by fear? Those empires had all fallen.

After considering these things, I spoke. "To the ends of the world, fear of Rome is like a blindfold that blocks out the light of truth. Along with every nation, we Jews have fallen because of fear. We have given up our freedom. Brutal men control our lives. We compromise our beliefs as long as it is others who are brutalized and not we ourselves. Terror is a powerful religion. The spirit of fear is a god that takes the human heart captive. But our God, the Living God of Israel, longs to fill our hearts with joy and freedom. That is what separates believers from all other people."

Samson tugged his earlobe. "It is written, somewhere, that the Romans pray to many gods … out of fear. In our Jewish worship the wail of fear gives way to the cry of 'Hallelujah! Blessed is he who comes in the name of the Lord.'"

"*Omaine!*" Porthos continued. "So what did I learn in Athens? That I must seek the one who will rule my heart and mind with mercy and love. Perhaps when I find him, I will no longer be afraid of anything."

"You were not afraid to help me the day I was beaten," I reminded him.

"But I was afraid. Indeed."

Though Porthos humbly denied his courage in helping me, I was well aware that he risked his life to come to my aid.

"Then why did you do it?" Samson asked.

Porthos did not answer the question. "I promise I am a coward. My knees were knocking as I carried David all the way out the gates of the city."

Samson asked again, "Porthos, if you are such a coward, why did you save David's life?"

Patrick raised his cup in salute to Porthos. "He did it because courage is when you are terrified to do the right thing ... but it is still the right thing to do ... so, you go ahead and do it anyway."

"*Omaine!*" Samson clapped Porthos on his broad back and congratulated Patrick. "Well spoken!"

Then we turned our conversation to the weather and the crops.

The morning dawned bright and fair. Porthos shared a final breakfast with Martha and me.

I walked him to the gate and embraced him. "Brother, on your return—anytime—you are always welcome here beneath my roof."

"There is rebellion in the air, David ben Lazarus. I have come far and now feel I must see for myself the courageous prophet who preaches so against Herod Antipas and his woman, Herodias."

"When I heard him speak, I felt there never was a man like John." I handed Porthos a pack filled with supplies. "Perhaps Elijah. But never before or since."

Samson brought around from the stable a donkey the color of dark red wine. "Here you are, sir." He presented the reins to Porthos, who bowed slightly.

"I will take the best of care of her," Porthos assured Samson. Then he turned to me. "A beautiful gift, brother." Porthos patted the beast's neck and stroked her ears. "My own two feet have carried me far. I am blessed now to possess four more feet for my journey."

Samson stroked the donkey. "Her name is Pleasant. And that she is. A filly from my old girl and trained by my own hand. She will wish to lay down beside you, sir, and sleep beside you on the trail. Just let her. Pleasant is warmth and comfort when a man travels far from home."

Porthos climbed onto the donkey. His legs dangled awkwardly, and his feet nearly touched the ground. He clucked his tongue once, and Pleasant walked out smartly.

"Remember," Samson called after him. "One cluck for walk. Two clucks for trot. And a long, smacky kiss for canter."

Porthos raised his hand in thanks. "Never fear! I will dismount when traveling uphill," he promised. Then he clucked his tongue twice, and Pleasant trotted away.

"Well," Samson declared with finality, "a good and brave fellow indeed. Pleasant will be a good friend on his journey."

Chapter 8

"I've written Mary. And she's answered me." I held a papyrus up for Martha to see. "The name of the Roman centurion, her friend ..."

"Her lover, you mean. Just say it without dancing around it!" Martha countered. "Our widowed sister, with her estate in the Galil, is a shame to our family."

"Mary writes that the man's name is Marcus Longinus. A centurion who has the respect of Pilate for his bravery in the wars."

"What of it?"

"Mary says he is a man of great courage ... with a keen sense of what is just."

"That may be so, even for a Roman, but what do you think he can do for anyone?"

"I will ask him ... ask if he will find the fate of Judah and his mother and sister. Perhaps he'll help us. At least to know."

"Have you no common sense? We've been warned to stop asking questions. Do you want to lose everything? They can take it all, you know. That is the lesson we are meant to learn from Judah ben Perez! And now you would go to a Roman centurion? David! There is nothing more you can do for them." Martha turned her back on me and stomped out of the room. As was her way, she decided she would have the last word on the subject of Judah and his family.

So I let my sister have the last word. I was silent. I did not answer her.

Leaving the house that morning, I saddled my mare and rode out without an explanation to anyone. Martha was right. The arrest of Judah was meant to instill fear in all of us who had any wealth or position. The tactic had been effective.

I cantered up the road to the great city, remembering what Porthos and Patrick and Samson had said about courage.

I was afraid but rode out anyway. Though I had sent dozens of inquiries, I had not been to Jerusalem since my beating. Sights and sounds and smells so familiar to me since my childhood now made my stomach churn. At the sight of soldiers on the ramparts, memories clubbed out of my mind came rushing back.

I passed through the gate and rode by the marketplace, up a steep street, and over a causeway. Ahead of me was the Antonia Fortress; the center of Roman military power.

Perhaps I looked too fierce in my determination as I approached the sentries. "I come in search of—"

They brandished their weapons. "Get off your horse, Jewish dog. It is the law that you do not address a Roman sentry from a saddle."

I opened my hands, showing I did not have a weapon, then stepped off my mare. Holding the reins, I allowed them to search me for a hidden dagger. The first was scrawny and the second built like a bull. Both were unwashed and foul smelling.

"He's unarmed." The big man wiped his nose with the back of his hand. "What's your business here?"

I answered, "I am in search of Centurion Marcus Longinus.

He is a … friend … of my family." The words nearly choked me, but for the sake of Judah I pretended.

"Centurion Longinus? A friend of a Jew?" mocked the thin fellow. "Well, everyone knows Longinus. Famous, he is. But he isn't here. Out on patrol. Rounding up Jewish rebels and …" He drew his finger across his neck. "Still want to talk to him?"

"When will he return?" I asked. My mouth was dry.

"Weeks, it could be. If you're a friend, why don't you know?" the first soldier taunted.

The second soldier's eyes narrowed as he sized me up and laughed. "Maybe you're an assassin, eh? Sent to kill him."

"No. You see I am unarmed. Marcus Longinus will not be pleased at the way you question me and mock me. What are your names? I will report to him …"

The mocking fell silent. They exchanged uneasy looks and became suddenly docile. "Now see here. How are we to know … you, a Jew and all, riding up and making demands from atop your horse?"

The change in their demeanor strengthened my resolve. I said fiercely, "I don't believe the centurion is on patrol. And if he hears I have come, and you have turned me away …"

The two men blinked at me for a moment, then one said to the other, "We … perhaps are mistaking who rode out this morning."

"I thought it was Longinus."

"Aye. Looked like him."

"But it was at a distance."

I mounted my mare and stared them down defiantly. "Go see if he is here. Tell him David ben Lazarus is at the gate on his horse."

My heart was pounding. Minutes passed before the first

sentry returned meekly following a muscled, compactly built officer with close-cropped reddish-brown hair and the fair skin of the people of the far north but sun-bronzed from his military service. He glanced at me with suspicion. From his accent I deduced he was a Briton by heritage. I understood now why my sister Mary found him exotic and handsome.

"Shalom, Centurion," I said quickly. "My sister Mary sends her greetings."

"Ah." He scratched his temple. "Mary's brother. Good man … David."

"Yes. I received a letter from her this morning."

"She is well? My Mary?"

I swallowed hard. "Our Mary … yes. She is well. I have news …"

"Welcome. Follow me to my quarters." He snapped his fingers, commanding the sentry to hold my horse as I dismounted.

I followed him across the cobblestone paved central court of the fortress. On my left was an open door, revealing a blood-spattered flogging post amid other devices of torment. I imagined my friend being dragged across this space. I thought of Jemima and Judah's mother in the dungeon beneath the fortress. I was also keenly aware that the ancient garments of the high priest of Israel were locked up within the Antonia and only permitted to be used on certain high holy days. It was as though even our religion was held captive by our conquerors.

Entering the stark foyer of the stronghold, I looked up to see the images of the emperor on shields adorning every wall. These shields, when first displayed publicly in Jerusalem by Pilate, had nearly caused a riot. *So*, I thought, *Pilate learned a lesson and kept the images of the Emperor-god Tiberius hidden from sight of the people.*

I repressed a shudder at the thought of dead bodies strewn

across the Temple Mount. I kept my eyes fixed on the back of the centurion's head.

Passing through a long corridor, we climbed steps to a chamber overlooking the Temple. The songs of the choir and the bellowing of sacrificial animals were heard clearly.

Marcus Longinus closed the door and indicated with a wave of his hand that I should sit. He poured a cup of wine and offered it to me, then poured one for himself. "So. David ben Lazarus. Your sister has spoken of you, David. May I call you David? She told me of your disdain for her ... for our ... friendship."

"I didn't come here to discuss my sister, Centurion." I ignored his appeal to my name and waited until he drank before I sipped very bad wine.

"You are a Jew. A religious Jew. Your sister once told me you would not be caught dead entering the abode of Gentiles." He waved his hand around the room. "Yet here you are."

"The ancient garments of the high priest are held captive here. And many righteous men and women are shackled to these walls as well. Their presence makes my reason for coming here a holy purpose."

He considered my words, took another sip, and placed his cup aside. "Our cup in this place is very bitter."

"Yes. Many will bear witness to that."

"What can I offer you instead?" he asked.

"Information," I replied.

"Sometimes information is also a bitter cup to drink."

"Better than dying of thirst."

He spread his palms and shrugged a Gallic shrug. "So? Ask me."

"The family of Perez? Judah ben Perez. His mother and sister?"

Longinus fell silent. He appeared uneasy, which was unusual for a Roman centurion unless being reprimanded by a superior officer. In the case of Marcus Longinus, his only superiors in Judea were a military tribune and Governor Pilate himself.

The Roman seized the goblet and drained it, then set it down with more force than needed. "They are dead."

"I don't believe it," I challenged.

Longinus frowned and narrowed his eyes. "Ben Lazarus, do you have any other family?"

The remark caught me off guard. "Only my sisters ... why?"

"Because it is better for you ... and for them ... to believe what I say about the House of Perez. Let it alone."

"Is that a threat?"

The officer shrugged. "Call it a warning." Longinus seized the jug and refilled his cup, offered me another, and when I refused, emptied his in a single, long swallow. He met my eyes squarely. "I have nothing against you, ben Lazarus. In a different time and place we might have been friends. But hear me: I had nothing to do with the fate of Judah ben Perez or his mother or his sister. But neither can I do anything to aid them. Nor can you. All you will accomplish is to bring the wrath of Rome down on your head, and Jove help you if that happens, for even your god with the unutterable name won't be able to."

Emotion swelled in my chest, threatening to choke me. "Judah's my friend, Centurion! Almost a brother. And he's innocent."

Longinus clenched his jaw, then raised his square chin until our eyes locked again. "I know that," he admitted. "And I admire you for your loyalty and courage. But leave it alone, for now. If there comes a time when anything ... anything at all ... can be done for them, I give you my solemn oath I will attempt it, but until then, let it go. For Mary's sake, you understand? Will you agree?"

Numbly I nodded, then left without speaking again.

※

I met with Joseph of Arimathea, the elder, a wine exporter, with ships sailing from Joppa. He had been a great friend of my father and had lived in Rome for a time. He became the chief exporter of Judean goods to the Roman colony in Britannia. Trade with the Gentiles had made him very wealthy.

Joseph had worked closely with Judah ben Perez and was well connected throughout the Roman Empire. With Judah gone now, Joseph stepped in to help those of us who did not have the connections needed to sell our produce. He was in his midfifties and from the tribe of Levi. Though his lineage qualified him for priestly duties, an accident in his youth had left him maimed and ritually unable to serve at the Temple. He wore a patch over his left eye and was missing two fingers on his left hand. He had focused his intelligence on business. His contacts with Gentile merchants gave him the ability to conduct his affairs without suspicion or interference from the Roman government.

Today's meeting was intended to ask Joseph's advice on pricing and marketing. We met in the storage caverns hacked out by my grandfather beneath the limestone hills.

The air at the surface sweltered with the midday sun, and I felt sweat trickling between my shoulders. But once inside the first bend in the tunnel leading downward, the atmosphere was noticeably cooler.

"Instant relief," Joseph remarked with admiration, "and the same all year round." He had visited my underground warehouse before and never failed to comment on how perfect it was for storing wine.

Samson stepped forward from the shadows to greet us. His wizened face and bent form suggested a barrel stave brought to life. "Always the same, if I may say so, your worship. It may boil or freeze out there," he jerked his head upward, "but the life of the vine rests in comfort beneath."

"Ah, Samson, still here I see, and as poetic as ever. Another year, another vintage, but like fine wine, you just get better with time."

My vintner beamed his gap-toothed smile under Joseph's praise. "Your pardon, sir," he corrected, "but the best wines don't really get better, they just get … different. A great vintage possesses fine qualities throughout its life but chooses to reveal them gradually as time passes."

"Samson has no need to prove his value any more than he has already," I said. "However, as I think you'll see, he's still revealing new abilities."

"Just a suggestion I made," the steward demurred. "Really the master's doing. This way, gentlemen, if you please. This way."

Leading us onward with a crablike, sideways shuffle, Samson directed our course past a series of side tunnels, each devoted to some aspect of my craft. In one rested the great fermenting casks.

In another branch, dimly seen by the light of a single flickering oil lamp, already filled shipping amphorae were being packed in straw-filled crates. Like shadowy wraiths, a pair of barely seen workers carried out their task. Their movements were hushed by the spilled stubble underfoot. Though never ordered to do so, even their conversation was carried on in hushed tones.

The entry to the third side passage was more brightly illuminated. Racks of wooden barrels higher than our heads formed a canyon stretching away in the darkness, like a corridor reaching through time toward an unseen future.

In the middle of the space rested a single barrel lying on its side in a cradle. The bung hole used for topping up the wine and for sampling the contents was already open. A glass chalice and a glass tube rested on a table.

Joseph sniffed the air. "Love the aroma in your storage caverns," he said. "But something's different ... what?"

Samson was almost skipping from side to side in his eagerness, but like the good servant he was, he deferred to me until I gave him permission to explain. "It's these barrels, if you please, sir," he suggested, grasping an oil lamp and bringing it near the staves. "See how much tighter is the grain, sir? And more uniform in color, not so streaky? Shall I tell him, sir?"

I grinned and waved for him to proceed.

"It's not acacia, sir," Samson said. "It's oak. The master paid for all new barrels two years ago."

"And the reason for this extravagant innovation?" Joseph questioned.

I took up the reasoning. "For one, it lets us age the wine longer. You know that more than a few months in acacia gives the wine a yellow tinge and a sharp aroma."

In his enthusiasm Samson shrugged off the leash of subservience. "Two years," he noted with pride. "Two years in these barrels. Topped off every month by me personally to make up for the angels' share."

"And was it worth it?" Joseph inquired.

"That's why you're here," I said, indicating that Samson should plunge the pipette into the barrel and withdraw a sample. The wine, a gloriously rich purple in color, foamed slightly as he released the contents of the tube into the cup. With evident pride he held it up toward a wall sconce before presenting it to the merchant.

The established protocol of tasting a new wine was simple: swirl, sniff, sip, and spit.

It was somewhere between sniff and sip that Joseph's face took on a transfixed appearance. He held the liquid in his mouth, closed his eyes, swallowed, then took another mouthful and yet another.

"Was it worth it?" I said, repeating his query back to him.

"I have never tasted such a perfect wine," he exclaimed. "The elegant and inviting scent … lavender? And the balance between tart and sweet. The smoothness. Extraordinary! Not even from the great vineyards of Dalmatia or Gaul have I tasted such. I taste ripe blackberries and figs and maybe a hint of pepper?"

"And our market?"

"To where they will pay the most," Joseph said conclusively. "You know how I warn you about the uncertainties of the market in Rome and the dangers of shipping, but this … this!" he said, swirling the wine yet again and swallowing another mouthful. "This is worth the risk. I want the lot, and I want to arrange it today."

Joseph was a fair, righteous man, and we settled our contract in the same terms I had enjoyed with Judah. As was the custom, at the conclusion of our business we rode back to my home to share a meal together.

The merchant of Arimathea knew my concerns and my questions before I inquired. He waited until my household servant had served us and left the room before he murmured, "I have news about our friend Judah."

I leaned closer. "Judah! Still alive?"

"A galley slave in a Roman warship. So, for the time being, alive."

"I will pray for him."

"Pray his suffering does not last too long." Joseph spoke the blessing, tore his bread, then dipped it into the hummus. "A man does not escape from such a living hell."

I pictured the torture my good friend endured: the whip, the hunger, chained night and day belowdecks without relief. "May God have mercy …"

Neither of us talked of the injustice of such a fate. Joseph answered, "Our ancestor Joseph was sold by his brothers as a slave in Egypt. Slandered by a woman, he was put in prison. How many years did Joseph suffer? I have pondered all these things, and the story of a good man's life does not end, even when he descends into the grave. Who he is and what he accomplishes will live beyond him, for good or evil. Does he who made the ear not hear? I tell you, the arm of the Lord is not shortened. Pray the Lord will make himself known to Judah, who is trapped like Jonah in the bowels of a Roman ship."

I nodded. "I have tried every way I know to learn the fate of Judah's mother and sister."

Joseph lowered his chin slightly. "They are dead." He answered plainly. "A Roman quartermaster told my steward as much when we delivered a load of wine to the Antonia Fortress."

Tears stung my eyes. I had not expected such news. "Tortured?"

"No. An illness. Some disease—a scourge of the lungs—swept like a wind through the women's cells. Prostitutes and righteous women like Judah's mother and sister died together. Buried by night in the potter's field. Jemima and her mother were swept away within days of their arrest."

Perhaps it was a mercy for these good women to be in Paradise together. "God has indeed delivered them from the hand of their enemies."

"*Omaine.* My thoughts," Joseph answered. "In such an evil world as we live in now, perhaps this is more merciful."

"Judah would be relieved to know his mother and sister are not destitute and locked away in a dark cell, but embraced and cared for by angels within the bosom of Abraham." Yet my voice was unsteady, lacking confidence.

Joseph was matter-of-fact. "I hired mourners to keen for them. There is no more to be done."

I thought of my wife and child and did not reply for a long time. "I will say *kaddish.* It is good that the suffering of the innocent ends quickly."

Joseph continued eating, though my appetite was gone. He moved on to other matters. "The prophet in the wilderness, John the Baptizer. Jesus of Nazareth. The Anointed of God is now among us. There could not be a better moment in all of history for the Deliverer to show himself. Like Moses of old, coming to free our fathers and mothers from Egypt ... we are little more than slaves in our own land."

"It is well with you, though, my friend?" I asked Joseph.

"It is well. Business flourishes. The Romans need my skill to feed their armies and their citizens." He hesitated a long moment. "Your sister, Mary of Magdala, has political connections in Galilee that may keep you safe from suspicion."

I tried not to let disapproval of my sister register on my face. "Mary goes her own way. It is not my way or the way of my family or of the God of our fathers."

"She is great friends with Johanna, wife of Kuza, the steward of Herod Antipas."

"Johanna and Kuza. Those two!"

"I have spoken with Mary at great length about her vineyards and her wine. Mary sells the wines of her late husband's estates at a fine price to the garrison in Tiberius. No need to export."

Bitterness consumed me. "Mary has sold her soul, Joseph."

"Her estates are in the Galil. The Messiah is there. Perhaps your sister's soul may yet be redeemed by the Redeemer."

"My younger sister was only trouble from the start. Not good and solid like Martha. A flighty thing. Pretty and spoiled."

"I remember her as a sweet and lonely child. Affected deeply by your mother's death. You married her to an old man for the sake of a business arrangement."

"A great opportunity," I shot back, "since Mary would not have had other offers in marriage. Mary should have been obedient and accepted with righteousness her purpose."

Joseph chewed a bit of roasted chicken as he pondered my judgment. "That may be. But even so, with Mary's husband dead now, she might welcome her brother's visit."

I shook my head slowly. "That would be too much for me to swallow. I have nothing to do with my sister. She is a shame to me and to my father's name."

I saw pity in the eyes of Joseph, who had seen much more of life and was thus more merciful. At last he said, "Your father was my dearest friend. After your mother died, he wed Mary's mother. It was plain to all that he did not love her. Nor did he look with favor on your half sister when she was born. When Mary's mother ... drowned ... there was speculation that perhaps she had taken her own life. Speculation that because your father did not love her, she waded into the water of the Sea of Galilee and put an end to her loneliness."

"That speculation and her sin branded us as a family," I insisted. "It left us few options."

"And it left your sister Mary ... beautiful little child ... alone," Joseph said swiftly. "Now I see, David, that you have your father's indifference. Perhaps you live in judgment of a woman who has spent her life looking for love." He stood. "I believe you will be attending your cousin's wedding in Cana? I pray that Mary will be there also ... and that you will show the mercy your father never showed."

The old man was honest with me. He had brought things to light that my own father had never spoken about before his death. And he was right in his conclusions.

My stepmother's suicide had affected us all. We had never spoken openly about the circumstances surrounding the death of Mary's mother. Little Mary had never recovered from watching her mother drown.

Joseph was also correct about my lack of compassion. I had never showed my sister any kindness. When the thirty days of mourning for my stepmother had ended, I had dismissed Mary's tears and demanded that the child "get on with life." And so she had. Bold and defiant, she had gone her own way. The kindness she did not find at home she sought in the arms of lovers. Her first lover had been Barak bar Halfi, the son of our wine steward. Even after the young man was joined to another woman in an arranged marriage, Mary pursued him shamefully. After that, I had married her off to an old man in Galilee to save her ... to save all of us.

Mary was a young and beautiful widow now, and she was rich, having inherited the estate of her elderly husband after his death. I hoped Mary would not dare to show her face at the wedding in Cana, yet I expected she would. I dreaded the encounter.

Chapter 9

It was seventy miles from Bethany to Cana, and the journey to attend the wedding would take almost a week. Alone, and on the white mare, I might have done the trip in three days by sleeping rough; two if I rode from dawn to dusk. With Martha along, riding in a donkey-drawn cart, even a full Sabbath-to-Sabbath span would barely be enough time.

We set out at full light on the first day of the week. I was comfortable leaving the vineyard in the hands of Samson and Patrick. Martha had her maidservant, Leah, riding with her in the cart, which was driven by my man, Uri. Going with us as a wedding gift was an amphora of the best vintage.

The most direct route to the Galil was directly north, through Samaria. That route was straight along the spine of hills flanking the valley of the Jordan. It was a good road and evenly planted with cities, but there was still a problem. As much as we Jews disliked our Roman overlords, there was even more animosity against Samaritans. We regarded them as apostates and traitors.

The pilgrim route avoided the problem by crossing to the east side of Jordan. However, I disliked it unless traveling with crowds going home from a festival in the Holy City. Crossing wild stretches, it was the most dangerous. So I chose to take us by the coast road. Parts of it, like that between Joppa and Cae-sarea, were still under construction, but it was patrolled by the Romans and safe. Subduing bandits was something Rome had brought to Judea, but at a very visible cost.

Just west of Jerusalem, before we reached Emmaus, we encountered three crosses erected beside the road. Mercifully, the occupants were already dead so we did not have to endure their pitiful cries for water or for death. The ravens had already been feasting.

The womenfolk covered their faces, but I forced myself to look. Crudely lettered, the indictments were attached above each head as part of the Roman economy of execution: one spike for each hand, one for the crossed feet, and a fourth so that the legal requirements were strictly observed. SIMON OF AIJALON, REBEL, one sign read. JASON, MURDERER, another. PHILIP OF HEBRON, CONSPIRATOR, noted the last.

I prayed for their souls and for their families and for my own.

We spent the first night of the journey at an inn outside Aijalon and the second at a caravansary in Joppa. The uncom-pleted road north from Joppa was no more than a cart track, but the breezes from the sea were bracing. As I rode, I watched fishermen putting out in tiny craft on the Great Sea of Middle Earth and marveled at their bravery.

A great Roman war galley passed us, coasting southward toward Alexandria. Its square sail was filled and drawing smartly, and the triple rank of oars were banked. The slaves chained to them were getting a momentary rest from the labor that would eventually kill them. It was said no one got away alive from being a galley slave.

It crushed my heart to think that Judah might be a prisoner

on that very ship. I asked Adonai to protect him, wherever he was, and to grant him release from the common fate.

It was while I was still pondering and praying that we reached a tiny village separated from the sea by a conical hill. I did not know its name. It might not have had one. It boasted no more than twenty rude stone buildings and a single well.

It was unremarkable except in one sense: it was empty. No one was beside the well. No children played in the street. A pair of goats badly in need of milking bawled from a pen, but no one came to attend them. No smoke rose from cook fires or ovens.

"David?" Martha said urgently. "David, what is it? Is it plague … or something worse?" Making the sign against the evil eye, my sensible, rational sister spit between her fingers.

"There are no bodies and no … smell," I said, trying to sound controlled while being far from easy in mind myself. With relief I spotted some movement beyond where the street curved around a rocky outcropping that had been too large to move. "Wait here," I directed, kicking the mare into a lope.

Outside a hovel, sitting on a wooden stool, was a toothless, elderly woman. In her arms was a sleeping infant. At her feet a little girl, perhaps two years old, played with stones and bits of stick.

"What happened here?" I demanded.

The crone shaded her eyes with a palsied, withered hand. "A penny, kind sir. Adonai blesses those who help the poor. Spare a penny?"

"Where is everyone?"

"Gone … all taken. Except old Bethulah. Alms?"

"Taken … how?"

"Taken. All of them, by the Romans." Old Bethulah made

a sweeping gesture that gathered up the missing inhabitants of her village and flung them over the hill toward the sea.

In singsong chant, the old woman's voice cracked as she droned over and over, like a sinister lullaby: "Taken by the Romans. Taken by the Romans …"

A chill coursed through me. What would the Romans do if a village was accused of harboring rebels? I did not need the vision of the three crosses to provide the answer, but it came just the same.

By now Uri had driven up with the cart. "Don't follow until I ride ahead and check," I ordered sternly.

Martha refused. "David, I'm frightened. I'm not staying here without you. Either we turn back or we go forward together."

The road curved around the hill, approaching the sea again from the southeast. As we cleared the obstruction, the incessant sound of hammering reached me. My worst fears seemed about to be fulfilled. Would the Romans crucify an entire village: men, women, and children?

Of course they would, if it suited their purposes. They would destroy an entire city to provide an example of Rome's stern, irresistible justice. At the fall of Carthage, Rome had pulled down every stone, sold fifty thousand people into slavery, and slaughtered the rest.

"Turn back," I said, gesturing to Uri.

The trail was too narrow to turn just then. We had to drive ahead to find a wider place.

The hammering grew louder. The drumming clashed with the rhythm of the breakers. I heard cries and shouts and demands for water echoed by the clamor of sea birds.

Everything I dreaded to see was about to be unveiled.

Before us the coastal plain rolled down to the water. Halfway between the hill and tide, on a level headland perched above the waves, fifty to seventy people toiled with picks and shovels … building a new road.

Under the lazy supervision of a Roman corporal, the entire male population of the nameless village scraped and raked and leveled. Children carried stones. Women toted baskets of sand. While an Imperial surveyor checked the perfection of his engineering, a squad of ten soldiers played at dice in a hollow out of the wind. They barely glanced up as we approached.

When I spoke to the corporal, he replied testily, "The new road will help that dump of a village grow. But do you think these wretches show any gratitude? Not a chance! All they can think about is that they only have to serve for two more days and then they go back to rotting in their hovels! No gratitude at all!"

He could not have guessed at the strange gratitude in my own heart at that moment.

The further we traveled toward the port of Caesarea Maritima, the more nearly completed was the Coast Road. Our pace increased with each perfectly level, expertly banked mile.

At Caesarea our route turned east toward Megiddo. Once across the Plain of Esdraelon progress slowed again on the climb up the Galilean hills. Nevertheless, we skirted Sepphoris and still arrived at Cana of Galilee a full day sooner than I expected.

I put the extra time before the wedding to good use.

The area around Cana was swampy. Where the marshes had been drained, and on the adjacent hillsides, there were orchards of figs and walnuts and pomegranates. These interested me, but not so much as the vineyards occupying the lower, southwestward-facing slopes.

The wines of the Galil had a special reputation in the world. Moist air funneled inland by the ridges of Mount Carmel cooled the mornings and left behind a heavy dewfall. The afternoon sun could be intense, bathing the vines in warmth and light that promoted lush growth.

I spoke with several growers about their efforts. One point on which all agreed was that wine grapes were the most awkward of crops. Vines on soft soil, positioned below springs, produced lush bunches in abundance … and watery tasting juice. Vines that grew on stony, barren hillsides produced the more memorable vintages. The yield from such a vineyard was much smaller, but the wine was much richer—bolder and more flavorful.

As Hiram of Rumah said to me when I visited his winery: "No winemaker, no matter how skilled or talented, can find something in the wine that God did not put in the grape. Great wines are truly made in the vineyard, not the winery. It is the vintner's job to let the wine be what it was created to be and not ruin it!"

Of course, when I explained about my investment in oak barrels, he remarked, "Too expensive. Never work out in the long run."

The wedding festivities began an hour before sunset. The aroma of meat roasting on spits made my mouth water. An immense crowd was gathering—far greater than anyone had expected. Apparently the Galil, having seen more than its share of forced conscriptions, floggings, and executions, was seriously in need of some laughter and good cheer, at least for one night.

I delivered my gift of the special wine to the father of the groom. At his insistence, I broached the barrel and allowed both he and the bride's father to sample it. They exclaimed over its quality. I was reassured to find that, even after the rough sloshing journey, it had traveled well. Both men agreed that the many toasts drunk that night would be memorable for more than just the speeches being made.

It was while I was visiting with a former vinedresser of mine who had moved to Cana to plant his own grapes that I received two shocks in quick succession. The first surprise was the arrival of Jesus of Nazareth. Since this wedding was an important event in the life of the communities west of the Sea of Galilee, it made perfect sense that such a celebrity—for that was what he had become since I'd seen him with John, being baptized in the river—would be invited to bless the gathering. After all, Nazareth, his home village, was a scant handful of miles away. He was almost a neighbor.

Because I had been so recently forcibly reminded of how Rome treated dissenters, I somehow expected him to remain in seclusion. Still, I had heard no tales that he preached sedition or rebellion. Such accusations were leveled against John the Baptizer, but so far, not against Jesus.

The second shock came so abruptly on the heels of the first that it drove my curiosity about the young rabbi out of my head. Unwarranted and unwanted, my sister Mary had indeed chosen to come to the festivities.

I could not believe it. Mary was an outcast from all proper society and flaunting a relationship with a Roman centurion.

Before I could collect my thoughts, Martha was at my side, bubbling with indignation and resentment. "David! You've got to do something! I will die of embarrassment! What if someone thinks we asked her to come? Make her leave, David."

Mary was camping in a grove of trees outside the town. It was before her tent, as it was being erected, that I confronted her ... quietly. I led her away from ears eager to absorb and tongues eager to repeat gossip. She was angry and resentful, but I also saw a flicker of fear in her eyes when I told her that if she stayed, the people would publicly shame her for the harlot she was and drive her away. They would make an example of her; it was already agreed to by the elders. I begged her not to stay—not to do this to herself or to Martha and me.

At last, as I gazed at her with sorrow—she still was my sister, after all, though she had humiliated all of us—she agreed to leave.

I returned to the feast, all my good feeling soured. Even Martha's praise for me did not relieve the sense that the evening, in fact the entire trip, had been spoiled.

It was then I had my next encounter with the rabbi from Nazareth.

"You were at the riverside with John," said a pleasantly resonant voice behind me.

Brown eyes containing dancing golden flecks regarded me as I turned. "Yes ... I ... his message is powerful ... perhaps, too powerful ... dangerous." I felt myself babbling. My friend Judah had been with me at the Jordan when we saw the Baptizer, and then he had been arrested and carried off to captivity and likely to his death. Unreasonable, I know, but in that instant I somehow blamed John for what happened to Judah.

That resentment spilled over into a sudden distrust of the Nazarene.

"A true prophet," Jesus said with certainty. "There is no one born of woman greater than John."

"He ... he speaks well of you also," I replied, scratching my beard to cover some confusion. Having heard the man in front of me identified as "the Lamb of God who takes away the sin of the world," how was I supposed to respond?

What were my choices? Did Jesus of Nazareth believe himself to be the Chosen One, the Deliverer? In that case, he was either a charlatan or a lunatic … unless …

Martha scuttled up to me, peered askance at Jesus, and plucked at my sleeve. "David," she urged. "They've asked you to offer the blessing over the wine. Come with me. The *chuppah* is ready and the bride is coming. Hurry!"

Jesus smiled at me as I let myself be hustled away toward the ceremony.

The groom, dressed in spotless white *kittel*, was already in place. Accompanied by her mother and her soon-to-be mother-in-law, the bride was conducted seven times around the groom while the cantor sang a passage from the Song of Songs:

"My dove in the clefts of the rock,
　　in the hiding places on the mountainside,
show me your face,
　　let me hear your voice;
for your voice is sweet,
　　and your face is lovely.
Catch for us the foxes,
　　the little foxes
that ruin the vineyards,
　　our vineyards that are in bloom."[1]

O Lord, I breathed, *how I miss my wife, my beloved.* In that moment I believed no one in the world had ever felt such grief and loss as I experienced.

Soon after I was called for, I shook myself out of my reverie. Handed a brimming cup of my own special wine, I held it aloft and recited: "Blessed art thou, O Lord God, King of the universe, who brings forth the fruit of the vine."

As I completed my duty, I caught Jesus of Nazareth watching me intently, as if my words contained a greater meaning than I perceived. It made me uncomfortable again. What was it about this mild-seeming man that provoked uneasiness in me?

The rabbi conducting the ceremony took up the thread and again pulled my attention away from Jesus. "Marriage," the rabbi said, "is like wine. When properly regarded and carefully matured, it goes through a miraculous transformation to become something wondrous that brings joy and flavors life with gladness."

"Well said, Rabbi," I heard Jesus acclaim.

The blessings continued with the new couple sharing the cup: over the new family being formed, over their future together, and over their future children. Thanks were returned to God for his wisdom in creating man and woman as two parts intended to form a miraculous whole.

The seven *b'rakha* being concluded, what followed was the witnessing of the *cheder yichud*. The new husband and wife were ushered alone into a closed room and left there together, which act concluded the legal requirements of the marriage.

Meanwhile the party began in earnest.

Apparently while I had been dealing with my sister Mary, fully half of the Galil had joined the festivities. Apart from the pilgrim feasts in Jerusalem, I had never seen such a boisterous, exuberant crowd. Platters of roasted meat held aloft by servants disappeared into the throngs and reappeared moments after, miraculously empty as by some conjuring trick.

Calls for "Wine! More wine, here!" echoed and reechoed around the community. Hiram of Rumah, standing beside me, noted, "That wine of yours, David? Excellent. Exceptional. Too bad it's already gone."

"Already?"

Hiram nodded, waving his arm over the mob that swarmed the village like locusts, even spilling down the hill into the orchards. "I don't think the wedding party expected this."

It was clear that the families of the bride and groom were disconcerted. I observed them from a distance, their heads together in animated conversation with the servants and the cooks. Much gesturing and finger-pointing followed.

Nor was there any letup in the cries of "More wine, here!"

At the far side of the scene stood Jesus of Nazareth, a nearby torch illuminating him, though all around was in shadow. Beside him was a pleasant-faced, middle-aged woman, whom I took to be his mother by the similarity of their features. That she was entreating him to do something was evident by her earnest, imploring look.

What could he possibly do to remedy this situation?

Involuntarily, I moved closer to see what would happen. I had heard that Jesus was a carpenter by trade. Could that information be wrong? Was he, perhaps, a merchant, with storehouses of wine that could be opened in an instant?

I saw Jesus shake his head, but he was smiling gently.

Proving that she did not take his refusal to heart, his mother summoned a squad of servants to her side. Gathering them around her as if she were the mother hen and they the chicks, she extended both hands. First she waved toward them and then in the direction of her son. Her command was clear: "Do whatever he tells you."

Jesus took the lead, marching ahead of the servants, who trailed along in evident confusion. I followed the file as it disappeared into the darkness down the hill, lighting their way with a pair of torches.

We soon came to a place with a well. The small, level plaza was surrounded by a ring of tall, stone jars designed to hold water for ceremonial cleansing. Each would contain some thirty gallons.

From a distance close enough to observe and yet not be seen, I heard Jesus say to the servants, "Fill the jars with water."

"But, sir ... ," one of them protested.

It was not a servant's place to question orders, but I know the attendants were as confused as I was. What was he doing? What could this exercise possibly accomplish?

The servants dropped the leather bag for drawing water into the well, then hoisted it aloft. Each pouch contained no more than five gallons at a time. The task Jesus gave them to fulfill was not easily or quickly accomplished. The women filled one jar, then hesitated. Surely he did not mean for them to fill all six! How would that remedy the problem?

"Sir, we have trays of food waiting ..."

When Jesus did not reply, the servants understood he had not changed his mind. He meant for them to continue.

Five gallons drawn from the depths of the well. Cranked aloft, each was carried to a stone jar and emptied. Six jars. Six waterskins each. Thirty-six trips from well to jars until water sloshed out the top of each.

Satisfied at last that his design had been fulfilled, Jesus said to the head of the group, "Now draw some out and take it to the master of the feast."

"But, sir!" the woman argued.

Once again, Jesus met the dissension with silent firmness.

With one of the empty wine pitchers in hand, the lead attendant shrugged. By loud sighs and rolls of her head and shoulders, she conveyed to her colleagues that the one giving the instructions was crazy, but what could you do?

She dipped the pitcher into the first stone container and filled it. She turned and marched with the stiff-backed dignity of manifest disapproval back toward the feast. Stepping back into the shadows, I waited until the servants had passed, then I returned to the festivities.

When we arrived the guests were still belligerently clamoring. The cantor tried to restore the lighthearted mood with more singing.

"You have stolen my heart, my completer;
   you have stolen my heart
with one glance of your eyes,
   with one jewel of your necklace.
How delightful is your love, my completer!
   How much more pleasing is your love than wine."[2]

He got no further, being drowned out by calls of "More wine!"

What happened next was incomprehensible to me.

I saw a trio of servants approach the master of ceremonies. Two of them combined in pushing forward the third, who carried the pitcher in her hand. That she was unwilling to carry out her assignment was plain by the way she hung back. At last the master of ceremonies noticed her and demanded what she wanted.

I saw her pour from the pitcher into his empty cup.

I saw him raise the goblet to his lips and drink.

Over his face came an expression of wonder and delight, mirrored in consternation and confusion on the face of the serving girl.

Soon relays of serving men and women were snaking through the crowd. Firelight danced and sparkled on the flow of wine, like streams of glistening red fire as they filled and refilled cups and goblets and mugs.

What had happened? From what secret trove had this new supply suddenly emerged? Why was the master of ceremonies slapping the bridegroom on the shoulder in evident congratulation?

I had difficulty getting the attention of one of the servants. Many guests, waving their goblets aloft, caught her before she got to me. I was fortunate there was even a mouthful remaining.

"Wait!" I demanded of her as she prepared to dart away. "What happened?"

"That man ... the one from Nazareth," she explained. "He had us fill the jars with water from the well, then told us to draw it out and take it to the master of the feast to taste, and ... see for yourself!"

At that moment the master of the feast said loudly to the bridegroom, "Everyone brings out the choice wine first and then the cheaper wine after the guests have had too much to drink; but you have saved the best till now."[3]

I raised the cup to my lips.

Incredible sensation! If my wine had a faint lavender aroma, this was like walking through an entire field of lavender and roses. This wine burst on my tongue in waves of exquisite tastes—powerful without being overwhelming. The flavors were the embodiment of an endless summer of ripe fruits—a banquet.

The most memorable wine I had ever experienced.

And meanwhile the cantor sang:

"Praise the Lord, O my soul!
He makes grass grow for the cattle,

and plants for man to cultivate—
bringing forth food from the earth:
wine that gladdens the heart of man,
oil to make his face shine
and bread that sustains his heart.[4]

"Return to us, God Almighty!
Look down from heaven and see!
Watch over this vine,
the root your right hand has planted,
the son you have raised up for yourself."[5]

Part Two

In the last days ...
everyone will sit under their own vine
and under their own fig tree,
and no one will make them afraid,
for the LORD Almighty has spoken.

MICAH 4:1, 4

Chapter 10

I was on my way into Jerusalem to make a fellowship offering at the Temple. Other services were for sin and guilt and forgiveness. These were somber in nature, as befitting their purpose. The fellowship offering was a joyful sacrifice of praise to the Almighty for answered prayers, or just to say thanks to the Lord of heaven and earth for his goodness.

As I strode along I sang:

"Ha'yadeh, l'Yahweh, ke tov, ke l'Olam Chessid
Give thanks to the LORD, for he is good,
   for his 'to forever love and mercy.'"[1]

In this instance I wanted to convey my gratitude for the success of the wine in the oak barrels. It was in my heart to establish the reputation of the House of Lazarus throughout the empire. This new vintage gave me exactly that opportunity.

How could I not be grateful?

In riding toward the Holy City, I passed by Bethphage and thought again of the loss of my grandfather's property and his life through the treachery of Bikri. The recollection was more bitter in my thoughts than sour wine in my mouth. My grandfather was completely innocent of wrongdoing.

It did not matter that Bikri had already endured decades of

suffering to repay his perfidy. As far as I was concerned, it still was not enough.

I had become increasingly convinced that there was much about the world and about my nation in particular that needed to be corrected. Since the days of the Hasmonean kings ended some one hundred years earlier, there had been no Jewish rulers over us. Either Roman puppets like Herod or Roman governors like Pontius Pilate had governed our country.

When would our state be restored? How long would it be before Jews again ruled the Land of Promise as the covenant with Abraham, Isaac, and Jacob promised?

When would the Deliverer come?

And could Jesus of Nazareth be the one for whom we prayed? It did not seem possible. Perhaps John the Baptizer could have filled that role, with his angry denunciations and powerful diatribes, but not the pleasant-seeming preacher from the Galil.

How could he ever redress wrongs? I heard he said things like "Turn the other cheek." This was not the justice for which I, or my people, longed.

All these thoughts mingled with my anger at what had happened to my grandfather and to Judah ben Perez. Though the two men had suffered abuse some forty years apart, they were now forever linked in my mind.

I met Nicodemus the Pharisee outside Nicanor Gate, on the plaza of the Temple Mount. Since the fellowship offering was the lone service after which the meat of the sacrifice was eaten by the participants and not just by the priests, I had invited him to share it with me.

But it was not to be.

"I'm sorry, David," Nicodemus said, gazing up at the lustrous hues of the Corinthian gold that formed the latticework of the gates towering above our heads. "I am summoned to a meeting of the council that cannot be postponed. It was already too late to catch you, or I would have sent word."

"It doesn't matter. I'll find someone to whom I can give the food. What's so urgent, if it's not a great secret?"

Looking around him as if anticipating the presence of spies, Nicodemus leaned close and whispered, "Lord Caiaphas is concerned about Jesus of Nazareth. He fears he will be blamed if Jesus leads a rebellion against Rome."

"The Nazarene rabbi?" I scoffed. "Have you heard him speak? There never was a less likely candidate to be a rebel commander."

"You've heard him, then?"

"I've met him," I replied. "He is altogether a gentle soul. Too simple and too genuine for this world. Perhaps Lord Caiaphas expects to find in Jesus a reflection of his own twisted, conniving soul."

"Shh!" Nicodemus urged. "I agree with you. In fact, I sought Jesus out myself to question him ... but I went at night and not openly. The walls have ears, you know."

A low, chuckling laughter erupted almost at our feet, frightening Nicodemus and startling me.

Tucked in an alcove of the gate was a thin, teenage beggar boy I recognized. His name was Peniel.

"Not only the walls, kind sirs," Peniel said, "but the floors and the nooks and crannies. I'm sorry to overhear your conversation, but then, I was here first."

Peniel, blind from birth, was a sweet-natured creature in spite of his disability. The son of a potter, he had a hard life, subsisting by begging for the charity of strangers.

"Don't look around," Peniel added, "but here comes Lord Caiaphas now."

He was correct. The sensitive hearing of the blind man had picked out the strident, pompous tones of the high priest before he and his entourage rounded the corner of the Court of Israel and hove into view. Watching them arrive was like being on the docks at Caesarea Maritima when a fleet of galleys maneuvered into port.

With a nod that barely passed for courtesy toward Nicodemus and a mere curl of the lip toward me, the high priest arrived outside the door to his offices. A swirl of sycophants orbited around him as if they were bits of wood caught in a current and he the drain toward which they were being drawn.

"Lord Caiaphas," one of the acolytes said in a fawning manner, "there's something I've been meaning to ask you." He waved a perfumed hand toward Peniel and spoke as if the boy were one of the gilded railings and not living at all. "Tell me your opinion. Who sinned—this man or his parents—that he would be so cursed as to be born blind and live such a wretched life?"

In sonorous syllables reeking of boredom, the high priest replied, "Probably all of them. Many generations of sinners, no doubt. He was utterly conceived in sin and born in sin and no doubt lives that way as well. Still, it's an uninteresting question, since one thing is absolutely certain."

"And that is?"

"He will never be healed. Never, since time began, has it been recorded that anyone ever opened the eyes of one born blind. See for yourselves that I'm right. All the authorities agree that it is hopeless—the ultimate in divine retribution and an example to us all."

With that the high priest and his flotilla swept on into the building. Over his shoulder he addressed Nicodemus: "Nicodemus, don't be late to the council meeting, or we'll have to start without you."

The door of his chambers banged shut behind him.

Nicodemus was seething. "Doesn't he just hope I'll be late. Because he knows my uncle and I are two of only a handful on the Sanhedrin who don't automatically support him in all he says and does." Turning toward the blind boy and stooping low, he said, "That was disgraceful and cruel, Peniel. I'm sorry you had to hear that."

Smiling, Peniel replied, "I've heard much worse, really. And I am an object lesson, you know. I like to think that when folk come to the Temple to pray, and they see me, that they are reminded of all they have to be thankful for. Besides, once a year Lord Caiaphas sends each of the Nicanor beggars a silver coin."

"Once a year …," Nicodemus sputtered. "Here, boy, are five silver coins, and I regret I have no more with me."

"I am going to make a fellowship offering," I said. "Would you like a haunch of mutton when I come back this way?"

Peniel's face beamed. "Very much! Thank you both, very much, kind sirs."

"I must leave you," Nicodemus said to me. "Perhaps I'll ride out to visit with you one day next week. You should be on the council yourself, you know."

"Not me," I protested. "I have no desire to get involved with politics. It never leads to anything good."

"Amen to that," Peniel concurred. "That's why I keep my ears open and my mouth shut."

❦

I selected the ram for my fellowship offering from the preapproved flocks available for purchase on the Temple Mount.

Because I shamelessly used Nicodemus's name, I was not seriously overcharged, as were all the unsuspecting pilgrims from the Galil and elsewhere.

The eastern expanse of the Temple plaza was entirely given over to the noise and smell of commerce. Entire herds of bleating goats and sheep competed with lowing bullocks. Flocks of twittering doves responded to the cries of vendors hawking their wares. All these noises mingled with the chants of the psalms. The air was punctuated by the sharp, metallic odor of blood and the aroma of the meat charring on the altar.

I gathered with a group of other men who all had a *todah*— a thank offering—to perform. One had been in a shipwreck and survived. Another had received word his only son had been killed while on a journey to Ecbatana, but the rumor was proven false when the son returned unharmed. Still another had recently seen the birth of his firstborn son and was celebrating with his friends. I swallowed a flood of returning grief and offered my congratulations.

A chorus of Levite singers began the hymn: "Give thanks to the Lord and call upon his name."

"Give thanks to the LORD, proclaim his name
   make known among the nations what he has done."

At which point those of us gathered around the altar of sacrifice joined in:

"Sing to him, sing praise to him;
   Tell of all his wonderful acts."[2]

A *todah* is a celebration of thanksgiving, but it is also a commemoration of past blessings and triumphs. It was a way to remind ourselves and others of God's faithfulness.

Even in the midst of being grateful, there was an undercurrent of longing because things still weren't all they should be:

"Cry out, 'Save us, O God our Savior;
　　gather us and deliver us from the nations,
　that we may give thanks to your holy name,
　　and glory in your praise.' "[3]

All the people standing around the altar and all the witnesses to the sacrifice or awaiting their turn to approach the altar, shouted, "*Omaine!* Hallelujah!"

Once the ram was slaughtered and roasted, half the meat became the property of the priests who performed the sacrifice. The rest, two quarters of roast mutton, was returned to me, wrapped for carrying home.

One parcel I immediately took to Peniel.

"Thank you, sir," he said as I approached.

"I hadn't even spoken yet. How did you know it was me?"

"I heard the Hallelujah sounding. When I smelled the delicious aroma coming directly toward me, I knew it was you ... or at least I hoped!" He stood, begging bowl under one arm, and I placed one of the parcels in his hands.

"Will you stay until they close the gates?" I asked.

"Ordinarily, sir, but not today. Between the generosity of Lord Nicodemus and yourself, I want to go home right away and share my good fortune with my family."

"Would you like me to guide you?"

Peniel smiled. "Not necessary, sir. I know every twist and turn between here and home."

"Then go and be well," I said. "We'll see each other again ..." I stopped in consternation at my ill-chosen words. "I mean, I'll see you ..." That was even worse.

The blind beggar laughed. "Not to worry, sir. People are always getting their tongues tangled around me, it seems. Perhaps it means the message of my life is getting through to them."

"*Shalom*, Peniel," I replied. "And yes, it does mean that."

As I exited the Temple Mount and made my way back toward the Bethany road, I pondered Peniel's cheerful good nature. What a bright, shining soul to live in constant darkness! If my sight were taken from me, would I still be grateful for my life, or would I be swallowed up in bitterness?

How many varieties of blindness were there in the world?

How blind were the Temple authorities, who had less regard for the beggars of Jerusalem than for their own comfort?

How blind were the people around me, so immersed in the struggles of each day that they could not thank God for anything?

How blind were those who listened to the words of John the Baptizer, or Jesus of Nazareth, and felt only curiosity, or nothing at all?

How blind was I if I let grief or worry or bitterness or anger overwhelm me?

So deep was I in these musings I did not notice where my steps took me. I had already passed out the Sheep Gate, beneath the frowning shadow of the Antonia, the Roman fortress, and reached the edge of the Pool of Bethesda.

The twin reservoirs together known as Beth Chesed, the House of Mercy, were also called, by some, the House of Shame. So far had the more extreme sect of Pharisees prevailed that to be crippled, blind, ill, or debilitated in any way meant that there was sin in the life of the afflicted. God punished sin, they said. They concluded that the more severe the punishment, the more flagrant the sin. Since the House of Mercy was a place where invalids gathered, hoping for a cure, it represented a collection of the worst sinners, unsurpassed in all of Jerusalem.

When I thought of Herod Antipas and the cronies of Lord Caiaphas, I had to disagree with the Pharisees, with one exception.

Surrounding the pools were white limestone colonnades supporting red tile roofs. These four porticoes, together with a fifth that divided the body of water into two parts, were another reason the structure was linked with Mercy. For cripples who had no ability to move from blistering sun or chilling rain, these covered spaces represented the only shelter many would find.

Reaching the terrace along the east side of the columns, I could not help myself. I turned in, expecting to see exactly what my eyes beheld.

Across the pool from me, crouching against one of the pillars, was Bikri ben Zimri—traitor and wretched talebearer—who had caused my grandfather's death.

His skull-like head lolled forward on his thin, sunken chest. Dank, faded yellow hair hung across his face like discarded scraps of tattered cloth. His legs, useless and twisted, coiled beneath him like the snake he was. Only his arms showed any evidence of the hale and strong young companion he had once been to my grandfather. His shoulders still displayed some muscles near his neck. His hands were bound in leather strips, since they were Bikri's only means of transport into shelter, or out to beg along the highway.

I was glad he was still there. I was not ready for him to die yet. He had not suffered enough.

Besides shelter from the elements there was yet another reason why the ill and infirm congregated at Bethesda: the possibility of a miracle. Every now and then, without warning, the water bubbled and roiled in the pool. It was said that an angel troubled the waters. In that instant, whoever was the first to enter the water would be healed … instantly cured.

I do not know if it was true or not. I had never met anyone who had been healed by the waters of Bethesda, but I hoped it was true. It gave me great satisfaction to know that Bikri, crippled as he was, would never, ever, be the first into the water. I wanted him to witness others being cured, being restored to their friends and family, while he lived on, alone, unloved, and hopeless.

If he lived to be a hundred, instead of the sixty that he now was, he would do so as a miserable lame man, despised by many, pitied by few.

In his case I truly believed the Pharisees had it right.

Shifting the remaining haunch of meat to my other arm gave me an idea. The amount and quality of the meat was more and better than a beggar could hope for from one year to the next.

I could walk up to Bikri, announce my name and identity, and offer it to him … only to take it away and give it to someone else. Remembering Peniel's keen sense of smell, I knew I could add another layer of torment to Bikri's existence.

Suddenly my stomach was sour, and I tasted bile in my mouth. Enough!

Approaching the nearest beggars at random, I handed over the mutton. "Share this," I said.

"God bless you," they chorused. "God keep your worship. What a good and kind man you are."

The sickness did not leave me until I passed the crest of the Mount of Olives and tasted the sweet air of home.

Chapter 11

Notorious! Jesus of Nazareth and my sister Mary of Magdala shared that title for different reasons. Jesus was slandered for his persistent righteousness. Mary was justly shunned for her flagrant sin.

Mary's presence in Jerusalem was something I dreaded, even though she was counted as dead to our family.

It was the morning of the final day of the high holy days when I happened upon my sister and Jesus of Nazareth by chance.

I rose early and made my way toward the Temple for the morning sacrifice. It was cool. The sun had not yet warmed the stones. The wide porticoes and courts were almost deserted. Only one place was crowded. I spotted Jesus seated on the steps near the treasury. Two hundred people were gathered around to hear him teach.

Curious to know what he was saying, I was drawn toward him. Suddenly there was a commotion at the gate. Temple guards and Pharisees dragged Mary forward. She was weeping and clothed in her nightdress. I did not need to ask why she was being brought to this place of judgment. There was a blush of shame upon her cheeks and her bare shoulders. Her feet were bare and bloody, her hair unbound. They threw her to the pavement at the feet of Jesus.

The rabbi leapt up and, in a posture of protection, stood between her and the men who shamed her and plotted her execution.

With great effort she raised herself to her knees and crouched there. Her hair hung down, almost obscuring her face, but I saw her shoulders heave with sobs.

I felt as though I would choke. My heart ached for the sister I had loved ... whom I still loved. In that terrible moment, I remembered Mary as a child. Pretty. Sweet and innocent. Now here she was before a cadre of men with stones in their fists.

Yet I made no move to protect her.

A priest challenged Jesus, "*Rebbe!* This woman was caught in the very act of adultery!"

The crowd gasped. Jesus looked at Mary with compassion. He did not move from his place, physically shielding her from the stones in upraised fists.

A second priest continued, "In our Torah, it is commanded that such a notorious woman be stoned to death so that we will put evil out of the house of Israel. What do you say about it?"

I knew this trap was meant to discredit Jesus. The life or death of my sister was of no concern to the twelve priests who formed a circle around her and Jesus.

If Jesus spoke for mercy, then he would be denounced as a false teacher and a breaker of the laws of Moses. But if he agreed with the sentence of death for Mary, then all his teaching about mercy would come to nothing.

No one moved or spoke as the world hung on the reply that Jesus would give. What would the rabbi do? Would he discredit himself? Or condemn Mary?

I saw Jesus scan the accusers. Who or what did he focus on? I could not tell. It occurred to me this might be the moment when he called upon his followers to turn on the Temple guards and fight. Perhaps Mary, who had caused so much unhappiness, would spark the beginning of rebellion.

Then Jesus did something extraordinary. He gazed down at Mary for a long moment, then stooped beside her. His head was level with hers. If the judges threw the stones now, Jesus was as vulnerable as Mary. He would share her condemnation, take the stones that were aimed at her. The jagged rocks, meant to tear her to pieces, could not miss him.

"What do you say, Rabbi? How do you answer the laws of Moses?"

Unafraid, Jesus locked eyes with Mary. She studied him with wonder as he calmly smoothed the dust of the ground into an even surface.

The frustrated challengers repeated their demand. "What do you say, Rabbi? Sin should be exposed and punished according to the law!"

Jesus did not reply. Instead, he deliberately began to write Hebrew letters in the dust. The priests leaned forward to read what he wrote. And as the message became clear, they faltered and stepped back.

Slowly, Jesus stood, careful to stand as shelter over Mary. He searched the faces of her accusers. Were they not also his accusers?

"The one of you who is without sin," Jesus said, "let him cast the first stone at her."

His words pierced my heart like an arrow. I, who was her own brother, had condemned her. I, who had known her as a child and had married her off to an old man to save our family's name ... was I not guilty of sin?

While his words hung in the air, he stooped again beside

Mary. Her only advocate, her only protector, he stayed close as the stones fell from the fists of the executioners one by one. I was certain, as the crowd drifted away, that Jesus would have died there with her, defending her, rather than allow her to be harmed.

I stayed close enough to hear. All of them walked away. Only Jesus and Mary remained. Then he stood. His shadow fell over her.

Standing beside her, Jesus asked gently, "Where are they? Does no man condemn you?"

"No man ... Lord," she said, amazed. Ashamed before him, she bowed her head and her tears fell into the dust where he had written.

Jesus waited a moment longer. Then he stretched out his hand to help her stand. "Neither do I condemn you. Now go, and don't sin anymore."[1]

He did not need her to reply. Her ordeal was over. Jesus turned to go. She started to follow him, but then my sister raised her eyes and saw me standing there.

I did not approach her. We gazed at one another over a gulf. Her shame was great, but his forgiveness was greater.

She wiped her cheek with the back of her hand. I saw her lips move. "Forgive me."

I mouthed, "Mary, come home."

She did not reply but turned away, following after Jesus.

I did not pursue her.

At that instant, sudden lightning split the sky in the east. A raindrop struck my cheek. And then the rain began to fall in earnest. I saw my sister Mary holding out her hands, receiving it as if it were a blessing, a cleansing.

Chapter 12

*I*t was Patrick, my barrelmaker, who suggested I again go hear John the Baptizer speak.

Samson and I were in my wine caverns, tasting from the barrels of the latest vintage. He and I sampled the wine from Faithful Vineyard on the first day of every week. The oak had contributed much to the flavor and aroma of the new wine, but there would come a time when I needed to move the contents to clay jars. I did not want to let even an extra Sabbath pass untested, lest perfection be lost.

Since the barrels were his creation, Patrick was equally interested in following the progress of the wine.

As Samson drew out a sample from yet another barrel, I remarked, "I met Nicodemus the Pharisee at the Street of the Coppersmiths yesterday."

"A good customer and a worthy gentleman, if I may say so, sir," my winemaker suggested. "Not at all like most Pharisees, if you'll excuse my bluntness."

Patrick chuckled as he sipped a mouthful of wine.

"Will he be ordering his usual allotment?" Samson continued.

"I let him sample this," I returned, then paused.

"And?" Samson and Patrick simultaneously urged, though Samson added, "If you please, sir."

"Double last year's purchase!" I concluded triumphantly. "A great success."

"Congratulations, sir," Samson praised.

"Congratulations, indeed, but it goes to you and Patrick here. In fact, the only question remaining is how soon we will run out."

"Very true, sir," Samson concurred. "Especially after Lord Nicodemus lets his friends try it as well. I believe he is among the leaders in Jerusalem, isn't he?"

"A member of the Sanhedrin," I replied. "You are right that he is around the most wealthy and powerful men in the Holy City." I rubbed my forehead as I reconstructed the conversation. "In fact, I just remembered something he said that I wish I knew more about."

Samson and Patrick waited patiently for me to continue, as it would be impolite to ask the master to share his thoughts unless he volunteered them.

"Now I recall: it's said there is a rift between the Baptizer and Jesus of Nazareth. Some other Pharisees say John is envious of Jesus' success."

"And do you think that's true?" Patrick inquired.

Samson shushed him, as being out of line, but I waved my hand to show I was not offended by the inquiry. Slowly, thinking aloud, I responded, "Only if John was wrong about who he proclaimed Jesus to be."

"Why not …," Patrick began, then continued over Samson's protests, "why not go hear for yourself?"

And so it was arranged. Patrick accompanied me, while Samson continued to tend the wine.

John was baptizing at Aenon, near Salim, on the east bank of the Jordan. It took us a day to journey there, with me on the white mare and Patrick riding another of Samson's donkeys.

Aenon was a village located on a tributary of the Jordan.

Our route lay along the stream, which chuckled and laughed as it ran down from Mount Ebal. As the water reached the level of the valley floor, the rivulet slowed and spread out, forming a series of pools and ponds, perfect for John's purposes.

"Is the Baptizer safe here?" Patrick inquired.

I considered the matter. "I think so. More importantly, he must think so." Reining to a halt on a knobby hill, I raised my free hand to draw an imaginary half circle from west to east. "We are near the border of four provinces: Galilee and Samaria on this side of the river, Perea and the Decapolis on the other. Over there is Wadi Cherith, where the Lord sent Elijah the prophet to hide from wicked King Ahab."

"So he would be safer over there?"

I shrugged. "But on this bank he is near Salim … ancient Salem … where Melchizedek was both ruler and priest. Even Father Abraham honored the King of Peace and Righteousness."

Shading his eyes against the sun, Patrick said, "I think I see a group of people by that pond, there. And the man standing up to his waist in the water …"

"… is the Baptizer," I confirmed.

His beard and hair wiry and unkempt, he seemed leaner than when I had last seen him.

At opposite ends of the pond, their backs to us, were two knots of men. A handful, dressed much as John was, appeared to be his remaining disciples.

The group at the other extreme was better clad, with colorful robes and clean turbans: Pharisees, by the look of them.

Between the two opposing forces, twenty-five onlookers jostled with each other as they listened to the exchange.

Patrick called my attention to a figure at the edge of the audience. "Isn't that Master Porthos?"

It was the Greek, listening attentively to the dialogue.

"Where are your crowds now?" one of the Pharisees taunted. "The whole world is running after the Nazarene. What do you say to that?"

I could not imagine that rich men would come into this wilderness merely to mock someone they despised. What was their motive?

Another jibed, "He keeps company with tax collectors and drunkards and all manner of sinners. What do you say to that?"

"I say that you are a brood of vipers," John snapped back at them. "Who warned you to flee from the wrath to come? I tell you, he is already separating the wheat from the chaff." Leveling a bony index finger, John shook it in their faces. "Soon enough the chaff will be heaped up and burned!"

The Pharisee jeered, "Where have the rest of your own disciples gone? Maybe they prefer wine and feasting to eating locusts and drinking cold water!"

I was surprised that John's reply, though forcefully stated, was not shouted in anger. Shaking his head firmly, he responded: "He must increase, while I must decrease."

"And what about Herod Antipas?" another man in a brocade robe shouted.

Now John threw his head back and the old fire roared to life in his response: "That snake? The tetrarch knows full well all the sins he is guilty of! Does he merely add adultery to murder, or is it the other way around? The sword of judgment hangs over his head as surely as it fell on King Ahab of old and his Jezebel!"

What happened next was sudden and violent, and the reason for the taunting became clear. In the crowd were a half dozen Herodian soldiers, their uniforms hidden beneath nondescript robes.

As John was goaded into his rash comments, they threw off their disguises. Three of them rushed at the prophet in a body. Another three drew short swords and flung themselves at the crowd.

The audience and John's followers scattered ... except for Porthos. The Grecian Jew stood his ground, even as a stocky mercenary bore down on him, stabbing blade lifted high and glinting in the sunlight.

Then Porthos did the bravest thing I had ever seen: he ran toward the soldier, ducking beneath the descending dagger so that it missed his shoulder by a whisker.

Seizing the Herodian guard with both hands, he lifted the man fully off the ground and flung him into the other pair of attackers. They tumbled together in a heap of short swords and curses.

Still Porthos did not flee. Instead, he roared at the men surrounding the Baptizer and charged them as well.

The latter trio had not even drawn their weapons, believing no one would resist them. Startled by Porthos's sudden onslaught, one tripped on a rock in the pond and disappeared beneath the surface in unwilling submission to the Baptizer's message.

With Patrick at my side, I darted forward. The three guardsmen overthrown by Porthos blocked our intervention with whirling blades. "Back off," one of them snarled.

Porthos managed to land a fist on the jaw of one of the soldiers, then stopped fighting suddenly when the captain of the squad put the point of his dagger against the Baptizer's throat. "Stop now, or he dies," the man bellowed.

Porthos dropped his clenched fists and stood helplessly, shaking with barely suppressed rage.

That was the moment when the soldier who had been ducked in the pool emerged sputtering … and stabbed Porthos in the back. The Greek dropped face forward into the water and lay unmoving.

Two of Herod's assassins kept us at bay while the rest quickly bound John's arms behind his back. Dragging him bodily out of the creek, they soon disappeared in the direction of Aenon.

Even before they were out of sight, Patrick and I hauled Porthos, streaming blood from a gash in his back, out of the stream. We laid him on a mossy bank and turned him over. As the sunlight hit his face, he coughed weakly and his eyelids fluttered. He was not dead, then!

Patting his face, I said, "Porthos, brother, I'll get you some help. Don't worry."

His eyes opened, and he struggled to focus on my features. "Ah, David," he said, then was racked by a cough that brought scarlet foam to his lips. "Did you think … you had to repay me? I told you … I'm not … not a brave …"

And he died.

We located Pleasant the donkey tied in a grove of trees near what had been the Baptizer's camp. I used her to take Porthos's body home with me and buried him in my family cemetery, near the tomb that held my wife and child.

Chapter 13

Mary had traveled back to Galilee, transformed. With many other women, including Joanna, the wife of Herod's steward, Mary became a devoted follower and supporter of Jesus.

I was still unsure about the motives and true identity of Jesus. I wanted to know, yet I suspected him.

After Hanukkah the winter months were dark and cold and the vines dormant. This was the time of pruning. I set my workers to the task of cutting off the dead branches, gathering the dead wood, and torching the piles at the ends of the rows. Unless the dead wood was cut back, new growth would be stunted, struggling to compete with the tangle of old growth.

I was supervising in the field when Martha and the women servants came out to feed the laborers.

Martha's cheeks were ruddy with the cold. Her breath rose in steam as she puffed up the path toward me. "Brother!" she hailed me, but when she came near, she lowered her voice. "There's a rumor … about our sister Mary."

I imagined that, in spite of Jesus' admonition not to sin again, Mary had already fallen and was back to her old ways. "Well?"

"Madness," Martha whispered. "If it's not one thing, it's another."

The aroma of stew was in the air. I was hungry and impatient, but I knew Martha had to tell me everything. "So are you surprised?"

"I am surprised. She was such a greedy little thing. Spending money on herself and no one else. But this!"

"Get on with it, Martha!"

"She's squandering her dead husband's fortune! That's what. Squandering! Spending her money on feeding the poor. Opened her villa to house women—*unmarried women*—and their infants. A one-woman charity house! That's what she is!" Martha reported the news with such disgust that it took me a moment to understand exactly what she was saying.

"This can't be … our Mary." I accepted a bowl of steaming food.

"We've got to put a stop to it. She's gone crazy. One extreme is as bad as the other. Extreme, I say! She will spend all her inheritance and then …" Martha's mouth turned downward. "Then she will come home begging. As much a beggar as the people she cares for today. And we will have to care for her!"

Spoon poised between the bowl and my mouth, I considered Martha's report for a moment. "Yes," I agreed. "Without a man to advise and direct her …"

It seemed to me, Mary's generosity to the needy had become careless and profligate. She had no kinsman but me to bring order back into her life.

Shortly thereafter, I left the care of my vineyards in the hands of Samson. Martha and I, with our friend Nicodemus, made the journey to Galilee to question Mary face-to-face about the business affairs of her estate.

Pruning had only begun in her vineyards. Observing the swarms of workmen in the fields, I noted that Mary employed too many for the task. I made a note of this as we rode to the wide-open gates of Mary's villa. In the courtyard beyond, children squealed and played while their mothers boiled laundry in great kettles scattered about the luxurious grounds.

A lanky, red-haired teenage boy named Carta kept us from entering. "Halt here, sir. Women only permitted to pass, except by permission of the Lady."

"I am brother to widow Mary of Magdala, mistress of this estate."

"How can I know who you are, sir? Too many angry brutes, husbands of the unfortunates, come prowling for a way to get their women back. They want to make them servants again to wickedness and beat them upon a drunken whim."

Martha drew herself up in protest. "My brother is none of those things. I am Martha, sister of Mary. And this is our friend, Nicodemus. We have traveled far, from Bethany, and you will tell my sister that her kinfolk have come. And that we are weary and expect at least the hospitality she shows to these ... these ... this ... mob!"

"In that case, wait here. It's wash day, and the mistress is somewhere about the grounds. It will take a moment." Carta bobbed his head and sprinted away. Some minutes passed before he came again to the entry. "Names?" he demanded.

I replied, "David ben Lazarus. Martha. And Nicodemus."

"Correct. You may enter." Carta stepped aside and swept his hand toward clotheslines and flapping linens.

We entered. Martha's face became more sour. Nicodemus seemed amused. I was amazed at the clutter and noise that had overcome my sister's once elegant grounds.

We waited in the private courtyard of the house beside a fountain. Children played tag just beyond the door, but the place was clearly off limits.

Only a minute passed before Mary appeared at the doorway. Dressed for work in a coarse, pale blue dress, her thick dark hair was piled on her head. Brown eyes were shining as she stretched out her arms to welcome us.

"Brother! And Martha! Oh! And you ... Nicodemus! To see you all here! It is an answer to my prayer."

My embrace was reserved, but she held me tighter and laughed. Her welcome was as warm for Martha, though the two women had never been on good terms. If she noticed our hesitation, she did not comment on it.

Leading us into her private quarters, she summoned servants to care for us and ordered food for us.

Throughout the lavish meal, Mary talked joyfully about Jesus, whom she called Rabboni, and the women and children who had taken refuge in her home. "Carta was a servant to Marcus Longinus. Jesus healed him from a terrible injury. Now he's helping me here." There were 136 souls living within the walls of Mary's villa. Some women escaped abuse from husbands. Others had been prostitutes who had repented, turned to God, and become followers of Jesus. They had no place of refuge but this. Three new babies had been born in the last two weeks. Most important in Mary's narrative was the news that, from time to time, Jesus of Nazareth and his disciples lodged in Mary's guest house.

She radiated joy as she spoke of all this. I thought she had never looked so beautiful.

"But why have you come?" she asked at last.

Martha blurted, "We have heard that you are wasting all

your estate. Spending your wealth like water! You never could do anything with moderation."

Mary gazed at Martha for a long moment. Her smile wavered. "Ah. I thought ... I was hoping ..."

Nicodemus blushed at the confrontation. He stood and escaped to the veranda.

I tried to explain gently to Mary. "You see, sister, we are concerned that perhaps you are being taken advantage of. Giving everything ... everything to others."

She studied me. "Brother, for the first time in my life I am happy. Jesus teaches ..."

Martha scoffed. "Jesus! Yes. All or nothing. That's the problem. No moderation."

I asked, "But what about the inheritance that your husband left to you? Your estates? I see you've hired an army of workers to prune your vines. Half the number would do."

"Yes. But then half the number would be unemployed. These are hard times, brother. Hunger is at the door here in the Galil. Men and women need work."

"But what if all you have is gone and the coffer empty because you did not manage wisely? It makes no sense, Mary. If you give all to the poor, then soon you will number yourself among the poor of Israel."

Mary answered. "I am rich. My orchards and vineyards are blessed. There is plenty to share, brother."

I explained, "But if you are careless with giving away what you own, no matter what your rabbi teaches ... a good man, yes. But impractical."

Mary did not attempt to answer my charge but simply replied, "Come, brother. Come and meet the Lord."

She took my arm and led me out of her villa. To the east our view was the Sea of Galilee. It was calm and flat and reflected the enormous clouds that loomed on the horizon. To the west was Mary's vast vineyard. Workers moved methodically through the rows, pruning wild, leafless canes down to the trunk of the vine.

Mary gestured beyond them. "There he is."

I recognized him at once. Jesus and about twenty of his disciples sat beneath a large tree at the top of a hill overlooking the vineyard.

Mary led the way up the path. Nicodemus joined us. I followed, and Martha trailed behind.

At our approach, Jesus raised his eyes, then waved a welcome, looking directly at me.

"*Shalom*, Mary." Jesus gestured for us to join the lesson.

"Rabboni! These are my brother, Lazarus, my sister, Martha, and Lord Nicodemus of Jerusalem. They've come visiting."

"*Shalom* and welcome," Jesus said. "We are enjoying the day. Will you join us?"

We came into the semicircle of rough-looking Galileans who made up the core of Jesus' followers. I was between Mary and the disciple called Peter. We three were directly in front of Jesus, close enough to touch the hem of his cloak. An easy grin with straight white teeth. Square jaw. Hands calloused from years of manual labor.

He asked me, "What do you think of all your sister has accomplished in her vineyard?"

"My sister has hired too many laborers. She needs an adviser to help her manage her business."

Jesus smiled. "Mary gives everything into the care of her Father. Can she trust him?" He held me in his gaze for an instant, long enough for me to know that the lesson I was about to hear concerned me, somehow.

"What do you think?" Jesus asked me. "There was a man who had two sons. He came to the first and said, 'Son, go and work today in the vineyard.' And the son answered, 'I will not.' But afterward he changed his mind and went. Then the father went to the other son and said the same thing. And the second son replied, 'I will, sir,' but he did not go. Which of the two did the will of the father?"[1]

Peter raised his hand and blurted out the answer, "The first son! That's the one!"

Jesus smiled and again cast his eyes on Mary. "That's right. The one who does the will of his father ... or in this case ... the will of her father."

My smile froze on my face.

He gave me a look that gently warned me I was about to learn something. Then he directed his attention to the crew of laborers in the field. "Truly, I tell you, the tax collectors and harlots will get into the Kingdom of Heaven before the hypocrites." He paused. "I saw you by the Jordan the day you came to hear John preach. Our friend John came walking in the way of an upright man in right standing with God, and they did not believe him. But tax collectors and harlots did believe him. And the religious hypocrites, even when they saw that, did not afterward change their minds and believe John's call to repentance."[2]

I felt color climb to my cheeks. Just that quickly I had become the subject of a lesson. And just that quickly I had been humbled.

Jesus asked me, "I saw you then at the wedding at Cana."

I nodded. "The wine. I never tasted anything so rich. So full of character. I've wanted to ask you how ... from what vines? What soil? I've pondered the wine I tasted that night and have never come up with a logical answer."

Jesus replied, "Mary tells me you own vineyards near Jerusalem."

"I do. Not so many acres as Mary."

"Have you finished your pruning?" he asked.

"The work of pruning is never really finished. To come here I left the care of my vineyard in the good hands of my vinedresser. He will do the job."

Jesus nodded. "We're mostly fishermen here … and one carpenter," he added in an aside that made several chuckle. "We have no real knowledge of grapes and vineyards, or how the grapes become good wine or … bad wine. Teach us. And why must vines be pruned, my friend?"

I considered his question. Surely there was a trap set for me. "First, the dead canes must be cut off in this season when the vine is sleeping. This season … you see the workers there … the pruning is severe. Down to the trunk of the vine. Dead canes will not bear fruit and so must be cut off first. In another month or so, depending on the weather, there will be bud break. The vine will produce new, healthy shoots. New growth will bear fruit."

Jesus asked, as though he did not know, "Is the job of the vinedresser finished when he cuts away these dead branches?"

"Well … no. Through the growing season, we train the branches. Set them in the best position to expose fruit to the sun. Thin the leaves that block the sun from the berries; break off clusters that will never ripen evenly. They only steal the life of the vine from the good clusters. The vinedresser cuts away excess foliage to concentrate the life of the vine into the best berries that will make the finest quality wine. The vine can't nourish the new growth properly … the quality of the grapes is not as good … if the vine must also support the weight of dead wood or wild tendrils that don't bear fruit or only produce showy foliage. So, to answer your question, pruning goes on all through the life of the vine."

"Exactly." Jesus nodded and leaned forward to gaze directly into my eyes. More than that, he looked into my heart.

Then he spoke to us all: "I am the true vine, and my Father is the vinedresser. Any branch that doesn't bear fruit, he cuts away. And he cleanses and repeatedly prunes every branch that continues to bear fruit, to make it bear more and richer and more excellent fruit. Just as no branch can bear fruit of itself without abiding in the vine, neither can you bear fruit unless you abide in me. I am the Vine; you are the branches. Whoever lives in me and I in him bears only the best fruit. However, if you are cut off from me, you can do nothing. If a person doesn't dwell in me, he is thrown out like a broken-off branch. He withers, and such branches are gathered up and thrown into the fire and burned." He gestured to a tribe of little boys gathering the broken sticks and heaping them into a pile for burning.

Jesus continued, "If you live in me, abide vitally united with my life, and my words remain in your hearts, ask whatever you will and it shall be done for you. When you bear much fruit, my Father is honored and glorified, and you show and prove yourselves to be true followers of mine."[3]

From that time, though I doubted at first, I came to admire and love Jesus of Nazareth. And I knew he loved me. He connected my heart to his. Like the morning of bud break, when the first new green foliage breaks forth from the vine, I was far from bearing fruit. My faith was small, about the size of my thumbnail, like the tiny clusters in early spring. All the promise of fullness and quality exists within the cluster from its beginning. But everything depends on the branch remaining united to the nourishment of the vine. I could not say if I would be among the few who matured to the full richness of life in Jesus. Yet I clung to every word he spoke. I was thirsty for his truth, drinking it in.

My understanding of who Jesus was became clearer as the weeks passed. The light of his life among us was like sun shining on the new berries. His teachings were the water, nourishing thirsty clusters, making my faith grow and ripen.

I came to understand why Jesus, the True Vine, turned plain water into the most extraordinary wine that has ever been made. As a vineyard owner and winemaker, I could comprehend the powerful significance of Jesus' first miracle at the wedding in Cana. In the wine that Jesus created, I had tasted for myself the glory of what a life could become if it remained connected to the True Vine.

Later I witnessed with my own eyes the miracles, signs, and wonders that are written about by many others. Lepers healed. The lame dancing. Deaf mutes singing. The blind rejoicing in the sunrise and counting the stars. The greatest miracle of all was the day the twelve-year-old daughter of Jairus of Capernaum died. Jesus, with a word, raised the little girl from the dead and returned her to her joyful parents.

I once heard Jesus ask before he cured a paralyzed man, "Is it easier to say, 'Your sins are forgiven,' or 'Rise up and walk'?"

My heart echoed the question as I looked at the crippled man on the mat before Jesus and listened to the Pharisees object to forgiveness. I said to myself, "How very difficult it is to say to anyone, your sins are forgiven. Go and sin no more. Jesus must prune away the dead wood, the showy green leaves that produce nothing. He must break off the excess, expose the fruit to the light!"

I remembered how Jesus stooped in the dust beside my sister

on the day of her condemnation. Jesus had no sin in his life, yet the men who condemned my sister also condemned Jesus for his righteousness. He had placed himself in danger to save her from the consequences of her sin. And after all the stones had dropped from angry fists and Mary's accusers had slunk away, Jesus told her she was forgiven, not condemned. The only Son of God had bridged the gap between the penalty of the law and the true love and mercy of the heavenly Father. Forgiveness! Bud break! Jesus called it being "born again"!

The great miracle for me was the reconciliation and restoration of Mary to me and to my sister Martha. I asked Mary's forgiveness for my sins of omission. I had not loved her. Had not forgiven her. Had not protected her. I had rejected her utterly in my own self-righteousness. Yet my righteousness had been nothing but showy green foliage that blocked the sun and was incapable of bearing fruit.

When at last we embraced and all things were made new by love, Mary's eyes were clear and bright. Her words were without fear and bitterness when she spoke to me and Martha.

The healing of a broken heart, I thought, was very much like raising someone from the dead. Jesus summed it all up for me in the parable of the pruning: "I am the True Vine and my Father is the Vinedresser."

It is enough to say the accounts of miracles are all true, and I bore witness to them. It is enough to know that I, like many thousands of others, believed that Jesus of Nazareth was indeed the long-awaited Messiah, Son of David, King of Israel.

But the vast numbers did not follow Jesus because of his teaching about the Kingdom of God. They waited and watched as he made a blind man see or cured a rotting leper of disease. Yes, they were entertained and amazed by such happenings. But most of the mob followed Jesus for a different reason—they wanted bread.

The last miracle I witnessed in Galilee was just before a Passover. Jesus and his inner core of disciples had withdrawn to the wilderness for a time.

Would he come to Jerusalem for the holy days? No one knew for certain.

Mary had decided she would come home with us to Bethany. Martha and I set out ahead of Mary. We determined we would wait at an inn, and Mary would join us after she conferred with Centurion Marcus Longinus.

This centurion was a God-fearer. He now also believed in Jesus. Marcus told Mary that he was taking a Roman official to hear Jesus teach, knowing that Jesus only spoke to the people of peace. He promised Mary he would dedicate his life to warning Jesus of the plots hatched against him and help protect him from opposition.

After Mary parted from the centurion, she and her servants joined us at the inn for the journey to Bethany. We heard from a group of travelers that Jesus was teaching and healing nearby. I longed to hear the message of hope he would preach to those who were making pilgrimage to Jerusalem. I sent Mary and Martha ahead to Bethany with the servants.

The same morning at sunrise, I joined throngs of pilgrims flowing like a river uphill through Galilee—thousands followed thousands seeking Jesus. I walked quickly, passing carts laden with sick and crippled people. The story of Jairus's daughter was passed from group to group.

"Jesus is near Capernaum!"

"No, he is closer to Tiberias!"

"What if he's already gone to Jerusalem for Passover?"

"No! He won't go now. The Herodians and the Pharisees want him dead."

Zealots and rebels traveled with us. These men had dreams of crowning Jesus king of the Jews and rousing the multitude to arm themselves and fight for our freedom. I had heard enough of Jesus' teaching by then to be sure that he was not interested in supplanting Herod Antipas. Jesus had said many times, "My kingdom is not of this world."

None of us knew exactly what Jesus meant. Where exactly was his kingdom if not here on earth? Our existence was only in this world. Like everyone who followed him, I longed for Jesus to declare himself king in Jerusalem and restore Israel to the glory of Solomon. It was clear that the political leaders feared him. Soldiers and Temple officials walked the same road as we did, only for different reasons. I wondered who was at the front of our procession and if, indeed, anyone really knew where Jesus was.

If Jesus was from a different world, how could we be citizens of his kingdom? How could Jesus call on us to fight for a kingdom not of this world?

I was too far back to approach Jesus, but I heard his voice as I came to the edge of the great gathering. "What's the Kingdom of God like? It's like a mustard seed, which a man took and planted in his garden. It grew and became a tree, and the birds of the air perched in its branches."

Wildflowers and new grass were trampled on either side of the highway. I climbed the hill overlooking the natural amphitheater. The site was remote, an equal distance between Capernaum and Bethsaida. I guessed that the swale was carpeted with about twenty-five thousand men, women, and children. I reckoned there were at least five thousand civilian males of military age. More were gathered here in this wilderness than the population of any Judean city except for Jerusalem and Caesarea. Clearly the mustard seed had bloomed and grown into a tree. And the Kingdom tree was filled with flocks of birds.

Jesus' deep voice echoed in the hollow and reached the ears of all. "A certain man was preparing a great banquet for his friends. At the time of the banquet he sent his servant to tell those who had been invited, 'Come on. Everything is ready!' But they all made excuses ...

"Then the owner of the house became angry and ordered his servant: 'Go out into the streets and alleys in the town and bring in the poor, the crippled, the blind and the lame.' The servant replied, 'Sir, what you have ordered has been done, but there is still room.'

"Then the master told the servant, 'Go out to the roads and country lanes and make them come in, so my house will be full. I tell you, not one of those men who were invited will get a taste of my banquet.'"[4]

Though my countrymen were untrained in the art of war, I was also aware that our citizens vastly outnumbered the foreign troops who occupied our land. There were, in all, only about three thousand Roman legionaries in the entire territory. Their leaders were only men. With Jesus at the head of our army, certainly Pilate and Herod and Caiaphas knew we could over-whelm them.

I was certain our overlords considered Jesus' popularity as dangerous. It was nearly noon, and the hungry pilgrims were stirring when I spotted Marcus Longinus and a Roman tribune.

Both men were listening intently to the teaching of Jesus. The tribune's expression was grim as he surveyed the pilgrims. Perhaps it occurred to him that a Roman tribune would be among the first to die if this crowd rioted.

There was no place close enough to buy bread for such a mob. Jesus' disciples approached him. I could not hear the discussion, but suddenly a command was given.

"Sit down! Sit down! Groups of fifty and one hundred! Sit down!"

"But where's our food?"

"What will we eat?"

"There's nothing to feed our children!"

A small boy in a striped tunic was brought forward to Jesus. The child offered his meager bundle of food: five loaves and two fish. Jesus placed his hand on the boy's head and thanked him. Then he held up a pitiful barley loaf and broke it, raising his voice in a *b'rakhah*: "Blessed are you, O Lord, King of the universe, who gives us bread from the earth!"

The boy's loaves and fishes became a banquet. Jesus broke one loaf, and always there was more in his hands. As one lights a single candle and the flame is spread to others, so the five loaves in the hands of Jesus multiplied to fifty and five hundred and five thousand, spreading across the field.

I received my ration within minutes. The bread was warm and fragrant, as though it had just come from the oven. I tasted. Like the wine at the wedding, the taste of the bread Jesus provided was beyond comparison.

It was the final proof of Jesus' identity. The prophet Moses fed our ancestors in the wilderness for forty years, and here Jesus was doing the same. There was enough for everyone. From so little, there was so much remaining that twelve disciples with baskets were sent out to gather the excess. The baskets returned to Jesus, filled to the brim and overflowing with bread.

At the base of the hill, people began to chant, "Hail, Jesus! Our King!"

Others joined in until the mountains rang with the shouts that Jesus must be crowned.

I finished my meal and turned to go, hoping like the rest that Jesus would enter Jerusalem at the head of an army.

I made my way toward Jesus through the thousands. Some clutched remnants of bread. In every circle I heard voices exclaim:

"There is no doubt he is the prophet we have been waiting for!"

"This Jesus can feed us as Moses gave bread to our fathers in the wilderness!"

"We will never go hungry again."

"Declare him King! The Romans and Herod have no power over such a man!"

"Isn't it written in Torah?"

"Moses said plainly, 'The Lord your God will raise up for you a prophet from the midst of your brethren like me! To him you shall listen!'"

"Moses fed our fathers bread for forty years in the wilderness! Now Jesus will do the same!"

By the time I reached the knoll of the hill where Jesus had been teaching, the Lord had slipped away. I asked Peter, "Where did the Lord go?"

Peter stood beside the heaping baskets. "Gone. Off by himself. He knows they meant to seize him and crown him by force. He won't have it, so now he's gone."

The pilgrims dispersed and drifted away when they saw the Lord had gone. I stayed with the Twelve until evening. We waited until dark, and still Jesus did not return.

"Come on," Peter said to us. "My boat's there, on the shore. Let's sail home to Capernaum. There are the lights of the village across the water. An easy trip."

I believed that men who made their living fishing at night could easily navigate our craft across the lake. I followed the fishermen and climbed into Peter's boat.

I sat in the bow silently contemplating Moses' prophecy about the coming Messiah. Today's miracle of feeding the thousands was confirmation that Jesus was the Deliverer promised to Israel in ages past. I felt the first stirring of the wind. The sea slapped against the boat. My stomach began to churn with the rocking.

"Take down the sail!" Peter ordered. "The wind will tear it to shreds!"

Two others helped him lower the sail. I was violently seasick, vomiting over the side. I thought we might die. I was sick enough that I would not have minded being put out of my misery. Matthew, a former tax collector with a fear of the sea, crawled toward me. Side by side, we retched into the water.

"Row harder!" James shouted as the gale increased.

Peter, James, John, and Philip leaned their backs into the oars, but we were tossed like a toy on the violent waves.

Four miles out I scanned the horizon, hoping to see some friendly light close to shore. A wave splashed my face. Judas raised his head and shouted in terror!

Were we about to capsize?

"Look! Look!"

"It's a ghost!"

BODIE & BROCK THOENE

"God have mercy!"

"A spirit has come to take us away!"

I squinted at the moonlit surface of the roiling water. There, before our eyes, an apparition like a man walked toward us.

I opened my mouth to cry out like the others.

Then the familiar voice of Jesus shouted out to us, "It is I! Don't be afraid!"

Not a vision! Not an apparition! Not an evil spirit come to drown us! No! It was the Lord himself, walking on the troubled seas that threatened us.

"It's Jesus!"

"Jesus on the water!"

"Lord! Save us!"

Jesus approached the vessel at the bow. I reached out my hands and helped him into the boat. He sat down calmly between me and Matthew. The sea grew still as we blinked at him in astonishment. We were afraid to speak. Peter and the others silently set to the oars again.

Within moments we came to shore. The wind had fallen away. The moon reflected on the silver surface of the sea.

I remember someone drawing the boat onto the sand. Exhausted from terror and exertion, we fell asleep.

Chapter 14

*T*he next morning Jesus was up before us all. A fire was crackling not far from the boat. There was fish, roasting on sticks, and warm bread heaped on a stone as we staggered out of the boat.

Boatloads of people began to arrive from Tiberias and across the Sea of Galilee as word got out that Jesus was on the far shore. Others, by the hundreds, came on foot.

Commoners, paid by Temple officials and assigned the task of spying on Jesus, started to question him.

"Rabbi, there was only one boat on the shore, and you did not leave with your disciples. How did you get here?"

All of us who had been on the boat the night before knew the truth of what had happened. We were witnesses that not even a troubled sea could stop Jesus from traveling with us. But we did not speak. We did not dare ask, "How?"

Nor did Jesus answer their question. "There's no doubt that you came looking for me, not because you witnessed many signs, but because you ate the bread and were filled. Don't labor for the food that perishes, but for the food that endures to everlasting life. The Son of Man will give this freely to you, because God the Father has set his seal upon him."

Then they asked, "What shall we do, that we may work the works of God?"

Jesus did not hesitate. "This is the work of God, that you believe in him whom he sent."

There was a stirring of resentment. I felt it, like the first breeze over the water before the great storm last night.

"What sign will you perform?"

"We want to see a sign so we can believe you."

"What work will you do?"

A Pharisee chimed in: "Our fathers ate the manna in the desert. It's written, 'He gave them bread from heaven to eat.' "

Jesus fixed his gaze on that man, who should have known the full meaning of the words written in Torah. "I tell you, Moses didn't give you bread from heaven. But my Father gives you the true bread from heaven. For the bread of God is he who comes down from heaven and gives life to the world."

I knew Jesus was speaking of himself. He was the bread sent down from heaven; Jesus was the bread that gave us life on our journey.

They believed he was speaking of the miracle of multiplying physical bread. "Lord! Give us this bread always!"

Then Jesus stated flatly, "I am the bread of life. He who comes to me will never hunger. He who believes in me will never thirst. You've seen me ... and yet you don't believe. Everyone the Father gives me will come to me. And the one who comes to me I will never cast out. I've come down from heaven, not to do my own will, but the will of him who sent me. Of everyone the Father has given me, I won't lose even one. I will raise them up on the last day."

The questioners began to mutter among themselves, "Who does he think he is? How does he know God's will?"

"He will raise us up from death on the last day?"

"Who does he think he is?"

Jesus replied, "This is the will of my Father ... that everyone who sees me and believes in me may have everlasting life. I will raise him up on the last day."

The seas of opinion begin to stir. The Pharisees mocked him, and the mocking spread among the crowd.

"Isn't this Jesus, the son of Joseph, whose father and mother we know?"

"He says he is the bread that comes from heaven!"

"Son of Joseph ..."

"How can he tell us that he comes down from heaven?"

Jesus let the storm of opposition build and then answered. "No one can come to me unless the Father who sent me draws him."

I noticed that Jesus was making a particular point when he said for the third time, "And I will raise him up on the last day."

I pondered his words. Surely Jesus was speaking of the resurrection of those who had died. Yes, I had witnessed the return to life of Jairus's daughter, but she had not been dead long. She had not been laid in a tomb to decay. How could Jesus raise to life those who were long dead and decayed?

Jesus continued, "It's written in the Prophets, 'And they shall all be taught by God.' That means that everyone who has heard and learned from the Father comes to me. Only I have seen the Father. This is truth ... anyone who believes in me has everlasting life."

A gasp went up at Jesus' claim that he had seen the Father. Everyone understood the significance of this claim. God the Father was surrounded by a thick cloud called the Cloud of Unknowing. To enter it meant instant annihilation. Only the Angel of the Lord came and went from that cloud—doing the will of God the Father, speaking only the Word of God the Father. Jesus had just told us all that he was the Angel of the Lord … the visible manifestation of the Almighty. Jesus was the one who dwelt within the Cloud of Unknowing and came out to proclaim the Word of the Almighty. There was no mistaking that Jesus clearly told us that he *was the Word*, the tangible expression of the Word of God. Jesus was the only knowable form of a God so powerful that none in heaven or earth had ever seen him. I believed the miracles of Jesus bore witness to this. How could mere man do the things Jesus did?

I heard them whisper, "Blasphemy!"

Jesus heard it too, but he did not draw back. Instead, he brought the lesson full circle: "I am the bread of life. Your fathers ate the manna in the wilderness, and they're long dead … I am the living bread which, like manna, came down from heaven. If anyone eats this bread, he'll live forever. The bread that I give is my body. I give it for the life of the world."

The storm of the onlookers increased to violent fury. "How can this man give us his flesh to eat?"

Jesus set the keel of truth deep and sailed on into the storm. "Unless you partake of the body of the Messiah and drink the wine of his blood, you have no life in you. Whoever eats my flesh and drinks my blood has eternal life, and I will raise him up on the last day. For my body is bread from heaven and my blood is wine from heaven …"

A shudder and a howling gale increased among his accusers at his words.

He taught us that life-giving manna provided in the wilderness had come directly from God. A heaven-sent meal giving life to those who partook. Now Jesus had also fed miraculous bread to a multitude.

In a glimmer of recognition, I remembered again the wine at the wedding; extraordinary wine created by Jesus. He called himself the "True Vine." Like the bread, the miraculous wine that had been offered to us had flowed out from heaven through Jesus.

Jesus nodded at me, acknowledging that I was beginning to understand. "He who eats my flesh and drinks my blood abides in me and I in him. As the living Father sent me, and I live because of the Father, so he who feeds on me will live because of me. This is the bread that came down from heaven—not as your fathers ate manna and are dead. He who eats this bread will live forever."

Many of his followers deserted him that day. I watched them leave, shaking their heads. I remained with the Twelve and a handful of others.

We walked along the shore of Capernaum. "Does this offend you?" Jesus smiled sadly at our inability to grasp the significance of his teaching. "What if you see me ascend where I was before?" He summed up the lesson. "It's the Spirit who gives life to the flesh, not the other way around. The words I speak to you are spirit, and they are life. But there are some among you who don't believe."

I thought I saw a glance at Judas, who walked to the side, almost by himself. I wondered if Judas would leave Jesus as many others had done.

Jesus asked us, "Do you want to go away too?"

Peter answered for those of us who remained, "Lord, who would we go to? You have the words of eternal life. Also, we've come to believe ... we know ... that you are the Messiah, Son of the Living God."

Jesus walked on a few steps and remarked quietly, "Didn't I choose you, the Twelve, and one of you is a devil?"[1]

I did not know then who he was talking about, but a cold chill passed through my heart. How could any one of us close to Jesus still not believe in him?

The season of Passover was upon us. Jesus told us that he would not be going to Jerusalem. He instructed us to go ahead of him. I left Galilee for home.

Chapter 15

*T*he season from Passover to Pentecost, the giving of the Law on Sinai, extended for forty-nine days, and was called Counting the Omer. Each day as the season progressed, tradition called us to count the passage of days and recite this blessing: "Praised are you, Lord our God, Ruler of the universe who has sanctified us with his commandments, commanding us to count the Omer."

Jesus returned from Galilee to stay at my house right before Pentecost. It had been about a year since Eliza and the baby had died. The vines were in full leaf and very beautiful, and I missed her more than ever. Perhaps the Lord knew that my grief was almost a sickness.

After supper Jesus said to me, "Come on. Let's go walk in your vineyard."

We set out together through the cool, broad leaves on the vines of Faithful Vineyard. The clusters of fruit were just beginning to set.

I was silent, lost in my own thoughts. Eliza had walked with me on this day of the Omer last year.

Jesus looked at the sun about to set in the west. "All your vines are planted running east to west. Tell me why."

"The sun rises in the east and sets in the west. An arch

overhead. As it passes over the vines, the grapes on each side are exposed equally to the sun through the day. Otherwise one side would only receive morning light and the other would be scorched every afternoon."

Jesus touched a wild leafy tendril that shaded a bunch of berries. "What about this? No fruit on it. And doesn't it keep sun from the cluster?"

I stepped into my role as vinedresser. It was good to be able to teach Jesus something he was unfamiliar with. "Good observation. You would do well in my vineyard." I reached out and broke off the leafy branch.

Jesus smiled, "All show without substance, and it blocks the sun from the fruit, eh?"

"That's it."

He scanned the cloudless sky. "A long time 'til rain. You water the vines one at a time?"

"Grapes are the only crop I know that need to be stressed to enhance flavor. I make my vines work a little harder. When I water, I pour the water just beyond the reach of the roots so they stretch and grow and set themselves deep."

"I thought there would be more fruit on the vines."

"I've thinned some fruit already, you see. Plucked unripe bunches that are set too low and so will never fully ripen. They only hold a promise of a good crop, but in the end they take away from the best. Now the vine is pouring all its lifeblood into the fruit that remains."

Jesus nodded. "A beautiful vineyard, David ben Lazarus. You tend it with wisdom."

I blushed at the compliment from one who seemed to possess the purest wisdom. "I see my workmen were too easy on this row. Too many fruitless branches left to grow without purpose. And to the detriment of good fruit. I'll send my men through a second time to thin the leaves and cut away the canes to expose the fruit. It will go on all through the summer right up to harvest."

Jesus brushed his hand over the foliage. It almost seemed the leaves turned toward him as he passed by. I wondered what extraordinary wine would come from this vineyard because Jesus had walked through it.

I thought for an instant I smelled Eliza's perfume and heard her laughter. Tears sprang to my eyes and trickled down my cheeks.

He asked me, "Lazarus, why do you weep?"

"You know, Lord. My wife. My baby. A year ago. Seems like a day and also like forever."

"You'll see her again, my friend. Do you believe me?"

"Yes, Lord. On the last day, when all are resurrected. But for now, I feel like this leafy branch … cut off. Not much good to anyone. Not even to myself. I don't know why God took her. And our son. I prayed and worshiped, and I offered every sacrifice according to the laws of Moses. But even righteousness could not save the ones I love."

"You question God's will?"

I wiped away my tears. "She's gone. Plainly I can't question that it is God's will to take her. But I question why it should be God's will? Why take from me the thing I hold most dearly in all the world?"

I studied his profile as we walked. Eyes forward, he seemed to see something far away at the end of the row. He asked, "What's your answer?"

"I don't have one. I was hoping you would have an answer."

"When a good man suffers … perhaps it makes his roots reach deeper for the water?"

"I see that. Yes. The metaphor is perfect. The vine is stressed, and the berries grow with more character. But even so, Jesus, I am so alone. I am pruned down to the trunk and ... without my love ... without my friend. Why? What did I do wrong?"

"Through no fault of your own," Jesus concluded.

"Not my fault? Then why has this calamity come upon me? I have been searching for the answer for a year. My sin? What is it?"

"Suffering comes to all men on the earth. It is a fact ... from man's rebellion and separation from the Lord in the Garden. It is written that one day you will see Messiah wipe away every tear—no more suffering and no more death. Meanwhile those who love God are not exempt from pain. But for the righteous man to suffer? Think of it! Only the wise vinedresser knows what will make the best wine. The vine is stressed—it reaches deep for the water, the shoots are pruned, the clusters are thinned, and in the end the fruit is richer and the wine is full of character and grace. Though the growing may be difficult, God will be glorified at the end of every righteous man's story."

I nodded, but the floodgates of my heart were open now and I could not be silent. "There is a young man, a beggar at the Nicanor Gate of the Temple. He's been blind from birth. I heard some of my friends—religious scholars, not farmers like me—they discussed who had sinned to make this boy blind from his birth. They discussed this in his hearing as though blindness also made him deaf. It troubles me, this cheerful boy with his smiling face and his begging bowl. Jesus! I pray you answer my question! What purpose is served in their mocking and his suffering?"

Jesus smiled. "*Shabbat shalom*, my dear friend. Come with me to the Temple tomorrow."

The Mount of Olives was packed with family groups gathered outside the walls of Jerusalem. The road leading past the Pool of Bethesda was jammed with worshipers going up to the Temple. They would celebrate Sabbath worship before returning to their camps to spend the night studying Torah, as was traditional.

The travelers coalesced around Jesus when he was recognized in the throng. "It's him, I tell you," I heard all around. "The rabbi from Nazareth. Let's follow him."

As the multitude pressed in, I was glad I had already mentioned Peniel to Jesus. It was getting harder to move with every step.

There were several locations on the Temple Mount where rabbis and other scholars assembled to instruct their disciples. A columned arcade called Solomon's Portico was one such location. The Temple courts, which contained chambers for wood and spices, and containers to receive offerings, was another.

The building housing the Temple treasury was in the northeast corner of the Court of Women. It was on the top step of the entry to this structure that Jesus sat down to teach. Like waves spreading out from a rock dropped into a pond, concentric rings of onlookers knelt to hear him. The most eager shushed those behind and urged the slower ones in front to sit down so all could see.

"I'll be right back," I called as I parted from Jesus.

The blind beggar, Peniel, could always be found on the steps of Nicanor Gate, at the far western end of the same court. Like a lone fish swimming upstream in the face of the living torrent of those moving toward Jesus, I fought my way through the crowd.

I knew it was a Sabbath. I did not think Jesus would want to incur the wrath of the religious authorities by healing on a Sabbath. I just wanted the two to meet. I was certain Jesus would do what was right for the young man.

I could not see through the press of the worshipers, tripled in number as it was on this, the eve of Pentecost.

Behind me I heard Jesus raise his voice and begin to speak: "If you hold to my teaching, you are really my disciples. Then you will know the truth and the truth will make you free."

At last I reached the shaded niche where Peniel most often sat. The man in the alcove was an older beggar missing his right leg and waving a crutch at the passersby. "Where's Peniel?" I demanded.

"Who?" he returned.

"Peniel, the blind lad who usually waits in this spot."

"I don't know him," was the reply. "I just got here from Joppa. And a long, weary journey it was too, kind sir, on just one leg and a tree branch. Since it's the Sabbath, I cannot beg, but if you are moved to help, sir?" The cripple thrust out a wrinkled palm.

"You have not seen a young man, perhaps seventeen or eighteen … blind, as I say … anywhere about this morning?"

The cripple reflected. "The last blind beggar I saw was outside the Golden Gate."

"Oh, yes," I returned, feeling relief. "How long ago?"

"An hour. But sir, that man was older than me and could not be the one you seek." Again the hand flipped over and back, calling attention to the empty, outstretched palm.

I was disappointed and confused. I had felt so strongly that I was being urged by almighty God to bring Peniel and Jesus together. Had I been wrong, or was this a test of the persistence of my belief?

It struck me that while I had come in search of one particular beggar, here was one also in need of meeting Jesus. Perhaps I had been brought to this moment for his sake. "What's your name?" I asked.

"Jabez of Antioch," he replied.

"Have you heard of Jesus of Nazareth?"

"The charlatan from Galilee? Is that him over there?"

I looked across the plaza. On both flanks of Jesus' audience were knots of hecklers: Pharisees in tall headdresses and brocade robes in one group; austere, thin-lipped Sadducees in another; a file of scribes, scholars in the interpretation of religious legal precepts, in a third.

"I assure you, he's very real," I corrected.

Jabez made a sour face. "Real or not, and I don't admit he is, he's offended the authorities. 'Have nothing good to say about that Jesus,' they told me, 'or out you go.' You understand my position, sir?"

My frustration was growing even greater. "Wouldn't you rather be healed? At least see what he can do for you?"

"And lose my livelihood?" Jabez exclaimed. "Would you step aside, sir? The kind gentleman behind you is offering me a penny. God bless you, sir. God bless you."

Disappointed, I drifted back across the courtyard. At the back of the crowd, Temple police were accosting listeners, demanding names, and making notes on wax tablets. Many of the curious onlookers moved away under the stern, disapproving glares.

I arrived in time to hear Jesus repeat the core theme of his message: "You will know the truth and the truth will set you free."

A man at the back of the crowd shouted, "I am a descendant

of *Abraham!*" He tapped his barrel-shaped chest with a meaty thumb. "I've never been a slave to anyone. What do you mean, I can be set free? I *am* free!"

Looking right at the man, Jesus replied, "I tell you the truth: everyone who sins is a slave to sin."

The critic dropped his head and blushed, then scowled when the crowd laughed.

Resuming, Jesus said, "I know that you are Abraham's descendants. Yet here you are, ready to kill me because you have no room for my Word. I am telling you what I have seen in the Father's presence, but you do what you have heard from *your* father."

"*Abraham* is our father!" the heavyset man roared with exasperation, recovering from his momentary shame.

"That's right!" another heckler added. "Who do you think you are, going on about our father?"

"What are you trying to say?" demanded a Levite in the robes of his duty at the Temple.

There were a number of opponents planted in the group surrounding the steps. Some were there merely to heckle. Others were present to prod Jesus into making incautious remarks for which he could be arrested … or worse.

Suddenly I was afraid for him. If they accused him of blasphemy they might try to stone him. The authorities might kill him and blame it on an angry mob, even if the first stone was flung by someone paid by Lord Caiaphas. I hoped he would be cautious, judicious with his choice of words.

"If you *were* Abraham's children," Jesus said quietly. By lowering his tone, he forced the mockers to be still as well to hear what he said next. "If you *were* children of Abraham, you would do the things Abraham did."

What did that mean? Abraham was known for a life of faith and obedience, even against all human reason ... even to the point of trusting a God who asked him to sacrifice his only son.

"As it is," Jesus continued, "you are determined to kill me, a man who has told you the truth that I heard from God. Abraham did not do such things. You are doing the things your own father does."

The connection to the depth of Abraham's faith was overshadowed by the last challenge. A growling rose from the rabbi's opponents. Even his closest followers looked uncomfortable.

"We are not illegitimate children!" challenged a Pharisee. "The only Father we have is God himself!"

"If God *were* your father," Jesus replied, "you would love me, for I came from God and now am here. Why is my language not clear to you? Because you are unable to hear what I say: you belong to your father ... the devil!"

There was such a roar from the crowd that Jesus' words were drowned out. The biggest disciple, Peter, and two muscled fishermen, stood to form a protective screen between Jesus and the mob, but the Teacher pushed them aside.

He did not let up. "He was a murderer from the beginning, not holding to the truth, for there is no truth in him. He who belongs to God must do what God says. The reason you do not hear is that you do not belong to God."

As the rank of Temple police closed in, the rings of listeners scooted out of the way and the crowd started to dissolve.

Someone shouted an insult, "You're a Samaritan, aren't you?"

Another amplified the abuse: "You're a Samaritan, *and* you're demon possessed!"

"I am not possessed," Jesus called back calmly, "but I honor my Father, and you dishonor me. I tell you the truth: if anyone keeps my word, he will never see death."

151

That statement rocked me to my core: *Never see death?* What did that mean? Even if Jesus was a good man, a fine teacher, a great philosopher, and a gifted healer, who could say such an outrageous thing? My wife and child were beyond that very veil. Never see death?

Who was this man?

Jesus' critics verbalized and amplified my doubts. "Now we know you are demon possessed! Abraham died—"

"That's right, and so did all the prophets!"

"Yet you claim that if anyone keeps your word, he will never taste death?"

"Are you greater than our father Abraham?"

This was very, very near dangerous ground. Making oneself out to be greater than Abraham was almost blasphemous and certainly sacrilegious, given the reverence in which Father Abraham was held.

"Who do you think you are, anyway?"

"Yes, tell us! Who?"

Jesus made some other remarks I could not catch amid the bellows of rage and animosity, but then some words again came through clearly: "Your father Abraham rejoiced at the thought of seeing my day. He saw it and was glad."

"What?"

"Preposterous!"

"This is a madman!"

"Lock him up for his own good!"

"You're not even fifty years old, but you claim to know Abraham?"

"You've seen him? He lived ... twice a thousand years ago! What are you saying?"

What *was* he saying? My heart was pounding in my chest.

Was Jesus about to be stoned or gathered up bodily and thrown from the pinnacle of the Temple to the rocks below?

"I tell you the truth," Jesus said.

In other words, listen and I'll answer your question. Give me a chance to speak. Hear me out. Pay attention.

"I tell you the truth ..."

And then he spoke the fatal, unmistakable words, words that echo down through time, ringing in my ears to this very day. The unequivocal statement that Jesus was himself divine. No good teacher, no wise philosopher would ever, ever speak these words in Hebrew: "Before Abraham was, I AM."

He had said it! The very title almighty God spoke when Moses asked by what name the God of the children of Abraham chose to identify himself. God said: "Say this to the Israelites: I AM THAT I AM. Tell them, I AM has sent me to you."

My worst fears were being realized. With a collective howl of rage, while families scattered in all directions, scribes and Pharisees and Temple officials clawed out cobblestones. Prying loose the pavement with their fingertips, they prepared to stone Jesus to death! Jesus had saved my sister from this very fate.

Who would save him now?

What could his small band of followers do to protect him? What could they do but die with him?

"Where did he go?" the burly heckler demanded.

There was a rush up the steps of the Treasury, but Jesus was not inside.

"Toward Nicanor! After him!"

But Jesus was not by the bronze gates either.

Somehow he had slipped away.[1]

Each of the angry enemies stood pivoting in place until,

feeling foolish, they dropped their clods and rocks and broken chunks of tile and departed.

Baffled and exhausted, so did I. No one could assert Jesus never claimed to be divine. I saw it. I heard it. He was almost stoned to death because of it!

Chapter 16

I wandered about Jerusalem, lost in my thoughts. Who was this man from Nazareth? Who, in his right mind, would claim he was older than Abraham? That he was, in fact, divine, equal to the I AM?

I also reviewed what my own eyes had seen: the transformation of water into wine, the multiplication of the loaves and fishes, walking on the surface of the sea and calming the storm ... bringing Jairus's daughter back to life again.

Surely he was more than a charlatan. All these events could not be staged, could they?

I heard his teaching. I had seen the transformation of my sister Mary's heart—itself a greater accomplishment than changing water into wine. I already believed him to be a prophet sent by God.

What was the phrase used by the prophets to describe when God appeared to men as a man? *The Angel of the Lord*—that was it. He had visited Father Abraham, wrestled with Jacob, appeared to Joshua, guided Gideon, proved himself to Samson's father. He was Almighty God, referred to as an angel but looking human.

But Jesus was human. I had eaten with him, tasted wine with him, walked beside him when he had to stop and pull a pebble from his sandal.

What could it mean?

I scarcely knew where I was going and did not know where Jesus had gone. Perhaps he had already returned to Bethany.

Eventually I discovered I had crossed the viaduct into the western city. I needed someone to talk with, and that sent me to find Nicodemus. If there was anyone with whom I could pour out my confusion, it was the learned Pharisee who was also wrestling with the same issues.

As it happened, I located Nicodemus and Jesus together. Deep in conversation and accompanied by a ring of Pharisees not yet convinced Jesus was more than a fake, they were outside the wall of Nicodemus's home, near a famous gardenia bush now grown as large as a tree.

I also found Peniel at the same moment. The blind man sat in the shade of the gardenia, his cloak spread out to gather alms, should any be offered.

One of the Pharisees singled out Peniel to challenge Jesus, to see what the rabbi would say. It was a familiar argument that made me cringe to hear: "Being born blind is about the worst thing that could happen to anyone. So who sinned? This man or his parents?"

What response would Jesus make? I felt myself holding my breath. Much, it seemed, depended on his reply.

Stooping beside Peniel, Jesus touched the beggar's forehead, brushing back a lock of the young man's hair. It seemed as if the two of them communicated without speaking. Then Jesus said: "Neither this man nor his parents sinned. This happened—" Jesus straightened and answered his challenger by addressing Peniel—"this happened so the works of God might be displayed in your life. As long as it is day, I must do the works of him who sent me."

The antagonistic Pharisee bristled visibly at the word *work*. I remembered suddenly that it was the Sabbath day. Nicodemus put out a restraining hand. Let Jesus continue, the gesture suggested.

Jesus knelt again, stirred up a pile of earth under the gardenia bush with his fingers, and spat in it. As he mixed it into mud, he said, "Night is coming, when no one can work. While I AM in the world, I AM the light of the world."

There it was again! Claiming the authority of God, claiming equality with God!

With a gentle touch, Jesus applied the clay first to one of Peniel's eyelids and then to the other. He took his time, smoothing away wrinkles and folds until he was satisfied with the workmanship.

Standing, Jesus brushed off his hands. As if he had no audience, he spoke to Peniel alone. "Now go. Wash in the Pool of Siloam."[1]

Peniel rose to his feet, trembling. Putting out a shaking hand to locate Nicodemus's wall, the boy took two hesitant steps, then steadied himself and walked purposefully away.

I suddenly realized he might need assistance locating the pool of which Jesus spoke. It was below the Temple Mount toward the south. "Peniel," I called after him. "Can I ..."

It was Jesus who touched me on the arm. "Let him go. I want you to stay with me."

We chatted together for about two hours, sitting in Nicodemus's courtyard. It was an amiable discussion, despite the efforts of a couple Pharisees to catch Jesus saying something in opposition to the Law of Moses. They were clumsy, and he was clever.

Toward the end of the visit, one grew exasperated and accused Jesus of trying to become famous and popular with the common people.

Jesus replied, "I am not seeking glory for myself. But there is one who seeks it, and he is the judge. If I glorify myself, my glory means nothing. My Father, whom you claim as your God, is the one who glorifies me."

The Pharisee harrumphed at these words, and it looked like there would be another explosion when an out-of-breath messenger tumbled into Nicodemus's yard with a summons. "Master Nicodemus, you must come at once. Joseph of Arimathea asks for you."

"Where and for what purpose?" Nicodemus returned. "You see I have guests."

Truthfully the courier's eyes bulged when he recognized Jesus, so he stammered and said, "There is an urgent meeting of the Pharisee brotherhood in the Chamber of Hewn Stone."

"And the subject of this urgent meeting?"

"I don't ..." The messenger cast a worried glance between Jesus and Nicodemus as if unsure whether he was violating a confidence.

"Speak plainly," Nicodemus urged. "We are all friends here."

Visibly swallowing his nervousness, the messenger answered, "There is a man ..." Stopping, he corrected himself. "It has been reported that a man born blind ..."

"Go on, man, out with it!"

"This blind man ... can now see! He says he was healed today, on the Sabbath! He is being brought to our council to answer questions about how it happened. We need to investigate whether it's fraud or sacrilege!"

Nicodemus muttered under his breath, "And those are the only two responses the learned council can imagine?" He stood, dismissing the courier with a curt, "Tell Joseph I will come at once." To me he added, "You should come and witness this, David. I would like someone besides myself to hear and report fairly." Next he faced Jesus but said nothing.

With a shrug, Jesus offered, "I don't think my presence will be wanted at your council, friend Nicodemus. We will visit further later."

"Indeed we will ... Lord."

❧

When Nicodemus and I reached the Chamber of Hewn Stone on the Temple Mount, an uproar was already in progress. Peniel, eyes wide open with bewilderment, was at the center of an inquisition.

Eyes ... wide ... open!

Astonishment overwhelmed me! In place of wizened flaps of skin covering useless, flattened sockets, bright eyes sparkled and gleamed. Like a bird in flight, Peniel's gaze flitted from ornament to ornament, lamp to lamp, tapestry to chair to mosaic tile to the face of the man in front of him.

From that moment on, Peniel concentrated his study on faces, as if he were searching for someone.

But how could someone who had never, ever, seen anyone's face before possibly know when he had located the one he sought?

"Who are you really?" one of the Pharisees demanded.

"I'm Peniel, the potter's son," the boy responded. "I beg at Nicanor Gate."

"Liar!" another shouted in Peniel's face. "That fellow was

born blind! Since the world began, no one has ever opened the eyes of a man born blind!"

Peniel shrugged. He was not belligerent, but neither was he intimidated. "And yet I am he."

"Perpetrating a religious fraud is a crime akin to stealing," the first interrogator bellowed. "Or else it's blasphemy. Now which are you guilty of?"

"Neither. I have been blind all my life ... until today. Here in the room with me are my parents and some of my neighbors. They all know me. They know I've always been blind."

"Then how do you explain the change?"

Peniel reflected before answering simply, "A man put mud on my eyes. I washed, and now I see."

"It's a hoax," the first questioner muttered.

"And it's sacrilege," the second intoned. "Healing on a Sabbath? Whoever did this, he can't be from God. He doesn't keep the Sabbath. Sabbath-breaker! Lawbreaker!"

Peniel closed his newly functioning eyes. He stood completely still. He had retreated, it seemed to me, into a place of safety in familiar darkness. Out here in the light was beauty but also anger.

Peniel had been born blind. Through no fault of his own, he had lived cut off from much of the world. He had lived a gracious, gentle life, bearing up under a weight that would have crushed a guilty man, let alone an innocent one.

And now that he was healed?

Peniel was still not guilty of anything. He had not caused the healing. He had not demanded that anyone break the Sabbath laws. Blind or healed, Peniel was still guilty of nothing yet judged by the Pharisees to be guilty!

If the veins in the necks of the Pharisees had not bulged so badly already, I would have laughed at them with scorn! How could they be so completely wrong on both arguments? The evidence that Peniel had been blind and now could see was right before their willfully blind eyes!

So their alternate challenge was, "Even if this is true, it's still a sin! It should not have been performed on a Sabbath!"

One was a deliberate, stubborn refusal to face facts.

The other was arrogant, self-serving self-righteousness.

Nicodemus was even more incensed than me. He roughly shouldered between the two inquisitors and planted himself in front of the boy. Leaning close to Peniel's ear, he said reassuringly, "Peniel. Open your eyes."

Speaking to the boy as if the two were alone instead of in front of a hundred onlookers, Nicodemus gently inquired, "How did it happen?"

"The man who put the mud on my eyes ..."

"Jesus of Nazareth," Nicodemus supplied.

"Yes!" Peniel's face lit up with joy. "He told me to go to the Pool of Siloam."

"And after?"

"Afterward, I went home, seeing!"

The two Pharisees flanking Nicodemus could not be restrained any longer. Darting at Peniel from either side of Nicodemus, they demanded, "What have you to say about him? This sorcerer?"

"Yes, what? It was your eyes he opened. What do you say?"

It filled me with angry amusement to watch these men, who believed themselves to be scholars—lifelong, pious students of Torah—awaiting a reply from the potter's son. The whole room leaned forward to hear what the formerly blind beggar of Nicanor Gate would say.

"Well," Peniel said, "he must be a prophet. How else could he perform such a miracle?"

Both of Peniel's antagonists threw up their hands in disgust. One swung around and leveled an accusatory finger at Peniel's father and mother, hustled to the front of the mob, and cowered there. "Is this your son? Is this the one who was born blind? How is it that he now can see?"

I saw tension and sorrow creep into Peniel's face, and I shivered. He was afraid his own parents would betray him for fear of the Temple authorities.

"We know he's our son," Peniel's father said slowly, as if by stating the obvious he could escape some sort of trap.

Peniel's mother added, "Yes, he was born blind. But how he can see now, or who opened his eyes, we don't know. How could we know? We weren't even there, were we?"

If Peniel's father was a man of few words and less courage, his wife made up for any lack of verbiage while managing to still disown her boy. "Why ask us? He's of age. He's a man. Ask him. Go on, ask him. We haven't done anything wrong."

Peniel gazed at the floor with the bitter knowledge that his mother and father would not speak up for him. They would sacrifice him to preserve themselves. Nicodemus grasped Peniel by the shoulders and gave him an encouraging squeeze.

Through gritted teeth the prosecutor said, "We ... know ... the man ... who did this ... is a sinner."

He managed to make it sound so vile and hateful that I expected Peniel to also recoil and denounce Jesus.

Instead, he lifted his chin to the light and raised his beautiful, clear, brand-new set of eyes toward heaven. In a voice that rang throughout the chamber and carried even beyond the door to the plaza outside, he declared, "Whether he is a sinner or not,

I don't know. One thing I do know: I was *blind* ... completely, totally, and utterly blind ... *and now I see!*"

"But how? How did he do this?"

Peniel let a little exasperation creep into his tone when he replied, "I already told you, and you didn't listen. Why do you want to hear it again?" A sly smile played across Peniel's lips when he added, "Do you want to become his disciples too?"

With that they bundled him toward the exit, all the while heaping abuse on him. They demanded more answers, then howled with rage when he would not admit Jesus was a sinner and a lawbreaker. They offered excuses for their unbelief, growing less and less coherent, while Peniel grew ever more confident and sure of himself.

When argument failed, they returned to the original imprecation, having nothing left to offer: "You were steeped in sin at birth. How dare you lecture us?"

And they threw him out.[2]

"Let's go after him," Nicodemus urged, "and see that no harm comes to him. He and his grace-filled faith are worth more than all the rest of these pious imposters put together."

Sometime later I learned that Jesus went looking for Peniel and found him. Peniel, the man born blind, became one of the most fervent disciples of Jesus of Nazareth and a living witness to the reality of his power. Because of his love for stories, the former beggar of Nicanor Gate became Peniel the scribe, recording the deeds of the one who gave him sight.

Part Three

Then the LORD was jealous for his land
  and took pity on his people....
The trees are bearing their fruit;
  the fig tree and the vine yield their riches....
I will repay you for the years the locusts have eaten.

JOEL 2:18, 22B, 25A

Chapter 17

The beheading of John the Baptizer was proof that Herod Antipas feared his wife more than he feared God. Like Ahab and Jezebel, the two brought judgment on the land just as John had warned. It was a difficult year for the righteous and the unrighteous together.

First, news of the approaching plague came in the heat of high summer. A hard-riding messenger was sent to us from our sister Mary in Magdala. Covered with the dust of his journey, he arrived before sunrise. His horse was lathered and near collapse.

"Open the gates! I bring urgent news from the Galil! Call Master Lazarus!"

I was already awake when Martha knocked on the door of my bedchamber. "Brother! A rider comes from Mary! Bad news, I fear!"

I dressed quickly and hurried to the courtyard.

Martha was beside the fountain. "Perhaps Mary is ill."

A single locust buzzed into the courtyard and fell to the stone floor at Martha's feet. She gasped and jumped to the side. I glanced into the fountain and scooped out three dead insects. The largest was half the size of my index finger.

I examined them in my palm. "For several days our vineyard workers have been killing locusts. Frying them for supper.

A delicacy. This time of year there are always a few stray locusts from the desert. Never so many that they can do harm."

Martha frowned. "Cook is from Ethiopia. She saw such plagues with her own eyes. She told me of the famine and misery that followed."

I hurried toward the stable where the rider waited. Remembering stories of biblical plagues, I reasoned that the sins of Herod and his wife could well bring a heavenly judgment on the land.

Samson and Patrick and two dozen workers gathered around me as I read Mary's warning aloud.

Greetings, my brother and sister,

I send this letter in hopes you may devise a plan to save your vines. I know harvest is near, yet still the grapes cannot be ripe enough to pick. Judgment comes from the north. Swarms of locusts, in clouds so dense that they darken the sun, are flying south. Do what you can to save your vines. In hopes you are well, your sister, Mary.

The rider sat on a heap of hay and filled his cheeks with bread. "They're coming, for certain. They'll eat every green leaf and shoot by the time they're done. A swarm in Syria, miles wide."

I asked the exhausted servant, "And Galilee?"

"Thousands north of the sea. Landed upon the grazing land, and when they flew away there was not one blade of grass left. Everything. Down to the bare dirt. Vineyards destroyed. Your sister says if you act now, you are a clever fellow and may have time to prepare."

I looked to Samson for wisdom. The old man's face was grim. He inclined his head toward Patrick.

"I set Patrick onto this last week when the very first rumor came from Tyre. Aye. The lad's got something to say, if you don't mind, sir."

Patrick cleared his throat. "I saw such a plague come when I served with the Roman army in Egypt. They stripped every tree and flower. Destroyed every crop before they left. Crawled into the beds of the mighty and tormented the poor. Drove the livestock mad. Fell into the water and the children's milk. Ate the fodder for the cattle. Stripped the vineyards clean. Leaving nothing behind but hunger, sir."

"What is to be done?" I spread my hands wide.

Samson spoke up. "Me and the lad have been thinking on this, sir. In case the rumor's true. There may be a way to save some vineyards and possibly a portion of the fig crop."

Patrick agreed. "The vines, yes. Partly. The orchards will be more difficult."

"If you can help us do this, Patrick, you will be well rewarded."

He tucked his chin. "I will do this for the good of fighting such a mindless, faceless enemy, sir. But since you offer, I will ask one reward, sir."

"Name it."

"My freedom."

"Done!"

He continued. "And not just myself, sir, but the girl Adrianna, Samson's adopted daughter. She is sixteen years old thereabouts. As near as she can figure. Old enough to marry. I'd like her as a wife. And her freedom too."

Samson nodded his approval.

It was an offer I accepted gladly. I clapped hands with Patrick in a bargain. "Before the Lord God of Abraham, Isaac, and Jacob, you shall be a free man."

"For such a prize I'll do all I am able."

Samson seemed pleased. "Patrick has fought these flying devils before. God has sent him to you to save what can be saved."

The Galilean messenger warned, "Unless there is a miracle, you have perhaps three days before the swarm overshadows Judea."

With a walking stick, Patrick etched our battle plan in the dirt. "We must cut firebreaks between the vines. We must sacrifice some. What you choose, we will attempt to save."

"How do we decide between them?" I looked to Samson.

The old man replied, "The hoppers will ride on the wind. The prevailing wind. From the north."

I considered the logic of our situation. "The decision is simple, then. The vineyard on the northwest hill faces the wind. It must be sacrificed. Those vines produce more grapes, as you have said, but weaker … less quality."

Samson nodded. "A wise choice. We concentrate on saving the best first. Then, if there is time, perhaps the others."

I caught the vision. "Then the Faithful vines on the south hill."

Patrick agreed. "Yes. We erect tall poles at both ends of the vine rows. At the top of the hill, dividing north from south. Suspend palm fronds, coated with pitch, upon the posts."

Samson scratched the ears of his goats. "You'll need to hire more laborers."

Martha, who had been pale and silent through it all, at last said, "Three days. Is that enough time?"

Patrick nodded. "Just. If we begin this instant."

Her chin jutted in determination. "We must do our best."

Samson concurred. "We must focus on vineyards. Harvest the figs that are ripe today. All else must be let go."

Patrick agreed. "Locusts can eat their weight in foliage in one day. When the monsters land on your pastures and begin to feast, we must set fire to the fields."

I considered the loss of grazing land in Galilee and Judea alone. What would that mean to the livestock in the coming year?

Martha was somber. "The women can help."

Patrick instructed, "Every hand, man, woman, and child must cut and gather palm fronds. And coat them with pitch." He turned toward Martha. "The men must be fed and cared for."

Martha took up the challenge. "Feed an army? This I can do."

Samson tugged his beard in deep thought. Raising his eyes heavenward, he said, "We must pray as we work. Hell has opened and spewed forth destruction."

❧

Samson set two dozen men at work, cutting a firebreak between Faithful Vineyard and the north vines. They started at the top of the rocky hill, stripping away branches to separate that which we would fight to save and that which we would give over to the evil.

I knew the fig groves could ultimately survive the locusts and severe pruning. Samson marked the best trees. Fruit had ripened on the sunny west side. Three teams of two men each began harvesting ripe figs, placing them in clay jars, and leaving what was not ripe. Others followed with pruning hooks to hack off leaves and limbs and unripe fruit for fodder to feed my flocks.

Oxen dragged the dead wood into strategic piles heaped up and prepared for the torch.

Patrick began construction of the frameworks that would support our shield against the enemy.

While I saddled my horse, Martha organized the feeding of our workers.

I rode to the village. In the marketplace, news had already spread about the scourge that was descending upon all Israel. By noon I had hired seventy-two strong men and sent them to the estate, promising each a denarius for a day's work.

Speculation about the cause of the scourge had begun. "God's judgment upon Herod for the murder of John the Baptizer."

"Aye. That's it. The Baptizer lived on locusts and honey, they say. So the locusts are sent for revenge." In Galilee the fields of Herod Antipas had already been devoured, but the vineyards of many righteous had also been consumed.

"Herod and the Romans will be after stealing any crops that are saved when their own are gone. Wish the Almighty would just smite the wicked for their crimes and not let all of us suffer ill."

Though I understood their feelings, I knew the Lord had given us sound reasoning and ways to defeat such a plague. I said, "Come to help only if you have faith strong enough to stand and fight."

When I returned home, I brought with me an army preparing for battle.

Chapter 18

The following morning there was still no sign of imminent doom. I rose before dawn after a fitful, sleepless night. To the west, hanging above the Mount of Olives, the star Vega shone like a blazing torch in the midst of King David's Harp. I prayed for courage and strength. As I faced about toward where the sun would soon punch its way over the heights of Moab, the orange eye of Aldebaran and the kindlier twinkle of Capella studied me from the placid heavens.

It was the northern sky that drew my attention. The breeze in my face was barely a whisper. I sniffed as if trying to catch the odor of trouble above the aroma of blooming flowers and ripening figs.

Was there an acrid tinge to the otherwise sweet morning air, or was I imagining it? I had eaten roasted grasshoppers before and did not care for them. There was a bitter, almost metallic sensation connected with the taste and smell, but perhaps that was a result of the oil in which they were cooked.

Was I truly scenting a locust horde on the wind? Or was it merely my nervous mind playing tricks on me?

The men I hired to help defend the vines slept wrapped in their cloaks at the end of the rows in case the plague arrived during the night. Now it seemed as if I had paid for an expensive set of unneeded guests, some of whom had helped themselves to grapes and figs from my crop.

Martha awoke also and came to stand beside me as gray light spread upward in the eastern sky. "There's fresh bread and cheese," she offered, gesturing toward the cookhouse behind our home.

I shook my head. "No, thank you. I'm not hungry."

"What about the men?" she asked.

"Let them rest. If the locusts come, we may not sleep again for days."

"Do you think they might not come this way, David?"

"It's whatever the Almighty wills," I said, shrugging. "If the breeze has shifted and is blowing more out of the west, then the hoppers are right now crossing Jordan to eat the Perean vineyards of Herod Antipas."

"And well does he deserve it," she concluded. Martha pointed toward the Judean hills in the direction of Shiloh and squinted. "The wind must be getting stronger. I think I see a dust cloud rising up."

I stared toward the north as the sky's pale blue luminescence increased and the stars faded. "I see it," I finally agreed. "You have good eyes, sister. A brown smudge against the ridgeline. To left and right the hills look more sharply defined. In the middle they are blurred."

"A dust storm would be a help, would it not?"

"Sweep the locusts away like Elijah's whirlwind, eh?"

Samson joined us at the front gate of the estate. "The men are waking, mistress. Are the trays of bread ready?"

That was when I first noticed a persistent rushing sound in my ears, like the noise of surf sliding up and back a sandy shore.

I shook my head. My lack of sleep was already affecting me. I'd be better after bread and a cup of pomegranate juice.

"Bread for the men, of course," Martha agreed. "My women and I were baking most of the night. There's plenty." The hissing noise increased. Now it sounded like the rasp of a pumice stone smoothing a board in a carpenter's shop.

Over the next moments the rush became a roaring and the rasping noise grew in volume and intensity. A wind storm indeed was approaching.

Samson cupped his hand around his right ear and leaned forward. "Your pardon, mistress. What did you ..."

I saw horrified realization bloom on Samson's wizened face at the same instant the identical thought struck me. Together we faced Shiloh and stared at the dirty brown wave now obscuring half the northern horizon.

"That's not dust," I said grimly. "Martha, get inside and bolt the shutters. Put all the food into cupboards and cover the jars. The plague has arrived. Go!" I nudged her toward the house, and she obeyed as Samson lurched away toward the vines, but I stayed transfixed at the sight.

The force of the wind above the trees was stronger than at ground level. The leading edge of the locust swarm dropped first on vines belonging to Herod. My orchards and vineyards would be next.

Samson moved in a shambling lope toward the crops, shouting for Patrick as he went. "Patrick! Light the smudge pots. Light them now!"

The middle rank of pests arrived. I felt the rush of air all around me. It was not a gentle breeze but the vibration of uncountable wings.

The first of the flying invaders pattered against my face and clothing like raindrops blown sideways. I brushed them away, only to have my hand encounter a half dozen more in midflight.

I turned to race toward the vineyards.

We had taken the precaution of buying tubs of tar. The pitchy substance, collected from the shore of the Dead Sea, was used to seal rooftops against rain. Ignited, it burned with an oily, smelly sputter that produced great volumes of thick black smoke. I hoped the stench and the heat would discourage the locusts. Even if it did not kill them all, perhaps the rest could be deflected into going elsewhere.

At the same time I had to trust I was not killing the vines by trying to save them! Thick dust or soot killed grape leaves. Intense heat would wither tender shoots and destroy the unripe fruit. Had we placed the pots of tar close enough to protect the vineyards and far enough away at the same time?

We would soon know.

Patrick raced in one direction, hopping at tremendous speed on his wooden leg. Samson pitched forward at a breakneck pace around the other perimeter. Both men were swinging firepots, clay jars of embers kept alive by being in constant motion at the end of rope slings.

As each man reached a smudge pot, he paused only long enough to set it alight, then raced on to the next.

With the arrival of the swarm, it was as if the sun had risen and then immediately retreated below the eastern horizon.

Already the thorn hedges around my home and the jasmine vines twined around the pillars of my porch were covered in locusts. While my ears continued to be assaulted by the hum of wings, the din was increased by a new raucous sound: chewing.

The pitch pots were fully ablaze. Swirling plumes of black vapor rose to bar entry into my choicest vines. It was working!

As the horde of hoppers flew toward the fields and confronted the fumes, they diverted to either side.

It sickened me to see how quickly they destroyed the first row of unprotected fig trees. Settling on the branches like a myriad of tiny pruning hooks, they changed summer's lush growth to wintry barrenness.

In order to save the Faithful Vineyard, other parts would have to be sacrificed. Nor would protecting even a remnant be easy.

The grasshoppers were a crafty foe. Like an enemy force unable to advance by one route seeks another, so too did the grasshoppers. They could not fly through the foul reek of the blazing tar, so they landed in front of my defenses.

The battle to save Faithful Vineyard began in earnest.

I shouted, having to cup my hands around my mouth and turn downwind to keep from inhaling a mouthful of pests, "Drive them! Drive them!"

Each of my seventy-two laborers was assigned a row of vines. With an empty grain sack in each hand, a man charged in, flailing on both sides.

The grasshoppers launched themselves into the air where the strengthening breeze caught and propelled them toward the opposite end of the planting.

Some flew directly into the sail-like rigs of palm fronds coated with pitch and were trapped there. Others rose on the wind and disappeared into the distance. The plan was succeeding but required unrelenting effort. Each of my human warriors moved ahead, holding the enemy at bay.

"We need more workers!" I urged Samson. "We must send a second wave to follow the first. Go to the market square and hire more."

"How much shall we offer them?"

"Still a denarius, if they will come now. Go!"

I soon regretted not eating breakfast at my sister's urging. There was no chance for even a bite of bread.

A water container with the lid left barely ajar was soon filled to the brim with drowned hoppers or those staying alive on the backs of their fallen comrades.

And still more of them came.

The pitch-covered traps worked so well they sagged beneath the weight of the captured locusts.

I ordered Samson, "We've got to replace those screens immediately, and we must send a third wave of men with sacks to keep driving."

The wail of a woman shrieking came from my home. I ran to investigate.

Martha answered my pounding summons by dragging me quickly into the front hall. She slammed the door again before no more than half a hundred grasshoppers entered with me.

"What's happened?" I demanded.

"Don't worry," my stalwart sister returned. "Someone failed to latch the shutters properly to your office. I sent her in there to fetch something, and when she opened the door … I'm sorry, but there's a regular Pharaoh's army crawling on ceiling, walls, and floors. It scared her, but I got the door shut tight now so they can't reach the rest of the house."

"But my papers? My manuscripts? They'll be devoured!" Then I bowed my head and laughed at my own foolishness. "Perhaps they'll eat the bills. After today there may not be any way to pay them!"

"I'm sorry, brother."

"Never mind. I'd happily give them my office to save the vines."

"How is it going up there?"

"Holding our own. At least, I hope so."

A cry of "More tar! More tar, here! The smudge pots are going out!"

Racing back out, I heard Martha jam the portal shut behind me.

As the orchards of Herod Antipas were consumed, still we held the perimeter of Faithful Vineyard. I had hoped that as the sun set and the day came to an end, so would the horror of the plague, but it did not let up.

The later quantity of tar we purchased was more volatile than the first. Instead of merely smoldering, sheets of flame shot upward as the pots were ignited. Blazing tongues of fire licked each column of smoke. Locusts blundering into them became squirming, burning embers tossing on the breeze.

It was a scene straight from a prophet's vision of Gehenna. Sheets of flame briefly illuminated flapping apparitions of men keeping locusts from landing. Workers staggered into view, flailing at the air as if battling phantoms, then plunged back into the darkness of the rows of vines.

A blazing grasshopper landed on the pitch-covered sailcloth. The entire device caught fire in an instant, becoming a fiery torch too hot to approach. Thousands of invaders were incinerated. A cheer went up among the men.

As the trap erupted in flames, we left it to become ashes. Like a captain on the deck of a burning ship, Patrick dashed about, giving the orders that hurriedly erected another and another.

Amid the darkness and the fumes and the commotion, there was no ability and no time to see if we were actually accomplishing our goal. We were killing myriads of locusts, but could we ultimately save the best vines?

Only daylight and a final relief from the plague would tell.

I staggered from row to row, alternately waving a flickering torch to chase away the locusts and stooping to check for damage. My eyes burned from the smoke and lack of sleep. My throat was parched from shouting orders.

The smudge pots were going out again. "Samson," I croaked, "more tar."

Putting his mouth near my ear, he rasped, "Begging your pardon, sir, but there is no more. We used it all."

This unwelcome news shook me awake. "Then send Patrick to the village to buy more! Don't wait."

As he raised his chin toward the light of the burning brand, I saw it quiver. "That's just it, if you take my meaning, sir. There is no more to be had. None."

That could not be right. We could not have worked so hard to be defeated now. "Then in Jerusalem," I argued. "Send men to the Street of the Roofers. They will have more."

"Already tried, sir. The man I sent came back an hour ago. Seems all the vinedressers followed your example. There is no tar to be had in all Judea." Samson sounded as though he were about to cry.

I clapped him on the shoulder. "We're not finished yet. Just give me a minute to think."

I tugged at my beard again in thought, and for the first time since the previous morning, I did not encounter a kicking insect. The significance did not dawn on me for a time, and then I noticed: the space around my head was momentarily clear of winged pests.

The torrent of airborne pests was actually slowing. Even the breeze carrying the invaders dropped, then backed around into the south, like an unseen hand pushing the grasshoppers out of my estate.

Had the relief come in time?

Fearful dawn crept up from over Jordan, disclosing three things. First light revealed whole swathes of orchard and vineyard almost completely devastated, plucked cleanly ... but these were the areas we had not tried to save.

As I rushed to the brow of the hill, I learned the second revelation: Faithful Vineyard had been spared. Around the edges of the field the vines had been gnawed, but the bulk of the leaves were intact; the crop was saved.

The third sight meeting my eyes was this: while no more locusts were arriving, the rows were still full of crawling pests. Battered from the sky and stunned by smoke, they were still a menace.

And my troops were as exhausted as the winged ones. My hired men displayed haggard faces and weary limbs.

There was a stirring of air on the side of my face toward the south, and a rustling on the breeze. Then I saw another wave of black specks dotting the sky.

The flapping increased and a shadow once more fell across me from above.

I hung my head in utter defeat and exhaustion. We had lost. It had all been for nothing.

Then I heard the sounds of cheering and laughter erupting from my workers, accompanied by shouts of "*Selovs!* The *selovs* are coming! The *selovs* of the desert are here!"

Quail! Flights, schools, armies of round-bodied birds from the wadis of the Negev and Sinai converged on my vineyards. Spiraling inward as if I had summoned them, their cries encircled me, the hilltop, and Faithful Vineyard. They pounced on the locusts and feasted, snapping up insects on all sides. My new allies plucked grasshoppers from leaves and unripe fruit with savage delight and perfect accuracy.

Later that day we learned that many of the vineyards and orchards of Judea had been saved by hard work, smudge pots, and the miracle of the quail.

The vines of Herod Antipas were not so fortunate: none of them were spared.

"Master!" Patrick exclaimed. "It's a miracle!"

"A true miracle," I agreed. "But you are wrong about one thing."

"Eh!"

"Call me David. I am your master no longer. You are free!"

꧁꧂

It was rumored among the rulers in Jerusalem that Jesus had called forth locusts from the abyss to devour the fields of those who approved of the execution of John the Baptizer. Herod Antipas, whose orchards and vines had been devastated both in Galilee and in Judea, alternated between rage and terror at what had come upon him.

I received a message from Mary that wherever Jesus was welcomed in Galilee, the locusts did not come. Mary's vines were untouched, and her crop would be plentiful this year. She wrote that the Lord and his disciples were coming to Judea for the harvest and that she had invited them to stay with our family through the high holy days.

So it was that Jesus came down from Galilee with his disciples to Judea to stay with us at Bethany.

Seventy of his close followers labored beside us to gather and crush the grapes of Faithful Vineyard. That was when young Carta, British slave of Centurion Marcus Longinus, another of the Lord's healed, came to live with us and apprentice as a winemaker.

Jesus worked with the men, shoulder to shoulder, harvesting the crop.

After all the grapes were harvested, with great joy Jesus waded into the wine vat to tread the grapes beside me.

It was, for those of us whose vines had survived the ravage, a time of great celebration. A wonderful banquet was prepared for all who had worked so hard to save my vineyard. As music played, we feasted on quail fattened by the locusts. I noticed when Jesus left his place. He stood on the hilltop where the frontline battle against the locusts had been fiercest.

Bringing a plate heaped with food to share, I joined him.

We sat on the hewn stump of a fig tree and ate as we surveyed the vineyards and orchards beyond my property.

"You fought and won a hard battle. Well done, my friend."

"I lost about a third of the harvest."

"You saved two-thirds." It was like Jesus to measure the positive. "But look over there."

The stripped vines of Herod's holdings were a sharp contrast to the still lush foliage of Faithful Vineyard.

I said to Jesus, "In Jerusalem and Tiberias, they are saying you called down a curse on Herod Antipas because of John."

"The wicked call a curse upon themselves. The righteous live in the midst of blessing, though everything around them be devoured." Jesus swept his hand toward the devastated fields. "Whose vineyard is that?"

"The vines once belonged to my grandfather. The old butcher-king Herod trumped up charges and stole the land."

"How do you feel seeing your grandfather's vines destroyed?" he asked me.

"Sad. I think of the dreams my grandfather had when he planted those vines. He would not have imagined it would come to this."

"How did your vines survive and Herod's did not?"

"We fought to save them. Patrick, my servant, fought because now he's won his freedom. Samson, my vinedresser, fought because he loves me and loves these vines as if they are his own. We didn't give up. And when the oil for the smudge pots was gone and we could do no more, the Lord sent a wind and a flock of quail to eat the locusts."

Jesus focused on the contrast. "How is it that the vineyard of Herod is completely stripped? Not a shred of green remains. All his crop lost."

It was a simple question. Easy to answer. "The laborers hired by Herod's overseer gave up before the battle began. When the insects dropped down, the men didn't fight to drive them off. They were paid to work, but they have no love for the vineyard. No care for the outcome. It's nothing to them if everything is lost."

"The hireling doesn't care, but the one who owns the land and plants, and the vinedresser who tends the vines, now there are lions who will fight to save the vineyard!" Jesus began to sing the old psalm:

"Restore us, O God;
  cause your face to shine,
  and we shall be saved!

You have brought a vine out of Egypt;
You have cast out the nations, and planted it.
You prepared room for it,
  and caused it to take root,
  and it filled the land."[1]

I joined him in singing. Jesus' voice was a clear, sweet baritone.

"The hills were covered with its shadow,
  and the mighty cedars with its boughs.

She sent out her boughs to the sea,
    and her branches to the river.
Why have you broken down her hedges
    so that all who pass by the way pluck her fruit?
Return, we beseech you, O God of Hosts,
    look down from heaven and see."[2]

In that moment I noticed for the first time that the places in my vineyard where Jesus had walked before had remained completely undamaged during our war against the locusts. The song continued:

"Visit this vine
    and the vineyard which your right hand has planted,
    and the branch that you made strong for yourself.
Let your hand be upon the man of your right hand,
    upon the son of man
    whom you made strong for yourself.
Then we will not turn back from you;
    revive us and we will call upon your name.
Restore us, O Lord God of hosts;
    cause your face to shine,
    and we shall be saved!"[3]

The song came to an end, but I did not want to stop singing. I sang the last line of the chorus alone.

Jesus crossed his arms, his face shining. He said to me, "Lazarus, do you understand?"

I nodded once. "Yes, Lord."

Then he said, "My Father is the Vinedresser. It is written by the prophets and it is true, 'The Lord will restore the years the locusts have eaten.'"[4]

Chapter 19

*P*atrick was given his freedom, but there was much more to my promise. He had asked for a wife. He had asked for freedom and the hand of Adrianna, the cook's helper.

Samson was Adrianna's foster father. The winemaker came to me in the company of his round and robust wife, whom he called Delilah because she had so captured his heart. Samson was a free man, yet his wife was a second-generation slave in the House of Lazarus. It was known that the House of Lazarus had the finest winemaker and the finest cook in the land. The couple had adopted Adrianna when she had arrived at my estate as a small orphan of about five years of age. Adrianna had possessed no skills. She was a shivering, lonely little girl when she came to us. Samson begged me for the favor of bringing her home to his childless wife. Little Adrianna became a part of the family, learning the culinary skills of Delilah, and was grafted into our faith and our ways.

Delilah and Samson stood before me on behalf of their daughter. "Sir, Patrick is a good man, as we all know. And now he has asked for the freedom of himself—"

"Which I have granted," I said proudly.

Samson continued, "And for the freedom and the hand of my daughter."

I nodded. "A fair bargain, considering the saving of Faithful Vineyard."

Samson's eyebrows went up slightly as he considered what he wanted to tell me. "Though he is not a Jew, as we are, he believes in the God of Abraham, Isaac, and Jacob."

I agreed with the good character of Patrick. "And so your daughter, who is also not descended from Abraham, is a good match for him."

Delilah shifted uneasily and did not speak, though her lip trembled. "Sir, neither am I a Jew, but am descended from slaves of Gaul. Yet I would not return to my forefathers' homeland if I were set free."

I did not understand the emotion in Delilah's face. The fear in her eyes. "What is it, good woman?"

Samson put his hand on Delilah's arm. "Sir, Patrick is a Briton. Yes, he fears our God, and yet now that he has his freedom, he says he may take my daughter far, far away from this place and her mother. We have no child but Adrianna."

"Perhaps, sir," Delilah blurted, "he will take my girl back to his own kin in Britannia."

Samson continued, "Here she is a slave in the household of a kind master, at least. But when she belongs to a husband, I will have no way to protect her if ..."

I suddenly understood. I had pledged the hand of Adrianna to Patrick without knowing all that was in Patrick's mind. It had not occurred to me that I might lose my barrelmaker and, much worse, they might lose their daughter. "Has Patrick said he wished to return to his own country?"

"Not in so many words, sir. I was supportive of the match, but now I'm frightened. He speaks of his family in the great city of Verulamium where Isis is worshiped. Britannia is a godless place, sir, if you don't mind my saying so. The Romans enforce their own ways upon the people. And if Patrick takes Adrianna away, we will see her no more."

"Grandchildren," Delilah whispered. "All I ever prayed for."

"I gave the lad my word." I stared at the seal upon my signet ring. "Patrick is a free man. And I have prepared the document to free your daughter." Opening a leather folder, I displayed two documents. The first declared Adriana's freedom. The second was the contract of marriage pledging Adrianna to Patrick. "Here. A *ketubah*."

Delilah started to weep softly. "Oh, my baby girl. In a land of human sacrifice and demon practices!"

Samson patted her gently. "There, there, my dove. My angel. The Lord must surely go with her. Surely there are Jews in Britannia! Surely a synagogue among the pagan temples."

The woman wept, drawing Martha to the door to gaze at our little gathering in sorrow.

Delilah cried, "But, sir, what shall I do? Oh, what shall I do without my baby girl near me?"

I could say no more. I had given my vow to Patrick in exchange for his efforts to save Faithful Vineyard. "I am at a loss how I can help. I gave my promise. If Patrick wishes to return to the far north ... he will do what he will do. And there is nothing I can do to change what is."

From the shadows, Martha cleared her throat. "Brother!" she declared. "There must be a way." She stepped into the pool of light and set her hands on her broad hips in her determined way.

Delilah's eyes shone with tears. Samson stared at her in surprise.

"Martha," I greeted her.

She motioned for Samson and Delilah to leave us. "Shalom. There is work to do, Delilah. Supper to cook. Company coming. I will speak with my brother."

The couple shuffled out of my chamber. Martha closed the door and whirled to face me. "Brother! What have you done?"

I defended, "He asked me, and I—"

"He asked you!"

"To save the vines."

"To save the vines, you sacrifice the wine? You are purest fool. Oh, you heartless creature! What have you done to sweet Delilah? And have you asked Adrianna if she wishes to be the wife of a pagan, one-legged barrelmaker from Britannia?"

She had me there. I had not thought to ask anyone. The girl was property, and I had the right to do as I wished. Freedom seemed a great gift. "My intentions were good. For the best, sister."

"Ha!" She snorted, pivoted on her heel, and made for the door. "Come up with something fast, or you'll have mutiny in the ranks."

❦

I had celebrated the end of a plague of locusts, yet now my house was a house of mourning.

At supper that night, Joseph of Arimathea the elder and Gamaliel, a great Torah scholar descended from a family of honorable Levites, sat at my table and feasted on lamb with mushrooms and wine sauce as we sipped the finest vintage yet created on my estate. Lamb, courtesy of Delilah and Adrianna. Wine, created by Samson, cured in barrels made by Patrick.

We had saved the vines, but now everything good and familiar seemed about to dissolve around me. I sucked the wine sauce from my lamb chop with a heavy heart.

Gamaliel commented, "Herod Antipas believes that Jesus of Nazareth is John the Baptizer raised from the dead."

Joseph concurred. "The locusts fully destroyed the tetrarch's vines. He is casting around for who he can blame. Jesus is a sorcerer, some say. Did he cast a spell on the vines? Antipas, like his father, is driven by fear: fear of his Roman masters, of Pilate, of Caesar. Fear of what the people will do. Rebellion? Fear of his wife, Herodias. And now, after severing the head of a prophet at the demand of this woman, he fears that John the Baptizer is again alive and may do to him what Antipas himself has done to others."

Delilah, eyes red with weeping, entered and cleaned away the main course. My guests pretended they did not notice her. As was proper, they complimented her as if she were not in the room. I tried very hard not to glance at her.

"Most excellent meal," Gamaliel said to me. "I heard the Roman tribune mention the quality of your wines and the reputation of your cooks. A mother and daughter, is it?"

Delilah sniffed and wiped a tear with the back of her hand.

Joseph agreed within Delilah's hearing. "Any household in all the empire would envy such a cook as this. You must never let the Gentiles suspect the skill of such a cook. They will steal her away to some far corner of the world."

I replied. "Yes. A gift from God, she is. She has always been with our family."

I heard a choked sob as Delilah padded quickly down the hallway.

Joseph leaned in. "Is she all right?"

I tasted the sweet honeyed pastry of our dessert. "Her daughter will be wed soon."

Gamaliel licked his fingers. "Emotions of mothers run high in such times."

Joseph returned to the subject. "This Jesus is truly a wonderworker. My son is fascinated by him."

Gamaliel nodded. "The vineyards and orchards of Antipas. Stripped. I do not believe Jesus called down this plague upon him, but he will certainly be blamed for every calamity from now on. Good men are always suspected by evil men."

"I myself saw Jesus perform several miracles." I sipped my wine. "Here's one you'll appreciate. It seemed unmistakable. At a wedding, it was. He turned water into wine."

Gamaliel laughed. "A trick. And if not a trick, then sorcery."

I studied the deep red contents of my cup. "But no. I tasted it. Unlike any wine ever made. More delicious than—"

Gamaliel laughed again. "So Jesus is your competition, eh?"

"Jesus," Joseph mused aloud. "A cousin of John the Baptizer. I wonder if he'll raise up a rebellion to avenge the death of such a righteous man."

Gamaliel nodded. "Caiaphas has put forth to the council that Jesus' works will lead to the deaths of many. That is, if there is another rebellion. Another preacher claiming to be the Messiah! I cannot think of a worse time than now for this Jesus to be preaching the coming of Messiah to redeem the people."

Joseph raised his cup. "There will never be wine as good as yours, even if the Kingdom of God comes to earth."

My guests spoke long into the night about the events unfolding in Galilee with the followers of Jesus. They recounted the rumors of miracles that daily streamed in to the priests and Temple authorities. It was indeed a dangerous time for Jesus.

I was relieved when the evening came to an end, and Gamaliel and Joseph retired to their bedchambers.

Weary, I made my way toward my study. The certificate

of Adrianna's freedom and the marriage contract were on my writing table. I sat down and studied them with regret. Surely my cook and my winemaker would never smile again. I resolved that in the morning I would talk with Adrianna to hear her thoughts on the matter.

Chapter 20

I did not feel it was my place to speak alone with the daughter of Delilah and Samson. Nor did I feel the girl's parents should be present to influence her. I had hardly ever noticed the presence of Adrianna. She was a plain little girl when we brought her home from the slave auction. Plump, with brown hair and wide-set brown eyes, she rarely uttered a sound in my presence. Now, at age sixteen, she had become the focus of all interest. I needed the help of my sisters to sort this out.

Mary, Martha, and I sat on the wide veranda with the girl. Mary knew much about the love of a woman for a man. Martha knew nothing. I only had the perspective of a man.

Mary, whose gentle eyes brimmed with compassion, leaned forward and took Adrianna's hand. "Patrick has chosen you to be his wife."

Adrianna clasped her hands together. "Yes, ma'am."

When no other words came forth from the girl, Martha asked. "Well?"

One corner of Adrianna's mouth curved in an almost-smile. "Well? What? Ma'am?"

Martha was impatient. "We brought you here so you could tell us what you think about it."

Adrianna answered, "I don't know. I never thought about it."

Mary patted the girl's arm. "Do you love him?"

Adrianna tucked her chin. A blush flowed up her cheeks. "I don't know about that, ma'am. But my father often said what a good fellow he is. A hard worker. I find him pleasant enough. Almost handsome. I don't mind the wooden leg. But ..."

"But what?" I asked, unconsciously echoing the girl.

She looked startled at the sound of my voice. Her gaze shifted nervously from me to Martha and then settled on Mary. "But ... he seems to wish to carry me far away. And though I am a free woman now, though I don't know what being free means, I am to be taken away from my mother and father and this ... my home. As if I am still a slave."

I tugged my beard and considered my hasty pledge to offer the girl in marriage. If she was to be set free, what right did I have to give her to a man in payment for saving my vineyards? "You are not a slave."

She held her gaze on Mary. "Then if I am free, why will I be married and taken away from my home and family?"

Martha asked, "Don't you like the fellow?"

Adrianna replied, "Like. Yes. But if I am free ..."

I interjected, "Even women who are born free have arranged marriages."

Mary shot me a disapproving glance. "Brother, what do you know of a woman's heart?"

Adrianna's eyes filled with tears. "Then I am not free."

Martha agreed with me. "What our brother says is correct."

Adrianna dared to blurt again, "But if he takes me to Britannia—a place I do not even know, nor do I know how far it is from my home—then if I am taken there against my will I am not free. You see?"

Of course we all understood the concept of freedom. We understood that women were not truly free to do as they wished. Mary had rebelled against custom, and it had resulted in the ruin of her reputation. Yet my concern was for the overall happiness of my household. My cook would never smile again. My winemaker would weep salt tears into the barrels. My barrelmaker would simply be gone.

I thanked Adrianna and sent her back to her mother in the kitchen.

"Well," I said to my sisters, "that was of no use to me. I have given my pledge to Patrick."

"No use at all," Martha concurred. "I came upon Delilah sobbing as she kneaded the bread this morning. Too much salt in her tears for the bread to bake joyfully."

Mary's pretty lips pressed tight, as if she was trying not to speak.

I asked her, "What do you want to say?"

"No one cares about the girl. All you care about is keeping your word to Patrick. A pledge that you gave upon the life and happiness of another human being. Upon the lives of several others, if you count your cook and your winemaker. And all the rest of us."

I argued, "She might be very happy in Britannia."

Mary tossed her hair. "I know something of that place. It is a land where none are free. And women are worth less than cattle. There is a custom among them that a wife or daughter may be taken away and used vilely at the will of the royalty and then, after the ravage, returned to her husband."

Martha's mouth twitched. She stared off at the vines. "A terrible revelation, sister. How could you know such a thing?"

"Does it matter?" Mary snapped. "Brother? Does it matter

how I am aware of such a terrible practice among the pagans of the north? I tell you, you must find a better way. If you have given Adrianna freedom, then she must be free. If she loves him but does not want to be taken from her mother and father, then you must find another way to keep your promise."

Patrick's hair was the color of the red donkey. *A matched pair,* I thought, as we rode toward Jerusalem. Only the donkey was not stubborn. And for the first time I thought that Patrick was in need of a beating.

Patrick's freedom had suddenly made him unmovable.

"I am a free man." Patrick lifted his chin. "I will marry Adrianna. I asked, and you said if I saved the vineyard I could have her. A promise is a promise, sir."

"But her parents. Samson is your friend. Delilah is … well … you cannot break the heart of such a good woman."

"I will go where I will go. That is what being a free man means, does it not?"

"But to marry Adrianna and take her away to Britannia! To deny the girl's parents the joy of raising grandchildren."

Patrick set his eyes on the road ahead. Herod's devastated vineyard was on our right. There was not one green sprig remaining. I remembered the sorrow Samson had expressed over what my grandfather had lost when his life was taken from him: he had lost the joy of knowing his grandchildren!

Sweeping my hand toward the ravaged vines, I said to Patrick, "Samson has been kind to you."

"Like a father."

"Then you would treat him thus? Stripping away his joy? To take his daughter and future grandchildren? To deny old

Samson the joy of dandling grandchildren on his knee? Then you send the locusts to devour his finest dreams of happiness."

Patrick frowned at my words, and for a moment I thought I was getting through to him. "And my family? In Verulamium. When I was conscripted to serve our Roman masters, I promised myself that I would return home one day. That if ever I was free, I would come home."

"How many years ago?" I asked.

"I've counted twelve years. Half my life lived in slavery. I was a lad of twelve when the soldiers took me from my father's shop."

I was silent for a time, wondering about the family who had remained behind. "Have you ever heard from them?"

"What? As in … a letter, you mean?"

"Surely you could send them a letter on one of the great merchant ships. Pay someone to carry it for you. And pledge a coin to the bearer from your family when they received word from you."

"A letter carrier receive coin from my father? To receive word from me?" He expelled a short, bitter laugh. "My father sold me for his debt. And besides, I do not read. Neither does he read or write. Not like you Jews who teach a toddler his numbers and letters. We have no time for such nonsense where I come from. So. To answer your question, I ask you … how could I hear from them? What would I hear? "

"I will help you send a letter. Your father owned a cooperage in the city of Verulamium, you say."

"Aye. That he does. He's not an old man. When he could not pay taxes, the Roman centurion came to draft my father as a smith, making weapons for the wars against the Celts in the north. Father begged them to let him stay home. They then selected my older brother, skilled with shoeing horses. Thranal is accomplished at making iron shoes. But my father knew my older brother was too valuable to lose. What was the blacksmith business without him?"

"Did they conscript him?"

"No. Father offered me and my younger brother, Oren, instead. Two strong boys. Two for one. Boys. Extra mouths for my father to feed. Worthless to my father. We would have been apprenticed out that year anyway. So. The Romans got quite a bargain. Except that Oren died the first winter. I lived on … as you can see. If you can call what I lived through living."

"So you will go home and comfort your father in his old age."

Patrick snorted. "He never liked me anyway. Always said I would come to no good. A worthless boy except that he could beat me and sell me. No. I will come home and show him. How, in spite of him, the great God of Israel gave me freedom and prosperity and happiness … and a wife. He will regret what he did to me."

"Your father's regret will make you happy?" I fixed my gaze on Patrick's bitter face. "Are you happy here?"

He nodded once. "For the first time in my life. Samson. And Delilah. Never two kinder … They have indeed treated me like a son …"

"Then why leave?"

He blinked as if it was the first time that question had ever entered his mind. "My dream to return. It kept me alive."

"Your dream?" I urged him to speak of it.

His eyes hardened. "My vindication. A sort of revenge. Showing my father that he sold the wrong son into bondage. Justice. Showing them—"

I held my hands out, imploring. "Patrick? What are you thinking?"

"If I don't go, my father will die never knowing how he consigned me to twelve years of misery."

"Before Samson dies, he longs for grandchildren to love."

"Until now. Until this place? I never knew a moment of happiness."

"Happiness." I weighed the concept in my right palm. "Or vindication." I weighed his goal in my left.

He stared at me in disbelief. Could it be that happiness was more important than revenge?

My grandfather's Bethphage vineyard was clearly destroyed. Vines he had planted. Desolate now and unyielding to the evil house of Herod the Great who had killed him to possess our heritage.

This was justice against the House of Herod, yet the sight of the devastation gave me no pleasure. I wondered as we rode past if there would ever be another vintage from my grandfather's estate. I considered Bikri, alone and friendless. Thirty-eight years begging for mercy and none to help him. Vindication? Revenge? It was not sweet to my eyes.

So I knew that returning home to Britannia would not ever bring peace to Patrick. "And now you have won your freedom. You left Britannia as an unloved boy with two legs and a talent for making things. You will return to your father's shop. You will show him that you have made your own life. Show him. A wife who loves you. A skill he did not teach you. Show him your worth?"

"That is my dream. My sunrise and sunset."

"But the sun shines upon you … here. Today."

"Then what will I do with all the dreams of revenge that I have cherished?"

"You can learn to cherish this day that the Lord has made. You cannot make sweet wine from bitter grapes."

"I imagine my older brother. What he received from my father's hand. Everything. While Oren died and I suffered at the hands of cruel masters." He studied the devastation beside us. "When the locusts came, I imagined my brother's life and wished such disaster on him. When I heard the news the locusts were coming, I hoped to help defeat the plague for you and win the hand of a wife and return home a free man."

"And will knowing the fate of your brother make you happy? Will you be happy if his life is as desolate as this field? As happy in revenge as you are here in a good life among people who love you and work that prospers you?"

Patrick's lower lip jutted out. His brow furrowed. "Ah, I see. I never thought of it. Aye. Different thought than I have had in these twelve years."

"Could it be that God has a different plan for you? That he has given you a new father who longs for you to stay instead of go? A mother who will cherish you?"

He looked at me, and his lips curved in wonder. "And perhaps an elder brother?"

I nodded and stretched out my hand to him. "Come. I have something to show you."

In silence, we rode up the slope that skirted my grandfather's vineyard. A narrow path branched off from the main road and the knoll of a low hill. A crooked trail led to a ruined cottage surrounded by an overgrown tangle of briars and a block of age-blackened, untended vines. Even after the locust plague, the wild foliage appeared to be unharmed by the insects.

I explained, "This is where my mother was raised by her widowed mother. It was a caretaker's cottage. Ten acres of vines and a few fig trees."

I did not speak of the thousands of acres stolen from my grandfather's estate. Perhaps Samson had already told the sad story to Patrick, for the young man's eyes filled with sorrow as he surveyed the wreckage.

"Right next to Herod's vineyard," said Patrick. "And yet not devoured. Just ... unloved. Neglected."

I took a deep breath. "It was a house of joy, in spite of sorrow. I own the cottage and the vineyard, though it has been deserted and uncultivated for many years."

"There is still life here."

"Samson rode out and walked the vineyard. He says the vines can be brought back to vigor. Two seasons, he says, if they are loved."

Patrick sat in silence. "And why have you abandoned this for so long?"

I shrugged. "It was a reminder of things long past. Though it is only a few minutes' ride from my Bethany estate, I did not wish to travel through the vines claimed by Herod to get here. So it has lain fallow these many years. These vines are the most ancient in the land. Grown from cuttings that go back to the time of King David. In my grandfather's day, the wines from this place were sacramental. Used for holy purposes. Perhaps that is why Herod the Great was afraid to touch them."

I studied Patrick's expression as he took it all in. I saw his thoughts race as he considered what a clever man could accomplish in such a place.

He did not speak. I clucked my tongue, urging my mount forward toward the house. Patrick's donkey followed.

One great vine, gnarled and as large as the trunk of a man, stood sentinel beside the flagstone path leading to the front door. "From that vine, the cuttings for many vineyards were taken. It is the ancestor of the wine of Israel. King David and Solomon drank from its fruit."

Patrick licked his lips. "I wish that I might … one day."

"The caretaker was a prophet, they say. He was one killed by Herod the Great in the rebellion."

"It is a beautiful cottage." Patrick seemed to see past reality. The roof was damaged, but the walls were strong stone blocks. The door hung askew on broken hinges. A barn and stone-walled sheep pens were intact. The well was covered by a stone.

I dismounted. "Samson says such a place would blossom under the care of a good tenant. One who would share eighteen percent of his crop with me on a ninety-nine-year lease … renewable on the same terms with future generations. Perhaps an arrangement with a bright young man … with a wife … and a flock of happy children."

Patrick stepped off the donkey. "Do you know any such fellow?"

"The only one I thought of is determined to leave for the far north of the world and never more return."

Patrick looked down at his hands. "Sir," he said slowly, "I did not ever dare to dream of such a paradise as this."

I surveyed the ruined dwelling place, the tangle of vines and briars. "Paradise." I repeated the word.

"Yes," he answered. "I say yes. If you will have me. I will stay. We will stay."

"I will contribute workmen to help you restore the house and clear the vines. And then it will be up to you and Adrianna and God to build a life."

Chapter 21

*T*he old cottage and still more ancient vineyard transformed dramatically, resurrected through the enthusiasm of Patrick, the energy of Carta, and the eager participation of Samson. The men divided their time between saving the dilapidated house and restoring the fields.

The cabin boasted only two rooms, separated by a wall containing the central fireplace and a space for cooking. I worked when I could spare time from my winery, and within two weeks the roof was sound, and the missing chinking in the walls repaired. Soon after, the chimney was repaired and the flue was drawing properly.

Inside two more weeks, Patrick and Carta had constructed a sturdy table and chairs for the front room. They added a clothes chest and a bed with a wooden frame and rope mattress for the back.

Patrick hung oiled-leather coverings over the two openings that served as windows. He also installed a new front door. It was strapped by leather hinges to a pole that rotated in sockets in lintel and floor. Thereafter he swept the paving stones and declared himself satisfied with the house.

He set to work repairing the water supply by cleaning the well and cistern.

While I had only visited occasionally, supplying such tools, lumber, and stone as the job required, I gave Samson leave to see to the property's vineyard.

One afternoon I rode over to inspect the progress. The rows in between the vines had been shorn of weeds. The trellis work had been repaired. Beside a cistern near the vines was a heap of debris, shoveled from its depths. Carta was dumping yet another bucket of dirt clods before dropping the pail back into the opening by its rope.

Samson greeted me as I arrived. He waved a cutting and summoned me to examine it. "See here, sir. If I may say so, there's life in this old vine yet." He split a cane with his knife and showed me a tiny fragment of green at its core. "Waiting, as it were," he said. "Dormant-like. It's as if it was waiting to be watered by its true master. Not give away its secrets to one as won't appreciate it, if you take my meaning."

I summoned Carta to join us. "I understand completely," I said, squinting at the hillside and the angle of the sun and digging in the soil with the toe of my sandal. "Afternoon sun. Limestone substrate. Good drainage. Fallow these many years. What you're saying is that this planting, brought back to production, may rival Faithful Vineyard for the quality of its produce. Not sure how I feel about that. What if Patrick sells his crop to a rival winemaker? What if he knows all our secrets and outdoes us? And you, my faithful winemaker, helping him surpass me?"

Samson looked stricken. "Sir, he never would. I mean, if I may say so, he never ..."

I smiled to show I was teasing, then clapped him on the shoulder. "You and I will have to make him such a fine offer for his crop that he is never tempted, eh?"

Carta chuckled to see the old man's chagrin at being caught by a joke.

My horse, tethered beside Pleasant the donkey to a venerable, thick-trunked vine, tossed up her head and whinnied.

Around the hill, striding rapidly into view with a no-nonsense manner, came a file of Roman soldiers, together with their decurion.

I was suddenly apprehensive, but not for myself. "Either they're looking for rebels or they're after——"

"Patrick," Samson muttered.

I turned in place, trying to appear unconcerned as the approaching Roman officer watched my every move. Barely moving my lips I said, "Where is he? In the cottage?"

Samson shook his head.

"God be praised, then. He's not here. We'll have a chance to warn him."

Samson hung his head. "No, we won't."

Now I looked around openly. "Where is he, then?"

Samson gestured toward a ladder's upright posts jutting out of the cistern. "He's plastering the walls."

I took in the situation. "Keep quiet and let me deal with this," I urged.

Then the squad of soldiers arrived and stamped to a halt.

The decurion, a swarthy man with a twice-broken nose and a cast to his left eye, greeted me. "You are David ben Lazarus, owner of this property?"

"I am."

"You have a slave named Patrick who has some skill with metal work? And we hear he worked out a way to turn back a plague from your vineyards. Clever fellow, we hear. Where is this slave?"

"He's now a free man," I replied. "No concern of yours." I felt myself begin to sweat.

The officer tipped the front of his helmet back on his low forehead and brought his right eye to bear on my face while his left wandered over the vineyard. He looked surprisingly pleased at my answer. "See, it's this way. Rome can requisition any freeman or any slave for the good of the empire. This Patrick is needed for the good of the empire's forges. But I don't have to explain anything to you. Where is he?"

"I haven't seen him," I replied cautiously.

"He has been seen coming to this location every day this week."

Who among my neighbors was spying on me for Rome?

I shrugged and said nothing further.

"Search the house," ordered the decurion. Five of the ten men surrounded the cottage to guard against escape, and the other five entered with short swords drawn.

The officer regarded me critically. "You wouldn't be trying to hide him from me, would you?"

"I said, I haven't seen him. Listen, Decurion, this is a mistake, and Centurion Marcus Longinus won't like it."

"Oh, ho," the Roman chortled. "Longinus, is it? Not a good time to use that name. He's in bad odor with the higher-ups, is Longinus. Stripped of rank and sent off to the wilds of Galilee to chase bandits, I hear. No, preaching to me of Longinus won't help you here."

The troopers emerged from the cottage. How long could it take to search a two-room cabin?

"No sign of him, sir," the leader of the squad reported.

I felt myself holding my breath. A few more minutes and they would march away. After dark we could rescue Patrick and send him away ... where? To my sister's estate in the Galil, perhaps. Somewhere until this could be straightened out.

"Look, Decurion, why don't I pay the bounty for you to hire a substitute?"

The Roman scratched the stubble on his chin and squinted at me with his left eye. "Not up to me. I've got my orders."

Leaning close enough to the decurion's powerful odor almost gagged me, but I said in a confidential tone, "Would it be better if I paid the bounty directly to you, Decurion? Cleaner and quicker that way?"

The Roman swayed, clearly tempted by the offer. I jingled my money pouch to indicate my willingness to shell out a bribe.

But the officer shook his head. "New chief centurion is a right unpleasant chap. Had the skin flogged off one of my mates for having a spot of rust on his armor at inspection." He looked regretful but determined. "Nope, can't chance it. I've got my orders. 'Bring in Patrick the smith,' and that's what I aim to do."

"Just not here and not now," I returned, trying to sound agreeable. "Look, it's a warm day. Why don't you and your men come inside for a moment? I have nothing to offer you but water, but you can have that before you march ..."

As soon as the word was out of my mouth, I saw my error, but it was too late. First one of the decurion's eyes, and then the other pivoted from well to cistern, taking in the ladder rails protruding above the rim.

Before I could blink, he whipped out his sword and held the point to my throat. "Search the cistern, men," he commanded.

As they marched Patrick away, a prisoner surrounded by guards, the decurion was laughing. "Don't need a cell for this one," he chortled. "Take away his peg at night, and he's good as pinned. Can't run far, now, can he?"

"Patrick," I called after him, "don't worry. I'll get this straightened out. I'll tell Adrianna your wedding is just postponed for a bit."

"Postponed is right," the decurion mocked. "I hear the legion's going campaigning against the Arabs next week. Maybe he can wave good-bye to his sweetheart as he goes away."

※

I rode north toward Galilee, leaving a household of mourners behind in Bethany. It was almost like death. Patrick was taken before the completion of the house and the wedding. All felt the ultimate loss for Samson, Delilah, and Adrianna.

My actions were tempered by the still vivid memory of Porthos's death. I was convinced there was no resisting our oppressors by force. If Patrick was to be saved, the answer lay with those we knew in places of influence.

I could not think of anyone but Marcus Longinus. The centurion was now suspect and assigned to duty far from Jerusalem because of his favorable sympathies toward Jesus. Even so, he was still honored and well respected among the rank and file of the legionaries.

His post in Capernaum was a journey of many days. When I arrived, I was aware Patrick could already be on the way to a military camp on the border of Parthia.

It was almost sunset, the beginning of Sabbath, when I arrived at the military barracks of legionaries lead by Marcus Longinus.

The Galilee outpost was established at the caravansary occupying the crossroads of the caravan route. Westward lay the port city of Caesarea Maritima, built by Herod the Great to honor Augustus Caesar.

Two sentries at the gate stopped me from riding in. "Halt!"

Remembering to dismount before I addressed them, I stepped off my mare.

"What's your business?" demanded a burly Syrian mercenary.

"I have traveled far to speak with Marcus Longinus, your commander."

The two put their heads together. "Our centurion … is a friend to these Jews," one muttered.

The Syrian demanded, "What's your name, then?"

"David ben Lazarus."

While the Syrian barred my way, the other soldier opened the pedestrian gate and hurried away. Through the portal I glimpsed a half dozen sweaty, unsaddled horses tied at the rail. I heard the clank of hammer upon hot iron coming from the blacksmith shop.

The smell of roasting pork and baking bread was in the air as the cooks prepared supper for the company. Off-duty soldiers roared and laughed as they played dice. Another honed his short sword and shouted at the stable boys carrying fodder for the livestock.

Minutes passed before Marcus emerged and tersely ordered the sentries to take my horse into the stable to be fed and watered. Marcus and I remained outside the gate. Only when they retreated did Marcus address me.

"Peace be with you," I said.

"And also with you," he answered with a question in his eyes. "Friend, is it well with you? With your … family?"

We walked away from the caravansary before I answered. To the west the deep orange ball of the sun melted on the far horizon. Banners of salmon and pink streaked the sky.

"I've been riding for days to reach you."

"Your Sabbath has begun. *Shabbat Shalom.*"

"*Shabbat Shalom.*"

"Mary? Is she well?"

"She is well."

"And Carta?"

"He has become a member of our family."

His mouth curved in a tight smile of relief. "Why have you come?"

"I need your help ... my friend."

"You have it, if I am able to give it."

"The officers from the Jerusalem garrison have conscripted Patrick of Verulamium. He belonged to Rome for twelve years. A blacksmith and a barrelmaker. He lost his leg in service and was put on the block. Once he was my slave, as I bought him at auction from the army. He is very useful to me."

"You freed him?"

"He earned his freedom by helping save my vines from the locusts. He is soon to be married."

"You say you purchased him, yet you set him free."

"A good man. A skilled fellow, Patrick. A Briton as you are."

Marcus rubbed his cheek. "Ah, Lazarus. What you don't know ... Patrick was safe from conscription as long as you bought and paid for him. As long as he belonged to you, they could not conscript him ... at least not without paying you his value."

"His value, slave or free, is incalculable to my business."

"Surely his fame as a clever fellow got back to the officers in Jerusalem. Herod Antipas and Pilate no doubt asked, how is it that the vineyards of the estate of Lazarus were saved and not the estates of Herod and the sympathizers of Rome?"

"Well, Patrick's gone. They took him by force, and we were helpless to stop them."

Marcus pondered for a long moment as a supper bell clanged. "I know your laws about the Sabbath. You can't enter the dwelling place of a Gentile ... my men are eating now."

"I cannot eat with you."

"But will you violate your laws to save a life?"

"My heart knows what is right."

"I have learned the Lord's teaching. You people accuse him and condemn Jesus for healing on Shabbat. Yet you will pull an ox from a ditch on Shabbat. Now, to save a one-legged blacksmith, will you come with me?"

There was no longer any question. "I came for that purpose." I followed Marcus through the gate of the outpost. The courtyard was now deserted. I heard the rowdy laughter of men eating in a dining hall to our right. To the left, the clank of hammer on iron continued in the blacksmith shop.

Marcus led me toward the forge. And there, bent and sweating over the red-hot iron, Patrick labored on. Sparks flew with every hammer blow. He did not look up. I saw the fresh bloody brand of a military slave with the number of Marcus's cohort burned on Patrick's forearm.

I stopped midstride as Marcus stepped aside. He addressed Patrick in the language of Britannia.

Patrick did not reply.

Marcus took my arm and pulled me forward into the light of the fire. "He has not spoken one word since he came three days ago. He barely eats. Speak to him," Marcus instructed me.

I said quietly, "Patrick?"

At the sound of my voice, he paused, still staring at the yellow glow of the iron. He did not look up. His eyes brimmed.

Tears spilled over and hissed on the metal as they fell. "I am dreaming," he whispered as he wept. "I hear the voice of my brother." His shoulders shook with silent sobs.

"Patrick!" I was at his side in two steps. The heat of the forge was on my face. "Look up! Not a dream!"

He cried out and flung the hammer away. Standing erect, he wrapped his arms around me and buried his face in my neck. "It's you! You came for me! My brother! My father!"

I wept with him. "My brother. My son."

"What's to be done? They'll never let me go!"

Marcus observed our reunion in silence for a time.

"How is my darling girl?"

"Adrianna weeps for you, her only love. Her hopes are smashed. Her heart broken."

At this news, Patrick could not control his grief. "Poor darling girl. Poor Adrianna. Better I never gave her hope!"

"Samson and Delilah try to comfort her, but they love you so. Like their own son. Delilah's tears salt our bread with sorrow."

"I am lost! All is lost! What is to be done?"

Marcus cleared his throat. "If you were the slave of the House of Lazarus, you could not be conscripted unless your master was paid fair value for a slave."

Patrick groped for a stool and sank down. He buried his sooty face in his hands. "It was all false! False! There is no freedom within the reach of Rome."

Marcus's eyes narrowed. He commanded, "Be a man. Stop sniveling. Look at him! David ben Lazarus! How can you call this creature worth his salt? Such a weakling is no good to Rome here in the frontier!"

I protested. "But ... but ... Patrick is ..."

Marcus growled, "A worthless weakling, I say! One legged. Mostly mute! He is worse than a woman!" He stepped forward, raising his hand as if to strike Patrick. "What good are you to Rome?"

Patrick looked at the heap of horseshoes he had forged. He blinked at Marcus in astonishment. "Sir ..."

Marcus shouted, "Why did you lie to the officers? Why did you tell them you were a free man?"

Patrick tried to speak. "But, sir, I am ..."

"Shut up, weakling! Liar! Your master has come for payment from us ... or to claim you." Marcus turned his fury on me. His voice carried across the courtyard. The clamor of soldiers in the dining hall fell silent. "All right, Jew. So! You identified him. This is the man. One leg! Ha! They send the rejects to me and expect me to manage! But you say he is your slave and has value to your estate. What then is the price for him?"

I could hardly think what price I could ever place on Patrick. "I ... I ... he is my barrelmaker and I ..."

Marcus bellowed. "Thirty pieces of silver? You demand the full price of a healthy slave? You must be mad! What use is he to Rome? You think I could justify paying such a price? What would my officers say if I showed them the accounts of this post and then pointed to a cripple and said, 'For this one-legged slave I was required by law to pay his master ...' They would take it out of my hide!"

At last light dawned. I fully entered the charade. "I will not take one denarius less! Thirty pieces of silver or I will appeal to the judges. Rome has stolen my slave and—"

Marcus roared back. "Take him! Take the sniveling creature!"

"I will!" I shouted.

Marcus lowered his voice. His expression softened. "Patrick, your life belongs to David ben Lazarus. There is safety in that. Do you understand?"

Patrick's chin jerked down once. His eyes were wide. He spoke in the tongue of his homeland. I guessed he was thanking Marcus.

Marcus took charge. "All right, then. Be of good courage. It's settled. I will prepare papers of release and put my seal on it while you saddle your horse and mine. It's Sabbath … your day of rest, but for the sake of Patrick, do not rest. Ride through the night. Ride like the wind. The fresh brand of a conscript slave is a danger to you. Blot it out. If you're stopped, the soldiers on patrol will likely be unable to read the words on my document of transfer. But show them my seal. I will come to Bethany to fetch back my horse. See you take care of him. Now hurry!" He pivoted on his heel and strode out of the forge.

"Come, Patrick. Let's go. Adrianna is waiting."

Patrick shook his head slowly from side to side. "Something to do first." He took the tongs and lifted up the red hot iron of the half-formed shoe. His eyes fixed on the coals of the forge for an instant. Then he moved his arm near to the fierce heat. In a single stroke, he pressed his arm onto the molten metal. Flesh hissed and seared, burning away the mark of slavery. Patrick made a low growling in his agony, then plunged his arm into a bucket of cold water.

He gasped. "Finished. Now. Home."

Chapter 22

News of Patrick's homecoming somehow preceded us, spreading from village to village in Judea. As we topped the rise of the hill overlooking home, two hundred people were gathered outside the gates waiting for us.

Patrick raised his arms to heaven and wept. "Home!" he cried. "Was there ever such a sight so beautiful in all the world?"

Smoke and the aroma of cooking meat filled the air.

"Look!" I laughed. "They're roasting the fatted calf! For you, Patrick! All for you!"

Strains of Carta's flute, of tambourines and drums, drifted up as we rode closer to home.

Patrick began to sing:

"For the horses of Pharaoh
went with his chariots
and horsemen into the sea!
Sing to the LORD,
for he has triumphed gloriously!
The horse and rider
He has thrown into the sea!"[1]

At the challenge of Patrick's rich baritone, the watchman on the walls lifted a shofar to his lips and gave the signal. Heads

215

lifted up, and suddenly there came a shout of joy so loud that the hills behind us echoed.

Adrianna came running, followed by Carta playing his flute at the head of a dozen skipping children.

"Look! Look! It's Patrick! Patrick and the master!"

"Master Lazarus has brought Patrick home!"

"Praise to God in heaven on high!"

"Patrick's home!"

Samson and Delilah followed with the three goats on their heels. And then came Martha and all the others, kicking up dust on the road as they ran.

Patrick leapt from the fine black horse. He bowed and kissed the ground, then jumped up and gave a whoop of delight as Adrianna, puffing and red-faced, fell into his arms!

He was instantly surrounded, swallowed up by joy!

"Patrick! How'd you get free?"

"Tell us what happened?"

"From front to back ... tell us!"

"Tell us!"

Flushed and grinning, Patrick glanced back at me over his shoulder and babbled. "The Master found me. Lost sheep that I was. He was very brave to be sure. He said I was his slave and demanded payment from the officer for me."

"Demanded!"

"Did you hear that? Master Lazarus demanded from a Roman officer!"

Patrick continued, "The fellow would not pay him the price. Said I am a one-legged reject and not worth it!"

This brought howls of laughter from the crowd. "Ha! Not worth it?"

"Patrick not worth it?"

Carta declared, "Now this is why Rome will one day fall! They do not know a bargain when they see one!"

More laughter.

Patrick finished the tale. "And so the master made a bargain with the Roman to take me home and never to set me free again! I am a happy slave in the House of Lazarus!"

This evoked cheers from all.

"Blessed be our master."

"… good master of the vines."

"Lazarus!"

"The Lord bless the House of Lazarus forever!"

"Our master went out in search of one lost sheep."

Carta yelped, "And he brought home the goat!"

I asked, "Adrianna, tell us. What are your thoughts of your betrothed coming home so soon?"

The girl blushed and tucked herself under the arm of Patrick. She gazed up at him with doe-eyes. He bent and wiped her tears with his thumb.

She tried to speak. "I think … I think that … I shall only be happier when it is my wedding day!"

Samson stepped up to me and bowed slightly. He whispered, "The cottage is all finished. We kept working even after he was away. We believed you would bring him back. Sir, if you don't mind me saying, by faith, our preparations for a wedding are well under way. A bath and fresh clothes are what Patrick needs, and then … we've got the guests. Everyone who loves us is here. And the food. There's plenty of wine. Here's the bride, my daughter … all blushing and filled with joy! And now the bridegroom has come to us. Can we not celebrate his return with a wedding feast?"

"Someone call the rabbi!" I commanded. "Tonight will be the wedding feast of Patrick and Adrianna!"

There was a cheer from all at the news. Adrianna burst into fresh tears.

Patrick beamed. "If I had known, I would have galloped all the way without stopping!"

Old Delilah embraced her blushing daughter. "My darling girl, my beautiful baby girl, come!" She commanded the children, "Hurry now. There are flowers on the hillside. Go pick flowers for the bride to carry!"

Samson shrugged. "Why wait? Why wait? You never know what tomorrow will bring."

I ordered that the finest wedding clothes be provided for Patrick. I longed only for sleep after my journey, but who could deny the momentum of joy? Giving my little white mare into the care of the stable boy, I hurried into the house.

As I bathed, the tempo of the music increased outside. Laughter spilled over the walls and splashed through my window. I glanced at the western sky. In the distance, Jerusalem crowned the mountain. I remembered my own wedding day. No day ever like it before or since. I imagined what it would be like when Messiah, the true heavenly Bridegroom, set his foot upon the Mount of Olives as the prophets foretold. The lion would lay down with the lamb. The Lord would teach our children in the streets of Jerusalem. Our oppressors would be cast out from us. Surely I would live to see that day.

I emerged into the twilight. The wedding preparations were complete. Children adorned the wedding canopy with flowers, and petals were strewn around the grounds. In the distance I saw Samson bringing the rabbi to our celebration.

I remembered Jesus at the wedding in Cana, blessing wine he had created from water.

"Blessed are you, O Lord our God, Ruler of the universe, Creator of the fruit of the vine ..."

It was Jesus who created the fruit of the vine that night. My thoughts leapt at the meaning of the miracle and the significance of the words of the prayer of thanks. "Blessed are you, O Lord … Creator!"

Wine from water? Impossible for mere man. But the light had shown upon Jesus when he recited the blessing and passed the chalice.

Without Jesus, water was just water. When I tasted the wine Jesus made, I knew his vineyard, like his kingdom, could not be of this earth.

As Patrick and I had returned home, in joy, I fully believed in the meaning of Jesus' miracles. No doubt remained in my mind.

Jesus was the True Vine. Jesus was the heavenly wine. Jesus was Messiah, the true Bridegroom of Israel, come down from heaven to redeem his people.

Martha was the commanding general, organizing all parts of the wedding with military precision. Never mind that Patrick and Adrianna were Gentiles by heritage. Martha ordered that the nuptials be executed like any Jewish wedding. There would be no mistakes. No dish underdone. No lamp unlit. No musician faltering in his song. It was understood by all that the festivities would be perfect and filled with joy … or else.

Patrick asked me to stand for him as groomsman beneath the chuppah. As the vows between Patrick and Adrianna were sealed by the rabbi, women wept. Men smiled behind their beards, and I noticed that Adrianna no longer looked plain and plump. Love, it seemed, had made her beautiful.

The wedding feast went on for hours, with dancing and song and many, many toasts.

At last the celebration culminated in the presentation of the dowry and gifts.

Samson swayed a little as he raised his glass in the toast to his daughter and new son-in-law. "And finally"—he was misty-eyed as he spoke—"for the little girl who came to us with such a kind and loving heart. Our precious, beautiful, sweet, intelligent, well-spoken, and ... beautiful Adrianna. Our dear daughter. Yes. So. Where was I?"

Delilah chirped, "Hurry up! The sun will come up soon!"

Samson raised his index finger as though testing the wind. "Ah. Yes. As I was saying. Adrianna. Dear, kindhearted, and precious girl. Leaving my home for another. So. Her mother and I wish to present to the couple ... the gift of ..." Samson spread his arms wide and waved his hand at Carta, who waited in the shadows. "Come on, then!"

A little off cue, Carta led out Samson's favorite wine-red donkey. There was much applause as the creature stepped forward and nuzzled Samson affectionately. "No. No, I say. You don't belong to me any longer." He stroked her ears. "You are a pretty little thing. The color of a fine glass of wine." He smiled at us. "Don't you think she is a pretty little thing? Served me well. Her name is Happiness. Now here is a double blessing. Happiness is pregnant and will soon bear a fine foal for the happy couple. Along with Happiness, I pray my son-in-law will do his duty so that many grandchildren will bless my dear Delilah and myself. May Happiness always be with you, my daughter, dear Adrianna."

Applause. Amens. Another ten toasts. And so happiness came at last to Patrick. Just after midnight, he lifted his bride onto the back of the beautiful donkey. We plucked our torches from the ground and began the procession to deliver the couple to their new cottage among my grandfather's ancient vines.

"My beloved has gone down to his garden,
 to the beds of spices,
to feed his flocks in the gardens,
 and to gather lilies.
I am my beloved's and my beloved is mine;
 he feeds his flock among the lilies."[2]

We serenaded beside the ancestor vine at the head of the path. Patrick bade us *shalom* and carried his bride into the house. He kicked the door shut.

"My dove, my perfect one, is the only one.
 The only one of her mother.
 The favorite of the one who bore her.
 The daughters saw her and called her blessed."[3]

Chapter 23

My sister Mary brought Jesus and his disciples to stay with us in Bethany for a time during the season of Omer. Peniel, the boy Jesus healed of blindness, was with us, full of joy and constant wonder.

For seven weeks we marked the days from the escape of the Hebrew slaves from Egypt until the revelation of the law at Mount Sinai. Our hearts commemorated the journey from slaves of Pharaoh to servants of the Lord. Seven times seven days from Passover to Pentecost; it was a holy number. Each of the seven weeks represented a patriarch and the divine attributes of that man:

Abraham — Grace, Love
Isaac — Severity, Respect
Jacob — Beauty, Compassion
Joseph — Foundation, Loyalty
Moses — Victory, Efficiency
Aaron — Glory, Aesthetics
David — Majesty, Surrender

I had witnessed and come to believe that Jesus summed up all these divine attributes of God. But unlike our Fathers, there was no vice or weakness in Jesus to taint the perfect purity of his spirit. He was truly the only one without sin among us.

On this anniversary of Eliza's passing, the Lord walked with me as the sun set over Faithful Vineyard. "Tell me, my friend, what has changed in your heart since last year?"

I thought a moment, then expressed what I knew but had never put into words. "I'm stronger now. Like Isaac. Even without my beloved. I've grown stronger through this long, lonely winter. Efficient like Moses. I have even surrendered to my loss … like David. But still not where I want to be, not altogether filled with the righteous attributes of the Fathers as I wish. Especially not filled with love, like Abraham. No compassion, like Jacob. So very far to go until I become …" I hesitated, feeling his gaze locked on me, listening.

"Until you become … what?"

"Until I am like you. All the positive qualities."

We walked on together.

In the swale, where it was cooler and less exposed to the sun, the Lord paused beside a leafless vine. "Lazarus, there are no leaves. No sign of life here. Is this vine dead?"

"No, Lord. It's alive but still sleeping. Its blood is only beginning to stir."

"But to look at it, it looks dead. To someone who doesn't know, it looks like something to be uprooted and burned." He laughed.

"The warmth of the sun will wake it up in a few days. The vine is waiting for the warmth of the sun," I answered.

"What will happen then?"

"Bud break. The vine will push out new growth." I pointed to the vines higher on the slope. "You see?"

Jesus strode up the hill to the place where green buds had just emerged. "Well, here. Yes. I see it. Tiny leaves. Knobs of growth no bigger than my thumbnail."

"The higher we go into the light and warmth, the more advanced the growth," I said, flattered that Jesus wanted to learn from my experience.

"But how do you know these bits of green will ever become leaves?" he asked.

I motioned toward the top of the hill. "Because. It will happen. I know it will happen. When you've lived among the vines … well, the vines always bring forth buds, then leaves, then fruit, then … every year it's the same. They grow. There … look."

Jesus set out ahead of me. Near the top of the hill, where the sun shone brightest, the vines had blossomed with new life.

"Lazarus." We paused by a vine whose buds were a few days old. "What do you see?"

"Bud break. Leaves and tendrils. See there …" I pointed. "By the end of summer, if I care for it properly, that will be a cluster of fruit."

"And by next year you will pour it into my cup," Jesus said. "What about the dead-looking vines in the valley?"

"A few days in the sun and they will look like this vine. They'll put out buds, then leaves, then clusters of berries … then wine."

"Faith."

"Experience."

"Yes. Faith …"

"Ah. Yes. I see what you mean. I believe what's coming. Bud break. Fruit and harvest. Even though it's a long way off."

Jesus clapped me on the back. "That's faith. Can anything keep the ripening or the harvest or the wine from our cup?" He touched the new leaves as though he could visualize the full, rich berries ready for harvest.

"Yes. Oh, so many things, Lord. A big wind might come along and blow away the buds. Or a late frost could burn them. Or drought. Too many cloudy days. Not enough sun. Or disease. Or insects. Grape growing is full of worries, you see. At every stage. It's never a sure thing until the wine is in the cup. And the cup is at your lips."

Jesus studied the infant buds. "So is the human heart in the care of the Father." He drew a deep breath. "What in your life prevents you from bearing the most excellent fruit? Is there anything that will prevent you from ripening to perfect sweetness ... becoming a wine worthy to be drunk at the King's supper?"

It was an easy question to answer. The image of Bikri beside the pool came to my mind. "Yes. There's a wicked man, a man who has done great harm to my family." Tears brimmed as I remembered all the wrongs that had come to my dear ones through the deeds of Bikri.

Jesus did not reply for a moment but waited for me to fully think through what I felt but had never expressed. Then he asked, "Lazarus, why do you weep?"

I continued angrily as tears streamed. "The hand of God's judgment rightly came upon him. He was struck down ... a cripple. And he's been a beggar, alone and friendless, beside the Pool of Bethesda for many years."

"What is that to you?" His voice was gentle.

I rattled off, "I rejoice in his misery. I celebrate his suffering. It comes to me sometimes when I go to the Temple to bring my offerings and I go to look at him. Just to look at him—loathsome, flies buzzing around his head, shriveled legs, unable to move."

"Surely he deserves his punishment? Not like Peniel, the cheerful blind boy you brought me to last year."

"Yes. Yes. Lord, this fellow deserves … every calamity." Tears of rage continued to spill over.

Jesus asked, "Then what is it?"

"I hate him so deeply! And … it's a blight on my leaves. I can't seem to let go of the wrong he did to us. The betrayal."

"So his sin continues to hurt you."

"Yes. I have no compassion for him. I can't forget—can't let go, let alone forgive. You say to love my enemy. To pray for those who despitefully use me. You command it, but I can't. Hating this man is a dark cloud that keeps the sun from ripening the fruit. I rejoice, you see, in his unhappiness. And so my fruit is unripe and bitter, setting my teeth on edge."

"What can be done, Lazarus? To end your suffering? So only sunlight shines on your heart?"

I inhaled deeply, knowing the answer. "Look. The sun is setting. *Shabbat Shalom*, Lord. Will you be going to the Temple in the morning to teach?"

❦

As the sun rose the next morning, I walked to Jerusalem with Jesus and his disciples. The city was quiet, the marketplace empty because of the Sabbath.

Jesus took my arm and directed his disciples to leave us and go ahead of him into the Temple. We watched them retreat. Peniel looked over his shoulder and grinned broadly. Perhaps he was remembering this was the anniversary of his healing. He waved cheerfully and matched Peter's gait stride for stride.

Sunlight beamed on the parapets of the vast sanctuary. A flock of mourning doves rose above us in a spiral, like the smoke of living incense.

"I love this time of day," Jesus said quietly.

"Yes. At rest."

"Except for the poor and the sick. The beggars at the gates. They can't rest."

"No." My reply was curt. My heart was pounding in anticipation of what was to come.

"So. Where are you taking me, my dear friend?" Jesus inclined his head.

Wordlessly I led him through the streets to the pool at the Sheep Gate, where the animals of sacrifice entered the city. Outside the entrance I halted, hardly able to enter.

"My enemy is inside. Beneath the third portico." I managed to choke the words out.

"And why did you bring me to your enemy?"

"He has no one to help him."

"What is that to you?"

My mouth opened. Emotion constricted my throat. "I want to forget about him. I want to let go of my joy at his anguish."

"Why have you brought me here?" Jesus asked again, more earnestly.

"I ... I don't ... I can't hold on to the past anymore. My anger. My heart filled with bitterness."

"What is that to me?"

"Help me, Jesus. Help me let go of the sins of Bikri the thief. The liar. The man who betrayed my grandfather for money."

"How can I do what you ask? Tell me. Say it aloud."

"I ask you to ... heal my enemy. Let him walk again."

Jesus nodded. "You will have to enter this place of suffering with me."

"I ... can't. I have never confronted him. Only watched him from a distance."

"You must show me the man, Lazarus, my friend. Take me to his place."

I knew Jesus meant for me to take an active part in this. I could not hide myself and simply hope Jesus would find Bikri out of all those who camped beside the pool.

I linked my arm with his, and together we waded in among the multitude of sick and lame who lay beneath the porticoes of Bethesda. I covered my nose against the stench.

Jesus scanned the sea of human misery displayed before us. Every space on the pavement was filled.

"He's over there." I lowered my voice.

"Lead on," Jesus instructed.

I picked my way carefully through the filth and rubbish of those who waited for a healing angel to descend and stir the waters. The beggars seemed not to notice us as we wound our way toward my enemy.

And then we came upon him. He lay at our feet. He looked up at me. A vague flicker of recognition crossed his face. Did he see my grandfather reflected in my eyes? Did memory of his sin flash through his mind? He smiled slightly with decayed teeth. Then he raised his bony hand, palm up, in supplication.

His voice cracked. "Mercy, young sir. Have mercy on a poor cripple. A blessing from heaven upon you in exchange for a coin. A mite will do. Anything."

He was an old man. Pathetic. It occurred to me that he had begged here for thirty-eight years. What would become of him if he could suddenly walk?

Jesus stepped between me and my enemy. A shaft of light beamed down on the Lord. Jesus gazed at him with pity. Studying the cripple, he then asked, "Do you want to be made well?"

The sick man seemed befuddled by the question. He gave the answer of one who had stopped hoping. "Sir, I have no man to put me into the pool when the angel stirs the water.

When it is stirred up, while I am coming, another steps down before me."

Jesus took in his explanation and said to him, "Rise, take up your bed and walk."

Immediately, Bikri was made well. He sat up, picked up his mat, and walked.

My eyes widened. I gasped and stood back as Bikri raised his mat above his head and roared to his fellow inmates, "Look! Look at me! Look! I am standing! Healed. Walking!"[1]

Jesus put his arm on my shoulder, and we quickly escaped the uproar of astonishment that followed.

"How?"

"What happened?"

"Did the angel stir the waters?"

As we retreated up the street toward the Temple Mount, the quiet Sabbath morning was shattered as their cries pursued us up the incline.

At the top of the hill Jesus stopped beside the potter's shop and turned to see what would happen next.

Carrying his mat, Bikri emerged from the entrance to the pool and was almost instantly accosted by two Pharisees on their way to the Temple.

"It's the Sabbath! It's not lawful for you to carry your bed."

I plainly heard Bikri's reply. "The man who made me well said to me, 'Take up your bed and walk.' I didn't want to argue … after all—"

The Pharisees demanded, "Who made you well?"

"Who did this?"

"Who commanded you to break the Sabbath?"

"Tell us!"

Bikri shrugged and deposited his mat at the base of a pillar.

"I don't know his name. No idea."[2] He squinted at his bed and muttered to himself. "No one will steal it. It's Sabbath after all. Who would pick up a beggar's mat and walk away with it?" He laughed. "Who would want it?"

"So! He healed you on the Sabbath. Commanded you to break the Sabbath." The Pharisee pointed his finger in the old man's face. "If you find him, report his identity to us."

Bikri shrugged. "How much will you pay me?"

Jesus and I turned away from the scene as more Pharisees joined the crowd.

When we entered the Temple courts, the disciples of Jesus waited for him on the steps near the Treasury.

"And now, my friend?" Jesus asked me as we walked.

"The leaves that blocked the sun are stripped away."

"Yes. The sin he committed against you and your family will no longer burden you. You have chosen the better part, and now the path to eternal life is his to choose or reject."

"I understand." I felt an enormous weight had been lifted. "Thank you. I suppose he'll pick up where he left off. Continue in his ways. Do just as he did when he was young."

"And what's that to you? What's important is that you've done the right thing. In bringing me to him, you've let go of him. Maybe he will repent and do good, or maybe he'll cling to his sin and do evil. If he does right, you've saved him from hell. If an evil man is warned and doesn't repent, then his blood isn't on your hands." Jesus raised his chin and fixed his gaze inside the Temple gate.

Bikri entered, looking frantically around the place. Spotting Jesus, the old man ran to him. Bikri grinned at Jesus with broken teeth. "Lord! Please tell me your name! They asked me why I carried my mat on the Sabbath, and I told them you commanded me to walk and carry my bed away. They want to know who you are ... a Sabbath-breaker, they say."

Jesus considered the man before him, then gave the warning, "See, you've been made well. Don't sin again, or a worse thing will come upon you."

I knew in the instant of hearing that Jesus was telling Bikri there would be no more chances for him to get it right. What could be worse than living as a cripple for thirty-eight years? Only one thing could be more terrifying: death and judgment.

Bikri insisted, "But what should I say to them that question me? About breaking the Sabbath and all?"

Jesus answered, "Tell them it was Jesus of Nazareth who told you to rise and walk and carry your bed on the Sabbath."

"Ah. Jesus of Nazareth. All right, then." Bikri did not stay to hear Jesus teach. He scuttled off to find the Pharisees who had questioned him.

I heard later that Bikri told them it was indeed Jesus of Nazareth who had broken the Sabbath by healing him. Jesus, who had commanded him to break the law when he picked up his mat.[3]

I heard also that they paid him to inform on Jesus.

But what was that to me?

Because Jesus had done good for a man on the Sabbath, the religious leaders dedicated themselves to persecuting him. But the truth Jesus lived out before us was undeniable. I wanted only to grow and ripen and become more like him.

My heart was at peace that day as I listened to Jesus teach.

"... The Son can do nothing of himself, but what he sees the Father do. For whatever the Father does, the Son does ... and he will show greater works than these that you may marvel. For as the Father raises the dead and gives life to them, even so the Son gives life to whoever he will. He who does not honor the Son, doesn't honor the Father. I say to you, whoever hears my word and believes in him who sent me has everlasting life and will not come into judgment, but has passed from death into life. The hour is coming, and now is, when the dead will hear the voice of the Son of God; and those who hear it shall live. Don't marvel at this; for the hour is coming in which all who are in the graves will hear his voice and come forth—those who have done good, to the resurrection of life, and those who have done evil, to the resurrection of condemnation."[4]

He aimed his message fiercely at the Pharisees who stood with arms crossed and fists clenched.

"I don't receive honor from men. But I know you, that you do not have the love of God in you. I've come in my Father's name, and you don't receive me ... There is one who accuses you—Moses, whom you say you trust. But if you really believed Moses, you would believe in me, because Moses wrote about me. If you don't believe his writings, how will you believe my words?"[5]

There was much more he taught that day that has been written down by other witnesses. These words of Jesus were guaranteed to offend the Pharisees even more than a beggar healed on the Sabbath.

After that, the religious leaders plotted all the more to kill Jesus because he said that God was his Father, making himself equal with God.

Jesus was serene in his purpose and in the truth. He saw clearly into the hearts of all people. The battle lines were drawn, but Jesus knew the end of the story.

Part Four

The scepter will not depart from Judah ...
    until he to whom it belongs shall come....
He will tether his donkey to a vine,
    his colt to the choicest branch.

GENESIS 49:10 – 11

Chapter 24

*J*esus came to stay with us again during the Feast of Dedication, which we call the Festival of Lights. It was the time of year after harvest when the vines are dormant, leafless, and unkempt. It was a cold, dark winter, and Jesus was our Light.

We all went together to the Temple to remember its desecration by the Greeks and the battles of the Maccabees to restore it. I believe this was the Jewish holiday our oppressors feared most. It was the holiday of rebellion and victory!

In every home along the route, lamps glowed in the windows facing the street. A drizzling rain chilled our faces as we climbed the steps, but we felt excitement in our hearts. When we reached the summit of Mount Moriah, the mist became flecks of snow that scudded on the wind.

Questions rang across the Temple Mount and into the halls of the mighty:

"Is Jesus of Nazareth another Judah Maccabee?"

"Will he call the people to rebel?"

"If the Maccabees defeated the Greek Empire, is it possible Jesus will rally many to defeat Rome?"

It was evening when we walked with Jesus in Solomon's Portico. A number of Jerusalem Sparrows, orphan boys of the city, guided us with torches. For the eight nights of the feast the Temple courts blazed with illumination. The glowing tribute to Almighty God could be seen for miles, as if the mountain were a beacon of freedom in a dark, weary world.

We circled the Temple courts in two files of worshipers. We sang with one chorus proposing and the other replying:

"Shouts of joy and victory
    resound in the tents of the righteous:
'The LORD's right hand has done mighty things!
    The LORD's right hand is lifted high!' "[1]

Jesus spoke to the boys of our forefathers and noted that most Jewish celebrations centered around freedom. Freedom from slavery. Freedom from sin. Slavery and sin were alike, were they not?

"No one can serve two masters," Jesus told us, "for either he will hate the one and love the other, or he will be devoted to the one and despise the other."[2]

Two Levite choirs continued the dialogue in song:

Open for me the gates of the righteous;
    I will enter and give thanks to the LORD.
This is the gate of the LORD
    through which the righteous may enter.
I will give you thanks, for you answered me;
    you have become my salvation."[3]

The Pharisees gathered around Jesus and began to question him:

"How long will you keep us in suspense?"

"If you are the Christ, tell us plainly."

Jesus answered, "I told you, and you don't believe. The works that I do in my Father's name bear witness about me. But you do not believe because you are not among my sheep. My sheep hear my voice, and I know them, and they follow me. I will give them eternal life, and they will never perish, and no one will snatch them out of my hand. My Father, who has given them to me, is greater than all, and no one is able to snatch them out of the Father's hand. I and the Father are one."[4]

The Levite choirs sang on in the background …

"Blessed is he who comes in the name of the LORD.
From the house of the LORD we bless you."[5]

The religious leaders were outraged as Jesus said these things. They picked up stones and were ready to stone him right then and there.

I whispered to Peter, "We've got to get him out of here."

But Jesus answered his accusers, "I have shown you many good works from the Father; for which of them are you going to stone me?"

Caiaphas stepped forward then. "It's not for a good work that we are going to stone you, but for blasphemy. Because you, being a man, make yourself God."

The priests and scholars could not match wits with Jesus. He quoted back to them from Scriptures, refuting every false charge they made against him. He ended the discussion that evening with this: "If I'm not doing the works of my Father, then don't believe me. But if I do them, even though you don't believe in me, believe the works. That way you'll know and understand that the Father is in me, and I am in the Father."[6]

The chorus continued singing:

"The stone the builders rejected
has become the cornerstone;

the Lord has done this,
    and it is marvelous in our eyes!"[7]

The council sent for the guards to arrest Jesus. But the Jerusalem Sparrows snuffed out their torches. People moved in, jostling and shoving, shouting back at the Temple guards. Jesus slipped away, escaping from their clutches.

We hurried back to Bethany, where the Lord spent one more night. Then he left us, crossing the Jordan River to safety where John the Baptizer had been at first, and there he and his close disciples remained.

Fame from his miracles reached far and wide. People came from everywhere to seek him. They said, "John never performed miracles, but everything John said about this man Jesus was true."

And many believed in Jesus in that place.

I rejoiced as the memory of a song of the Levite choirs at the Temple washed over me …

"You are my God and I will give praise you;
    you are my God and I will exalt you.
Give thanks to the LORD, for he is good;
    his love endures forever!"[8]

Chapter 25

It was in winter, just after Jesus of Nazareth and his followers departed for the region of Perea, that the strangling sickness came to Jerusalem. I learned the grim news when Centurion Marcus Longinus galloped his black stallion to Bethany in search of the Healer. Otherwise the Jerusalem Sparrows would die, Marcus said.

Plagues were common enough in Jerusalem, especially among the poor. And there were few who lived more desperate lives than the Jerusalem Sparrows, the Link Boys who resided in the ancient quarries. It was said, "Sparrows are sold two for a penny." The Link Boys were paid a penny for a pair of them to assist travelers in finding their way around Jerusalem by night. The Sanhedrin voted the orphans a charitable allowance: a supply of wood for torches. Such was the charity of Lord Caiaphas.

A penny earned might buy bread for a day ... but not much else. The Sparrows scavenged or begged for the rest of their needs. When fares were scarce and donations dried up, the boys were left starving and freezing.

Now this.

"They'll die by the dozens, and it will spread," Marcus reported. "I hoped to find Jesus ... to take him back there with me."

"It's because of threats against his life that we urged him to move away from Jerusalem," I said. "You know Lord Caiaphas has spies watching for him. So does Herod Antipas. Is there nothing we can do ourselves, so we don't have to ask him to return?"

Marcus looked doubtful. "I've seen such a plague take hold in Rome. Thousands died—mostly beggars and children—but anyone who cares for them will be risking the same."

"I'll go," I volunteered. "I'm no physician, but surely blankets and decent food will help. It's the least I can do."

Martha shook her finger in my face. "I'll not have you going alone. I'm coming too."

"We have lives to protect here," I countered. "Tell her, Marcus."

"He's right," the centurion agreed. "You have no idea how bad it is, Martha. The children Mary brought with her from Galilee must not be exposed to this plague. You and she must stay here and care for them. No one should go back and forth until the crisis passes. Only someone who can remain there should go."

"And that means me," I said firmly. "The vines are dormant. This year's vintage is in the barrels. I get restless this time of year anyway. I'll go, and Peniel can help me. Besides, Martha, you never had this illness. Mary and her servant, Tavita may be safe because they already had it. Peniel says he also had it as a child, but you never did."

❧

The underground caverns that were home to the Sparrows were gloomy and fearful at all times. Now the sounds of coughing and low moaning reverberated the length of the low ceilings.

It was terrifying. A score of children were already dead.

Threescore more were gripped by the plague: feverish, shivering, hollow-eyed, and listless. "Dear God of Heaven, where do we even begin?" I murmured my prayer of supplication even as my mind wrestled with the problem. "They must be moved," I decided. "These tunnels are too cold and drafty. They'll all be dead in days."

"I agree," Marcus said, ordering men to stir the meager fires and sending others to round up blankets. "But where can we take them? We don't want the plague to spread, nor cause a panic that one is spreading."

"Leave that to me," I offered. "Stoke the fires and get them some water. I'll be back as soon as I can."

The first three empty buildings I offered to rent suddenly became unavailable when I explained the need. Fear and superstition overcame greed.

It was not until I located an empty olive-oil storage warehouse outside the Damascus Gate that I was successful. The building had been vacant for a year. The owner was eager to see it earn some payment, his broker said, and in any case, the landlord lived in Antioch and never visited the property. "Make it worth his while and it's yours," the steward said, not even asking me my purpose for the space.

"Short term," I said. "I'll pay you three months' rent for two months' use if I can take possession today."

"Done," the steward said, stretching out his upturned palm to receive a pile of silver coins.

I recruited a team of beggars who were also eager to earn some of the coins from my money pouch. With their assistance, soon my hospital took shape. In short order I acquired braziers and charcoal to heat the drafty space, rope-strung sleeping pallets, cook pots and fresh water, and a supply of bread and beans.

When all this was organized and ready to receive the children, I sent my crew off to carry them back. Of the residents of Jerusalem, it was the beggars who had little fear of the plague. They had lived with near starvation much of their lives and often saw dreadful diseases up close. Finding their next meal was more important. This pestilence had no terror for them— at least, not yet. Unlike the wealthy, including Lord Caiaphas and Tetrarch Antipas, who escaped to safer locations, the poor had no means of escape.

The glowing embers of the braziers raised the temperature of the hall. Bubbling pots of stew scented the air. I made my way along rows of boys, spooning broth into mouths.

The first Sparrow, a lad of ten named Suda, was clad in little more than rags. He apologized for coughing. His eyes were bright with fever, but after a few mouthfuls of soup, he sat up and leaned back against the wall. "Thank you, sir," he said. "Will you give some to my brother now? He's only six and needs it more than me."

"What's your brother's name, and how will I know him?"

"Hiram," Suda replied. "He has a blue head scarf." Suda surveyed the warehouse. "I don't see him, but he was sleeping next to me in the caves."

Peniel touched my elbow. Drawing me aside, he said, "Hiram didn't make it."

Returning to Suda, I offered him more broth. "We'll see to your brother, boy. Right now you must eat and get well yourself."

Big tears welled in his eyes, and he turned away from me. "He's dead, isn't he? I promised to care for him ... and I failed."

With some difficulty, Marcus Longinus finally located a doctor who would come to our aid.

I was attempting to feed another of the Sparrows. Jason was his name, and he said his throat hurt too badly to swallow. "And ...," he gasped, "my chest hurts. Can't breathe good."

The physician, a Greek by the name of Sosthenes, asked another boy to open his mouth. By the light of an oil lamp held nearby, he examined the lad's tongue and throat. What he saw there caused him to narrow his eyes and frown.

Gesturing for me to follow him, he showed me the progression of the disease, from simple fever and cough, to constricted breathing and lethargy, and then to a third patient worse than the rest.

This boy—no one seemed to know his name—was barely responsive to the doctor's touch. His body was racked by spasms of coughing, and he shivered continuously. Each gasping breath made him raise his shoulders and gulp for air, like a drowning man ... or one being crucified.

More horror followed. Lifting the boy's head and turning it so the flickering light shown into his mouth, Sosthenes called for me to come closer.

What I saw caused me to draw back with disgust. Inside the boy's lips, his tongue and throat were carpeted with a grayish-green monstrosity.

"What ... what is that?" I demanded.

"Strangling sickness," the physician reported grimly. "They all have it, but this is where it leads if untreated. 'Leather-hide,' it's called."

"What do we do for it?" I asked urgently. It appeared some evil creature had crawled into the boy's throat and was choking him to death. "For him?"

Sosthenes shook his head. "For this one, it's already too late. He'll be dead by tomorrow."

"Can't you yank that ... that thing ... out of there?"

Marcus put his hand on my shoulder. "I saw this before. Even if you cut it loose, the boy would choke on his own blood and ... it grows back."

I shuddered, then turned to look around the hall. Every conscious soul seemed to be gazing at me, imploring me to save them. The echoing of coughing and sniffling multiplied and resonated as if the warehouse itself were in the grip of the disease. "Dear God, not all of them," I pleaded.

The doctor's manner was brusque and businesslike. "You won't save all of them," he snapped tersely. "But you won't lose them all either, if you do exactly what I say."

Sosthenes prepared a list of medications and a treatment schedule: lemon oil to be added to boiling water to steam the room ... oil of camphor in sweet wine, spooned into their gaping mouths ... another oil, whose name I had never heard before, used to paint throats three times a day ...

Just as the doctor was concluding his instructions, a Roman soldier marched up to Marcus, saluted, and presented a scroll sealed with the mark of Governor Pilate. Marcus read the message, grimaced, and said, "I'm ordered—*ordered!*—not to provide help. A Jewish problem, the governor says."

"Someone has pressured him," I said bitterly. "The Temple authorities want to use this as a trap to bring Jesus back to Jerusalem." I thought of the dozens of innocent lives being risked by the high priest's plot, and it made me angry and determined. "I know the power Jesus has," I said, grasping Peniel's wrist. "I know he told us to use his name in speaking to the Father ... and that's exactly what we'll do."

I expended my silver like water, buying supplies and medicine. Peniel hiked to my home and waited outside the gates. Martha filled a leather pouch with coins and carried on a shouted conversation about the progression of the disease. Peniel purchased what was needed and trudged back to the hospital.

Soon it seemed even that effort would not be enough to keep up with the plague's demanding maw. Roman soldiers rounded up Jerusalem's beggars at spearpoint and forced them into my shelter. Most were not ill, but since the plague had begun among the poorest of the citizens, the wisdom of the powerful was that the disease itself could be confined if the beggars were all imprisoned.

A ring of troopers surrounded the warehouse. They were not present to lend any assistance, only to see that none escaped … unless carried out dead.

The space that had seemed ample for the army of boys was now jammed wall-to-wall with a hundred patients.

I wrote a letter to Nicodemus, imploring him to ask the Jewish Council to send aid.

What I got in response—with Nicodemus's apology for the lack of caring on behalf of the Council—were four crones, matrons from the women's prison. They were greasy, surly, uncooperative, brutish wretches barely qualified to empty chamber pots.

Much of my time was occupied carrying out Sosthenes' instructions. He urged me to pay special attention to swabbing throats with the tincture he called *phytolacca*. It was the only means, he said, of stopping the progression of the disease into its acute phase.

My thoughts were haunted by dread of the malevolent olive-hued evil creeping down young throats and choking out their lives.

I dedicated myself to the task, though it was far from simple.

Eight-year-old Jason was braced against my knee as I sat on the floor. In one hand I held a bowl of the mixture. In the other I had a sprig of hyssop as a brush. Each time I attempted to paint his throat Jason would gag, cough, and spray phytolacca on both of us. Then he would apologize, and we would try again.

Meanwhile I was surrounded by pitiful cries for water. These were supplemented by the whimpering moans of children unable to care for their own sanitary needs.

"Rapha," I said, calling the senior of the matrons, "Rapha, do you hear? Can you attend the water, please?"

She and her sisters looked around at me like a herd of cows studies a passing rabbit, then resumed their gossiping. A phalanx of unfeeling, lazy flesh prevented the comfort of a charcoal brazier from reaching the patients. The women warmed their hands around the fire and studiously ignored me.

"Rapha!" I repeated more sharply. "I need your help!"

"But sir," she whined, "didn't you just tell me to stir the kettle so the stew don't burn?"

"How long does that take?"

She sniffed and sounded abused and unappreciated when she put her hand to the small of her back and said, "It's this cold and damp. My old bones don't move as well as they used to."

Her complaint provoked a chorus of sympathy from her cronies. They also made sure to let me know that all these duties were beneath their station in life. According to Rapha, performing chores for beggars was lower than keeping hogs.

"And besides," Rapha said, "none of us has no medical training. We wouldn't want to do something wrong and accidentally kill one of these boys."

The only success I had making them be of use was when I threatened to stop their food. Even that consequence only served before they had eaten. After sucking down a bowlful of lentils each, they were just as obnoxious and arrogantly slothful as before.

On more than one occasion I caught them stealing bites of stew that were supposed to go into the patients' mouths. They also hid bits of bread in their clothing.

In almost every instance it was easier for me to perform the tasks myself, unless I was free to stand right over the women as they worked. The only reason I got any work out of them at all was that the guards stationed around my hospital had orders that no one could leave, so they had no choice but to remain.

The physician had expressly ordered that the medication, the doses of camphor in sweet oil, had to go on around the clock. Otherwise, he said, we had small hope of saving any of the patients. For that reason I had to snatch a few minutes' sleep whenever I could.

It was not often. The rasping coughs and the cries for help kept me awake most times. If these sounds were not enough to prevent slumber, Rapha's snoring was.

After a few days I was exhausted, stumbling from boy to boy in a stupor almost as profound as the worst of the ill. In the morning I penned a note appealing to my sisters for help. I did not know what they could do, but I was at my wits' end.

The help that came in response to my note was more than I could ever have imagined. The day after I sent Peniel to Bethany with my appeal, my sister Mary and her servant Tavita appeared at the hospital. Within moments of taking in the situation, they also took charge.

"We will not risk asking Rabbi Jesus to return," Tavita said.

"And didn't Rabboni tell us to ask whatever we needed in his name and his Father would hear us?" added Mary. "So, we're asking! Almighty Father, we are not worthy that you should do anything for us, but in the name of Jesus of Nazareth, and by his direction, we do ask. Help us save these boys!"

Then Tavita added, "And we're going to keep on asking too!"

Mary whispered to me, "Putting the Almighty on notice is a new achievement, even for Tavita."

"She has always intimidated me," I confessed.

"Now that we're here you must sleep," Mary urged.

"But the next round of treatments—"

"Can wait for one hour," Mary replied. "You nap, and we'll organize. That's it. Off to the quietest corner with the cleanest blanket. There you go."

Truthfully, I did not require much urging. I think I was asleep while my feet were still moving toward my pallet.

I drifted off, listening to Mary stating her plans and Tavita barking orders. The last comment I remember before slumber claimed me was Mary observing to Rapha: "You will obey everything Tavita tells you to do, and you will do it immediately and without complaint. Or do you know what? I will see that you are returned to the prison as inmates for pilfering supplies! And you'll be confined in the lowest, coldest cell."

"Actually, you'll be thrown in with the prisoners you abused before you came here," Tavita added. "Wonder how that will turn out for you."

I slept with a smile …

When I awoke it was dark outside. I bolted upright in a panic: the medicine! The throat treatments! I was failing in my duty!

Mary reassured me otherwise: "Once Tavita got things organized, the rest was easy."

I scanned the warehouse. Before I slept, the patients had been arranged in long rows. Some were comfortably near the fires but others were chilled at too great a distance,

Now the boys were arranged in circles, like the spokes of a wheel, with a charcoal brazier at the center of each.

"Tavita, Peniel, and I have made the rounds with the medicine. We're starting with the throat painting now. You can help, if you're up to it."

I nodded, overwhelmed with generosity and hope.

"And they've all been fed," Mary added. "Rapha and her crew saw to that."

"How?"

"Let's just say Tavita found the right encouragement."

I mixed the phytolacca and prepared to show Mary and Tavita how to apply it. The boy I used for my demonstration was named Lamech. When I sat down next to him, his eyes were clearer than in days and his voice sounded stronger. "Please, sir. If it's all the same to you, I'd rather the lady dosed me," he said, pointing at Mary. "She told me part of a story when she gave me my tonic. I'd like to hear a bit more, if you don't mind."

Soon enough I was wrapped again in both a blanket and in slumber, confident that with Mary and Tavita in charge, my boys—I thought of them that way—were in better hands than in the previous week I had been caring for them. And that notion did not injure my feelings one bit.

❧

Telltale barking coughs still ricocheted around the ward of Jerusalem Sparrows. The plague would not lightly give up its grip on my boys.

What changed was the atmosphere in the hospital, meaning both the air we breathed and the spiritual sense too.

With only the prison matrons to assist us, Peniel and I had felt like drowning men. No task was ever completed; no dosage or feeding gave satisfaction.

We had been holding our own, but that was all.

When Mary and Tavita took charge, they insisted that any old, filthy rags be taken out and burned. The cheap charcoal we had been using was discarded; higher quality coals burned with more heat and less smoke. The crones were set to work sweeping and scrubbing floors with the steaming lemon water under Tavita's watchful eye.

The boys were bathed. The straw of their pallets was turned every day and discarded once a week, to be replaced with fresh stuffing. Tavita washed faces, cut and brushed hair, sewed new robes from blanket stock.

How she found time for all that and nursing as well I never discovered.

After another week, with rotating care provided by Mary and Tavita, it was clear that a true miracle was in progress. Not another death did we have.

Some, like Jason, were not only stronger, but they were gaining weight by eating regular, nourishing, hot meals.

Others, like Suda, who had been very low indeed, were brought back literally from the brink of the grave. Suda, who still mourned his lost brother, was able to swallow an entire bowl of broth and nibble a bit of bread.

Mary rocked the children. She sang to them and told them

stories about Jesus. "Do you know how, when our great-great-great grandfathers were in the wilderness, God sent manna … bread from heaven … to feed them? Well, Jesus did something just like that in Galilee. He fed thousands of people from just five barley loaves and two little fish."

"And then what happened?" they chorused.

"More later," she promised.

Disappointed groans followed her to her next circle of patients, but they were the sounds of boys on the mend, their strength returning.

Tavita also told every one of the Sparrows about Jesus of Nazareth. "In Capernaum there lives a girl named Deborah. She's about your age," the servant said, pointing toward a twelve-year-old. "Well, she got sick and died."

"Did she have the plague too?" piped a listener.

"No, something much more sudden," Tavita said. "But do you know what Rabbi Jesus did for her? He spoke to her, and she woke up and sat up."

"Was she really dead?"

Tavita nodded vigorously. "Really and truly. But Master Jesus spoke her name, and she came to life again."

Suda whispered, "I wish he did that for my brother Hiram."

Tavita folded the boy in her arms and rocked him. "Me too, lamb. But Hiram's in *olam haba* now. Who else do you know in *olam haba* who was there to meet him?"

"Mama and Papa," Suda said, his lower lip trembling. "They both died the same year we came to Jerusalem. That's how we came to live in the quarry."

"There now, my sweet boy," Tavita crooned, stroking Suda's forehead and cheeks. "Someday we'll go see them together, eh? What a reunion that will be."

At the other end of the hall Mary sang. She had a beautiful, lilting voice. "Listen! This is a song written and sung by my namesake, who was the Lawgiver's sister:

"Sing to the LORD,
   for he is highly exalted
The horse and its rider
   he has hurled into the sea.[1]

"Now I know," Mary said, "your terrible sore throats won't let you sing now. But I'll teach this to you, and soon enough we'll all sing it."

They all believed her and looked forward to joining her choir.

And so did I.

Chapter 26

*T*here came a morning when I awoke with a headache and a sore throat. In the reflection of a polished brass serving tray I inspected my tongue and saw two pale white spots there, each about the size of a denarius. I did not tell my sister, but she knew instinctively I was not well. I was shaky when I walked and halting in my speech.

The symptoms appeared on the same day word came that our departure from the hospital was abruptly ordered. A ferret-faced man named Ra'nabel ben Dives, who was secretary to High Priest Caiaphas, arrived at the head of a pack train of supplies.

It was more like a royal procession: a half score of donkeys were tended by twoscore servants and preceded by a crier and three men blowing silver trumpets.

"Make way for the high priest's retinue. These supplies are urgently needed by the suffering beggars of Jerusalem. Make way!"

Ra'nabel, head piously covered, walked behind the procession, praying loudly and thanking the God of Israel for the sacrificial generosity of Lord Caiaphas. By his prayer he informed the citizens of Jerusalem that this charity was absolutely essential to the survival of the Sparrows.

In truth the total supplies Caiaphas sent would only have required a single cart to transport, but they were welcome just the same. Or so I thought when one of the servants pounded on the door of the hospital, and Ra'nabel announced the gift.

While I spoke in a normal tone, the secretary continued stridently proclaiming to all Jerusalem the goodwill offered by Caiaphas. He made certain to make the aid sound massive and the plight of the "destitute and dying" very grim indeed.

I told him the help was very welcome. "And, thanks be to the Almighty, the danger is past. The boys are all on the mend, getting better every day."

Ra'nabel then informed me that our presence at the hospital was no longer required. "Lord Caiaphas thanks the House of Lazarus for its good service as you return to Bethany."

"Return to ... you're ordering us out?"

"Lord Caiaphas, mindful of his responsibility to the poor of Jerusalem, wants to take personal charge of seeing that the contagion does not spread. We will take over now."

In my foggy mental state it took a moment for me to comprehend these actions, and then it came to me. Word had reached the high priest, probably through one of the crones, that the Sparrows were improving as we worked and prayed in the name of Jesus of Nazareth.

If the boys had died, then Jesus could have been blamed, but he could not receive credit if they were made whole. The high priest had waited until a successful outcome was assured before seizing the credit for himself.

I started to reply to this takeover, suffered a sudden bout of coughing, and finally acquiesced.

When Mary protested, Ra'nabel's features lost their ingratiating aura. "You would do well to keep silent! We know the man from Nazareth is a sorcerer. It has come to the attention of Lord Caiaphas that incantations have been performed using the blasphemer's name. You are hereby ordered to gather your belongings and be out of here by tomorrow or be arrested for witchcraft."

With a hand trembling with both illness and emotion, I penned the news in a note to my sister Martha. I also asked that she prepare the disused building behind the barn for me to occupy.

Mary, reading my words, protested. "Brother, you're not well. When you get home you need your own bed."

"No," I countered. "I cannot be where I'm a danger to the others. I'll be fine in the old cottage. But only you and Peniel can come see about me. Please make it clear to Martha that I love her, and there is no way I will expose her to this disease."

Our departure from my boys was tearful. Laying hands on each child, we prayed in Jesus' name for their continued strength and full recovery. "Remember what we say: there is true power in Jesus of Nazareth. Not another one of you has been lost. Who has ever heard of such a thing?"

Mary kissed each boy's forehead ... then we were gone.

※

By the time we reached my front gate, my head was throbbing. I could not open my eyes wider than a squint because the Judean sun was unbearable. My throat felt parched, yet when I tried even a mouthful of water I could not swallow without a great effort to overcome the pain.

Because I did not want to alarm Martha, I said nothing about any of my symptoms. A few days of rest and good food, I reasoned, and I would be on the mend. In my deepest heart I knew this was self-deception at best. I was afraid to admit the extent of my illness for fear Martha would insist on summoning Jesus to help me.

The thought of being the cause of his arrest ... or worse ... was something I could not permit.

I pretended to scratch my beard, complaining that Mary and Tavita had made the Sparrows more presentable than I was. In reality I fingered the line of my jaw, the glands underneath alarmingly swollen and hot to the touch.

Martha met us and would have swept me up in an embrace, but I fended her off abruptly. "Need rest and quiet," I said brusquely. When I saw how my tone had hurt her, I added, "A few days ... right as rain." It was becoming harder and harder to speak at all. With every word either my throat seized up or I coughed, so all my phrases came between short pauses. "Fix your famous ... lamb and rice. See how ... fast I get ... strength back. But not today," I added. "Soup, today, please. Only Mary and Tavita should ... come near me, Martha. They ... had this illness ... got well, but you ... never had it."

"Neither have you," Martha murmured, alarm barely hidden behind a carefully neutral visage.

That night Martha prepared a savory broth. The steaming tureen of chicken soup filled the freshly scrubbed cottage with the aromas of cardamom and ginger.

As soon as I smelled it I felt my throat constrict. "Just put it ... down," I managed to rasp to Mary. "Sleep a bit. Eat later."

I did sleep then, but fitfully. My dreams were filled with images of a snake coiled around my neck, strangling me. When, in my dream, I struggled to free myself from its coils, it turned into a black cord knotted about my throat being tugged ever tighter by Lord Caiaphas and his scribe Ra'nabel.

Mary's touch on my forehead woke me. "So sorry, brother. You were making terrible noises, writhing on the bed. It sounded like you were calling for help."

"Just …" My throat hurt so badly I had to pause before adding, "… dreaming."

Her arms under my shoulders helped me prop upright. My head felt as if it weighed far too much for my neck to support. The least jostling filled my head with the sense a grinding stone was rolling around inside it.

She gave me a sip of water, for which I was grateful, but when she held the mug to my lips a second time I waved it away. Mary prayed for me then. In Jesus' name, she asked the Almighty to recognize how diligently I had worked to save the Sparrows and requested I be shown the same miracle of restoration as they.

When I opened my eyes in the morning, bright sunshine streamed in. Outside the cottage's window an almond tree displayed its exuberant rebirth in showy pink blossoms.

A trio of caregivers surrounded my bed. Mary, Tavita, and Peniel formed a knot of silent witnesses. Had they been standing over me all night? Was I so ill that they thought I was going to die? Or was I dreaming now?

Mary spoke: "Good to see you awake, brother. Martha sends her love and a pot of stew." She nodded toward Peniel, who raised the lid of the kettle he carried and inhaled appreciatively. "Smells wonderful, Master David," he observed. His stomach growled.

I had no appetite. My coughing was not as violent, but only because I had no strength left in my exhausted frame.

By what I knew to be a feeble gesture, I waved away the soup. With fragments of words I vowed to have some later.

"You must eat to recover your strength," Mary insisted.

Speaking required too much effort. I shook my head gingerly. I saw Mary exchange a worried glance with Tavita. When Tavita volunteered to coax me to eat, as she had successfully done with my boys, I allowed her to try.

I could not find any aroma or any taste in the broth, but that was of no concern to me. The liquid seemed to get stuck halfway down my throat. A pain built in my chest, as if I had swallowed a stone, and it was blocking the passage to my stomach. Each drop required a supreme effort of will to force down.

I could only manage a few swallows before I shook my head again. Between the soreness of my throat and the bouts of coughing, I feared I would choke. In any case I was not hungry.

The three of them left then, but I overheard their conference through the thin walls of the cabin.

Mary insisted I was getting better.

Tavita replied that Mary had not seen my throat or tongue. "We should send for Jesus. Now. At once. Send Peniel today."

I would have shouted and told them no, but I had no breath or strength for shouting. Feebly I called, but no one heard me.

Then I heard Mary complete my refusal for me: "My brother would never agree to call Jesus back into danger. We pulled all the boys through this. We'll pull David through as well. You'll see."

I lay back on the pillow then, as tired as if I had fought a great battle.

Outside the window a flotilla of clouds drifted past, like an armada of galleys coasting down the wind. I admired the lack of effort, the ease with which they floated. Of course they could not stop nor turn against the wind. All they could do is run before it until they piled up against a mountain peak or dissolved above the hot sands of the desert.

At the moment either choice was preferable to where I lay and how I felt.

Chapter 27

Was it morning or evening? Dawn or twilight? I could not tell. The light in the cottage was dim, but it seemed to neither increase nor decrease. I tried to lift my head to look around; failed. I tried to raise my hand to hold it in front of my face; failed again.

A dearly beloved countenance, almost as familiar as my own, bent over me. What was her name? Part of my mind wrestled with the problem. I knew I should know her name. Why couldn't I remember it?

A cloth dipped in warm water appeared. Gentle motions scrubbed my eyes, nose, and mouth. When it was lifted away from me, I saw it was stained red. Was I bleeding? It did not seem to matter.

"Poor, poor dear," a tender voice crooned.

Mary! That was the name. I vowed to remember it.

A spoon was inserted between my lips, and some liquid dribbled in. Where did she think the fluid would go? I could not recognize much, but I knew my tongue was now swollen until it completely filled the cavity of my mouth and throat.

No room! I wanted to shout. *You're going to choke me!*

"Come on, lamb, just a little more."

I clamped my lips shut. The wooden spoon clunked against my teeth. Some broth or soup or water dribbled on my chest.

Mary tried again to insert the spoon between my teeth.

By rolling my shoulders and flinging my emaciated frame to the left I managed to knock the spoon from her hand. *Leave me alone*, I felt like screaming.

Even thinking about screaming made my head ache.

"David? Brother? We must … must … send for Jesus. Now. Today."

A burst of coughing shook me from my head to my toes. Summoning all my reserve of breath and strength, I managed to croak: "No! Not safe! Don't!"

Then, like a crushed grape skin after the juice has been pressed, I folded back into the bed, lying flatter and stiller than I had before. "Promise!" I demanded.

❦

I was barely conscious of the ongoing efforts of my sisters and the physician, Sosthenes, to save me. I had no sense of time moving at all. I lived in a kind of perpetual suspense, waiting for something without knowing what.

I no longer opened my eyes. If I swallowed water or broth, it was without my knowledge, or perhaps in spite of it.

Only a few moments registered with me as taking place outside my mind.

The doctor, belatedly called to my bedside, forced open my mouth. He jammed a device in place to hold my jaws apart. Holding an oil lamp so close to my face I writhed away from the heat, he painted my throat with something far more foul and gagging than phytolacca.

I heard or perhaps dreamed Mary pleading with Marcus

Longinus. "Go find Jesus!" she begged. "Tell him we need him to come. For the sake of one he loves, he must come! Beg him to intercede!"

Such urgency was no longer relevant to me or my life.

Like spiders aimlessly wandering, my fingers plucked at the covers or at my beard. I scratched my own arms in the torments of trying to draw in air, but I was mercifully unaware of the struggle.

Chapter 28

*D*arkness. Silence. The sudden absence of pain.
I heard my sister Mary weeping. Calling my name. "David! Oh, David! Don't leave us! Don't leave ..."

I stood above her as she bent over the ashen body of a man. Who was he, lying there? Why did she weep for the stranger? She threw herself upon the chest of his empty shell. Her shoulders trembled with sobs.

I tried to speak to her. Reached out, but my hand could not touch solid flesh. I floated above the scene as others charged into the room. Martha shrieked and clapped her hands over her mouth.

I floated just above them. I studied the face of the dead man. I knew he had once been me. Strange that I did not recognize the face that had been my face in life. The thought came to me that I had gone through the days of my existence without seeing myself as I appeared to others on earth. My eyes had looked out upon others, but I had not seen myself as I was. I had smiled, and my sisters had returned smiles. I had frowned, and their faces reflected my unhappiness. But as I looked at my empty self, I did not recognize what I had been.

Martha rocked and beat her breast. "Oh, my brother! My brother! You have flown away."

I wanted to tell her that I had not yet flown. I still hovered in the room.

Mary picked up my dead self's hand and kissed it. I leaned close to look at it. Ah yes. I recognized the hand. It was familiar to me. I knew the scarred knuckles of old wounds won over the years working in the vines. I had used those fingers for everything. The hand was useless now. Limp and white. My body was now a dried cane, past its season, cut off and lying on the earth.

Mary's hair fell across the chest of the corpse.

"Mary, why do you weep? I'm here, Mary! I love you! All is well." But she could not hear me. There was no comfort in my silent testimony.

I heard the rustle of wings. I felt myself, my true self, hovering like a hawk, motionless on the wind.

A deep resonant voice said, *"Lazarus, you cannot help them now."*

I glanced up to see the angel. Tall, strong, wings folded at his sides, he was perfect in feature and form. Radiant white garments with the glow of a rainbow around him. I thought that he resembled me, only perfect.

"They grieve," I said.

"They loved you."

Mary cried, "If only Jesus had come! If only he had been here! Our brother would not have died!"

I said to my angel, "Poor Mary. Look at her. She has only just found me, and now I am lost to her."

The angel said, "Remember when Eliza left you. And the baby. Your sisters will go on. Life will go on."

"Well, then," I said, looking at my old self. "It was a good life."

My angel asked, "Are you ready?"

One last time I reached out to stroke Mary's hair. This time I felt it, soft beneath my fingers. She raised her head as though she felt my farewell.

"Well." She laid the hand across my old self's chest and patted it. "*Shalom*, dear brother." Not taking her gaze from the beloved face so familiar to her, she wiped tears with the back of her hand. "Look. He seems to smile. He was a good man. He'll be with Eliza and the baby now."

I felt the stirring of joy in me, like when music begins, calling one to dance.

"I'm ready," I said to the angel.

He reached out to me. Spreading his great silver wings over me, he clasped my hands. "Come on, then. They're all waiting for you."

"Who?" I asked.

Before he replied, I heard the rushing of a great wind as we moved through a tunnel of light at unimaginable speed. And yet I did not feel the motion of our journey. Earthly time was stripped away as we were immersed into eternal timelessness. I glimpsed my old life falling away like old work clothes.

I saw myself as a child playing among the green leaves of my father's vineyard. Then, as a young man, harvesting the grapes. Then, as a grown man, with a heaping basket on my shoulder carrying the fruit toward the crusher. Then I saw myself, the bridegroom, drinking the wine. Eliza smiled up at me. And I lay beside her, feeling the movement of our baby in her belly. Then there was Jesus and the blind boy at the Temple. I felt the eyes of my friend, Jesus, close upon me.

The light grew brighter and brighter before us.

I laughed. We emerged into a vast, beautiful vineyard that

swept across rolling hills crowned by a golden sky. In the far distance blue mountains reared up, taller than any earthly mountain. A great city crowned the peak. Light and music flowed from within it. My angel stood beside me as my feet touched solid ground. His wing was over me. A melody surrounded me. When I moved my hand, I heard the tinkling of bells, like the water of a brook. I inhaled the sweet perfume of flowers.

In the far distance I heard voices calling my name, as my mother had done when I was a boy staying out too long after dark.

"What is this place?" I asked my angel.

"You have seen it in your dreams. The Father's vineyard."

To my right and left, clusters of red, purple, and gold berries hung from different branches of the same vine. Ripe and unripe fruit, blossoms and new growth sprouted together.

The ripest bunches hung from eye level all the way to the ground. They appeared to be so heavy with fruit, so plump with juice, I imagined it would take two strong men to carry them on a pole.

"I admire this vineyard," I said to the angel as I placed my nose against the cluster and breathed in deeply. "Were there ever such grapes as these?"

I recognized the aroma of the fruit was like that of the wine Jesus had made for the wedding in Cana. Heavenly wine. I said to my angel, "So this is the soil that fed the Lord's wine."

"You have a good nose, David," the angel said.

I paused. "But … where is everyone? You told me they were waiting for me."

My angel raised his chin. "Look!" He lifted his hand and pointed down the long row.

I saw a group of people coming toward us through the vineyard. They wore white robes trimmed in gold with gold sashes embroidered with words I could not read. They were laughing and singing.

My mother and father walked at the front of the procession. My grandparents. Porthos. Judah ben Perez. His sister and mother and others I had known. The others stopped and sang as Mother and Father continued steadily toward me with their arms outstretched.

"My son," Mother called to me. "Oh, my boy!"

My mother. Young. Beautiful. Skin perfect and smooth, without a wrinkle. Teeth white and straight. Long auburn hair tumbled over her shoulders.

My father cried, "David! My son! Welcome! Welcome home!"

My father. A young man again. Strong. Handsome. Bronzed face aglow with delight. His shoulders were broad. Arms muscled. Black curls fell across his forehead. His dark eyes shone with happiness at the sight of me.

"Papa!" I called. "Mama!"

I ran toward them and they toward me. The ground beneath my feet was firm and solid. I glimpsed my hands as I reached out. Yes. My own familiar hands. But there were no scars. I fell into their arms and embraced them.

Burying my face in my mother's neck, I remembered the sound of her heartbeat against my back when she carried me in her womb. "It's been a long journey," she said, stroking my hair. "But you're home now."

"You've run the race well," Papa said.

I raised my face and asked, "Eliza and the baby? When will I see them?"

Papa answered, "My son, *when* is not a word we know here.

There is no time—no when, no before or after—there is only a perfect order to all things. So you say, 'This is first, and this is next, and this is after ...' You will see Eliza in the perfect order of all things."

"I am content," I said, sensing no urgency in anything.

Mama took my arm, and we three walked back to the place where I had first stood with my angel.

I saw now that the entry point was a tall arched gate reaching up to a misty height. The gate was adorned with a mosaic of palm-sized, multicolored stones. Sapphires, rubies, emeralds, and diamonds shimmered, refracting light as rainbows. Each color and its variant shades emanated a distinctive musical note. Music and color melded together in perfect harmony.

I hummed the color blue.

My angel was seated on a knoll where red flowers sang. A man sat beside him, watching our reunion with pleasure.

"David ben Lazarus!" He called to me, "Come up!"

Chapter 29

My mother and father remained at the foot of the hill. I approached the angel and the handsome young man I guessed to be in his midtwenties. The young man seemed familiar to me. I remembered on earth seeing my reflection as I drew water from a well. It was like that. My features, the set of my eyes, the curve of the mouth and shape of the face, only not myself.

The young man and my angel stood when I drew near. The young man put out his arms and enfolded me in an embrace. "My father," he said to me. "I am your son. Your heart named me Samuel the morning of my birth. And when I returned here, you wept for the baby named Samuel."

I said, "But my only son was a newborn when he died."

The chimes rang. The angel spoke: "There is only one age here. It is the age of perfection."

Samuel smiled. "I am the baby who lies buried in the garden beside my mother, your wife."

I gazed at him in wonder. We sat together on the knoll and held one another's hands and spoke of his brief journey into the world of man. "I was not sorry to return home … here. But I told my mother I would be glad when you joined us."

I studied the vineyards. "Where is she? Where? Your mother? My wife. Eliza."

"I am second in the order of those who have come to welcome you. It is proscribed: First, your mother and father—you are flesh of their flesh. I am your son, blood of your blood. It is right that I follow my grandparents in welcoming you. My mother will come to you after we have made our journey."

I nodded, comprehending the order of things. I felt no anxiety about when I would see Eliza. I was certain she would come when it was right. I was aware of the absence of time. The wonder of the meaning of *eternal*.

I told him about Bethany and all that I had done since I was a youth. I remembered the color of sunsets and described details of days and nights perfectly. He hugged his knees and drank in all the stories of my life as if it had been his life.

Samuel's face was radiant as he recalled his three days on earth. "My father, I only lived in the world such a short time. But I remember well how you held me close in your arms and whispered and called me your 'little man.' I recognized your face perfectly when you entered Everlasting. When we saw you, I said to Mother, 'Well, here he is!' Oh, my father! I remember your breath on my cheek and your fingertips brushing my forehead as you rocked me and prayed for me to stay on earth with you ... prayed for me to live and take up your mantle when you were old. And so ... look here! Here I am beside you! Alive as you asked. But it wasn't meant to be that I stay behind. Mother flew away home to heaven, and I was so small. I could not stay without her."

My true self was filled with joy at the beauty and wisdom of my son. Love for him engulfed me. I could no longer summon a memory of my grief at his loss.

I spoke to him of the majesty of Jesus now on earth among men. Samuel knew the Lord Jesus well and said all the angels and saints would be glad when he returned to his rightful place.

How much time on earth had passed since I met my grown son and recounted all the days of my life? Time was nothing, after all. I had no way to judge Forever. I guessed that many, many years had flown by on earth. Surely others of my loved ones would be joining us.

The rustling of feathers caused my son and me to raise our faces in unison. My angel stood before us.

"Lazarus"—my name floated to me like a song—"now you know your son. How do you feel?"

"Overwhelmed by love." I put my arm around Samuel. "I know what it means to be a father."

My angel nodded once, pleased by my answer. "As your father loves you, you love your son." The being closed his eyes.

The melody of many colors swirled around our knoll. Samuel gripped my forearm. "Look, Father! Look there! Joseph the Dreamer, Revealer of Secrets, comes!"

Suddenly a man dressed in a multicolored coat stepped out of a rainbow of refracted light. He was tall with dark hair and a braided beard. His teeth were white and straight, his lips curved in welcome. I recognized him at once.

He was Joseph, one of the twelve sons of Jacob the patriarch. His story had been my favorite in Torah school. Joseph had been the firstborn son of Jacob's beloved wife Rachel. He was the most beloved by his father. Because of this, Joseph was hated by his jealous half brothers. When Joseph was seventeen, they sold him into slavery, covered his multicolored coat with the blood of a slain goat, then told old Jacob that Joseph had been torn to pieces by wild beasts. But the Lord had raised Joseph from slavery to become the Prince of Egypt. He had saved the brothers who had betrayed him.

Joseph reached out to us in greeting with his hands palm up. "Ah. Blessed be the Lord, Adonai, who makes all things right! Look at you! It's Lazarus and Samuel. Parted on earth but now together. Was there ever such a beautiful sight? Father and son! Reunited after such a long time."

I knew Joseph spoke from experience. How many years had he lived the life of a slave before he became prince of Egypt and was reunited with his father?

The angel bowed to Joseph and stepped back.

Samuel and I also bowed low, but Joseph lifted us up. "Lazarus, master vinedresser ... honored friend of Messiah Jesus ... companion on his journey ... beloved of the Lord. I was also a son, like your boy. Am I not also a father, like you, Lazarus? I was also beloved by my father, who grieved every day after my elder brothers sold me into slavery. But my story is not mine alone. The details of my story also prophesy of the life of Jesus, Messiah, Holy One of Israel. Jesus, whose name means 'Salvation.' Jesus, son of ... Joseph. Come with me now and see what was, what is, and what is soon to come upon the earth."

"Where are we going?" I asked.

"Time is nothing. Walk."

Clasping my arm and that of my son, Joseph the Dreamer pulled us after him through the curtain of refracted light.

I heard the sound of mocking. "Climb out if you can!" A group of rough-looking desert shepherds gathered around an empty cistern. Flinging dust at some pitiful creature trapped beneath them, they shouted:

"Come on, then!"

"Show us what you can do, dreamer of dreams!"

"We, your brothers, are stars who bow down to you!"

"We are sheaves of wheat who pay homage to you, O Prince!"

"Show us! Climb out if you can!"

"Free yourself if you're so powerful."

Samuel and I recoiled, holding back.

The Dreamer did not let go of us. "You must come. My brothers cannot see us. It is myself in the pit … as I was the hour my brothers stripped me of my father's mantle and threw me naked down into the cistern."

We had stepped from perfect peace onto the hard ground of the violent earth. I smelled the sweat of the young men around the pit. Their clothes smelled like sheep. The burning heat of the desert beat on my head. Faces were contorted with a gleeful rage as they hurled insults and sheep dung onto their young victim.

The Dreamer said, "These then, were my brothers. Rachel, the beloved, was my mother. But we were all sons of Jacob, grandsons of Isaac, great-grandsons of Abraham, who was the faithful friend of God."

"May I speak?" I asked.

Joseph nodded. "They cannot hear you. They do not know we are watching."

I whispered to the Dreamer, "What has this to do with Jesus, who was sent from heaven to earth as Redeemer of all Israel?"

Joseph the Dreamer replied in a sad voice, remembering, "What was done to me will be done to him by his brothers. Everything means something." He inclined his head as the sons of Jacob left off their sport and left in a pack to eat their meal. Each of the sons of Jacob trampled on the beautiful coat their father had given his favored son.

"Listen to what they say," the Dreamer instructed us.

"Let's kill him," said one, tearing meat from the bone with his teeth.

"Aye," agreed another. "I'm for it."

"There are lions in this place. Our old father will never know it was us."

"We can say it was a lion. What do you say, Judah?"

The one they called Judah lifted his head from his meal. "Look! A caravan of Ishmaelites is approaching."

The Dreamer explained to me and Samuel, "They were from Gilead. Their camels were loaded with spices. They carried the balm of Gilead for healing and myrrh for burial. Even these spices were a prophecy of what must come for Messiah."

Judah stood and stretched, then said to his brothers, "What will we gain if we kill our brother and cover up his blood? Come, let's sell him to the Ishmaelites and not lay our hands on him; after all, he is our own flesh and blood."

His brothers agreed.

The Dreamer drew us near as the sons of Jacob pulled the young man from the pit and sold him to foreigners for twenty shekels of silver. We watched as the caravan receded in the distance and the brothers slaughtered a goat. Then they dipped the coat of their innocent brother in the blood of the goat and carried it home to their aging father.

I shuddered as I heard the terrible wail of Jacob's grief rising from the tent.

"My son! My son! My beloved son!"

The Dreamer lowered his chin and frowned as though the moment was fresh. "Oh! How my father, Jacob, wept! The grief of a father for his beloved son." We stood on a hill above the encampment of Jacob. The keening of the old man resounded like waves crashing against the rocks.

"I will not be comforted," Jacob cried. "In mourning I will go down to the grave with my son!"

So his father wept for him.[1]

As we listened to Jacob's sobs, the Dreamer thumped his heart with his clenched fist. "The sword of sorrow pierced my father's heart. I carried the weight of my father's sorrow away with me. I heard him weeping still, long after I was sold in Egypt."

The words of the Dreamer and his father's tears were too much for me to bear. I felt the grief of every father for every lost child. It pushed me down to my knees.

Joseph the Dreamer commanded me to rise, "Get up! The weight of the world's sorrow is too much for any man."

"I can't." My legs would not move. My shoulders trembled as I remembered the moment of holding my dead baby. Kissing his sweet forehead as I laid him in the grave. I began to weep.

Then Samuel, my son, lifted me to my feet. "Father, I am here. It's me … the son you lost."

I was able to stand. Able to breathe. I wrapped my arms around his neck and clung to him with joy.

"Come away." The Dreamer clasped my hand and the hand of my son, and we three stepped back through the veil of color. I was relieved as we departed the sorrow of the world. We left all that behind, entering again into the peace of the heavenly vineyard.

We sat on the knoll overlooking the vines. I thought to myself that surely many years had passed on earth since I had died.

I said to the Dreamer, "I never want to go back to the world as it is."

The Dreamer answered, "I suffered at the hands of strangers

for many years. I was thirty years old when the Lord lifted me out of prison and I entered the service of Pharaoh and became a prince in Egypt. The Lord revealed to me the famine that was to come upon all the world, and I stored the grain of Egypt for seven years. There was enough grain to feed the world."

The Dreamer raised his hand and pointed across the green and gold vines. "Look there! Time is nothing. My brothers, famished beggars, come seeking the help of one they do not know and will not recognize. They come to Egypt to buy grain from the prince of Egypt ... the brother they mocked and sold as a slave."

I saw in the distance a cloud of dust sweeping across a distant land. The cloud did not come near the vines of heaven.

The Dreamer commanded that we hold tightly to his sleeve. "Come!" he commanded. "Hurry!"

Suddenly we stood in the hall of a great Egyptian palace. The brothers of Joseph, older now, lean and weathered by sun and trouble, came walking as a group through the marble corridor.

We followed as they were ushered into the presence of a great man.

The Dreamer said to us, "That is who I became after all my suffering. They live in tents and tend my father's flocks. I am the prince of Egypt. I know my brothers, but they do not recognize me."

The eleven brothers bowed down before Joseph the prince, just as Joseph, as a boy, had dreamed they would. They presented him with gifts of frankincense and myrrh.

The Dreamer said to me, "There is my younger brother, Benjamin. We shared the same mother, Rachel. She died giving birth to the lad. I was present when he was born. He was a comfort to me and to my old father."

Samuel and I observed as the eyes of the prince fixed on Benjamin with such longing that I thought his heart would break.

Suddenly, the prince shouted that all his attendants should withdraw. As the Egyptians scurried out, the prince began to weep in front of his brothers. They looked at one another in confusion as Joseph's tears streamed down his face. "I am Joseph! Is my father still living?"

The brothers could not answer him. They were terrified at his presence.

He stood from his throne and descended. "Come close to me," Joseph entreated them.

They hesitantly moved toward him.

"I am your brother Joseph, the one whom you sold into Egypt. And now, do not be distressed or angry with yourselves for selling me here, because it was to save lives that God sent me ahead of you. For two years now there has been a famine in the land, and for the next five years there will not be plowing or reaping. But God sent me ahead of you to preserve a remnant on earth and to save your lives by a great deliverance. So, then, it was not you who sent me here, but God. Bring my father down here quickly!"

Then, as we watched, Joseph threw his arms around his brother Benjamin and wept. And Benjamin embraced him, weeping. Joseph kissed all his brothers and wept over them.

One moment more and I glimpsed the reunion of the old father, Jacob, with his son. Joseph held the old man in his arms, and the two wept for joy at their reunion.

The Dreamer smiled and turned away. "So many tears.

I wept for betrayal. For parting. For suffering. And for love. What my brothers meant for evil, God meant for good to save a remnant. The events of my life were but a foreshadowing of a greater life. He walks among his brothers now. But they do not recognize him. The prophecy is recorded by Moses in detail. As it was for me, so it is today on earth. Jesus the Messiah, only Son of God the Father, Deliverer and Redeemer of all the world, will soon be rejected by his brothers. Mocked, reviled, tortured, and stripped of glory. Jesus comes to be the Savior of all. What men intend for evil, God intends for good."

In the blink of an eye, we once again stood on the knoll above the heavenly vineyard of the Lord. And now the brothers of Joseph gathered around us. I recognized old Jacob, who, of all of them, still remained old in his appearance. His white hair and beard were an honored crown to a long life lived in sorrow.

The brothers bowed deeply before Joseph. Judah stood apart. It was Judah who offered to save his brother's life, I remembered.

Jacob approached Judah and placed his hand on his head. "Judah, like a good shepherd, you offered to give your life to save the life of your brother. It is recorded in Torah what I said to you. 'You are a lion's cub, O Judah! The scepter will not depart from Judah, nor the ruler's staff from between his feet until he comes to whom it belongs and the obedience of the nations is his. He will tether his donkey to a vine, his colt to the choicest branch. He will wash his garments in wine, his robes in the blood of grapes.'"

Joseph the Dreamer stood before Judah. "My brother, from your descendants and the tribe of Judah came forth King David, Israel's shepherd. From the descendants of David is born the Savior of the world: Jesus, son of David, son of Almighty God. The scepter is his."

Old Jacob turned to Joseph. "On earth, it is recorded that the father, the protector who raised up Jesus Messiah is a man named Joseph. Therefore Jesus is known as Jesus, son of Joseph. This is to honor you, my son. My blessing is recorded in Torah: 'Joseph is a fruitful vine, a vine near a spring, whose branches climb over a wall. With bitterness archers attacked him; they shot at him with hostility. But his bow remained steady, his strong arms remained limber because of the hand of the Mighty One of Jacob, because of the Shepherd, the Rock of Israel, because of your father's God who helps you, because of the Almighty who blesses you with blessings of the heavens above and blessings of the deep that lies below, blessings of the breast and blessings of the womb. Your father's blessings are greater than the blessings of the ancient mountains, than the bounty of age-old hills. Let all these rest on the head of Joseph, on the brow of the prince among his people.'"

I stood in wonder with my son in the midst of the ancient ones as they spoke of what was, what is, and what will be.

Love. Envy. Rejection. Betrayal. Suffering. Victory. Exultation. Reunion. Forgiveness. Salvation. Restoration. Deliverance.

The tears of Joseph were so great. The prophetic truth of what was to come upon Jesus, living out God's plan among brothers who hated him, was almost too much to bear. In the order of things, his story had only reached the tears of rejection ...

My son leaned close to my ear and whispered, "Look, Father! It's Mother. Mother is coming!"

The ancients parted for Eliza as she walked toward me. "Eliza!" I cried, enfolding my beloved in my arms.

Radiant at our reunion, she lay her cheek against my chest. "Oh, my love!" She sighed. "I have longed for you."

I had wondered if there could be longing in heaven. "Well, we are together now ... forever. Ever after is such a long time."

She raised her face to mine and kissed me. It was as I remembered her kisses in my dreams. Sweet wine. Together. Never more to be parted. No more tears. No more sorrow. I wished never again to see the world from which we had come, nor to remember the suffering that had been our lives.

I closed my eyes and drank her in. Eliza and I held one another for what I imagined was a century or two. It was calm and still.

And then all of heaven fell silent. The ground beneath my feet trembled as sound like none I had ever heard penetrated the peace of our garden ...

Chapter 30

*B*efore he called me forth from the grave, Jesus wept. His was not the loud, frantic keening of the women who mourned outside my tomb. His was a sigh and a groan and a single, salty tear. It was, at first, almost imperceptible, even to those standing closest to him.

But his sigh shook the universe, and the place where I was quaked. I stood in the midst of those who watched and waited for all things to be set right.

Jesus groaned, and the heads of angels and saints turned to look down upon the earth in wonder. His tear trickled down his cheek, and a spring burst forth at my feet. Pure, clear water spilled from its banks and flowed down a mountainside, leaving a myriad of new stars, like flowers, blooming and rising in its wake. I remember thinking, *On a clear night, constellations above the earth reflect on the still surface of the sea. But here? Only one of Jesus' tears contains a galaxy.*

My eternal companions and I listened. We heard his voice echo from Bethany across the universe! He commanded, "Roll away the stone!"

We all waited in anticipation for the next word from his lips.

Then Jesus spoke my name: "Lazarus!"

Surely he could not mean me, I thought. But all the same, I whispered, "Here I am, Lord."

Centuries have come and gone since his holy sob ripped me loose from timeless conversation with the ageless ones. Ten thousand, thousand scholars and saints have asked, "Why? What made the King of heaven bow his head and cover his eyes and spill holy tears onto the earth? Why? Why did Jesus weep?"

When Jesus called my name, it echoed in my head. His voice raised a shiver along my spine. Why was my hearing suddenly so muffled? A moment earlier every sound had been bell-like in clarity. Now all was indistinct, as if I had fallen into a well.

Worse yet, why was everything dark? From brilliant, joyful light I had passed into all-encompassing blackness, deeper than the deepest night.

Why was I unable to move? I could feel my arms but not move them. I sensed my feet but could barely wiggle my toes. It felt as if someone were sitting on my chest.

The aroma of myrrh and spikenard flooded my nostrils.

What had happened? What was wrong with me?

I suddenly recognized what it was Jesus had commanded me to do: "Come out."

He meant, "Come out of the grave!"

I was back in my body as it had been before the glories of paradise.

I was alive … but entombed!

As realization dawned, the emotion that overwhelmed me was not terror. It was sorrow. I had the most crushing feeling of disappointment and loss. *Eliza! Eliza!*

The only relief came in knowing that Jesus—Jesus!—had

called me. To answer his call, to be with him again, was the only cure for my pain.

Rolling my body, I bumped futilely against a stone wall. The opening to the niche in which my corpse had been placed was on the other side of the slab. It felt as if Mary and Martha had enclosed a hundredweight of spices in the grave clothes. I could barely move! Lunging, I almost fell to the ground. My legs hit stiffly, propping me up only because they were tightly bound together.

Coins over my eyes had a metallic coldness. My face, wrapped in a cloth separate from the one that locked my arms across my chest, gave me a little freedom of movement to turn my head.

From which direction had Jesus' voice come? Turning toward the memory of his call, I shuffled forward.

I heard shrieking cries. Mary? Martha?

Then I heard Jesus again: "Take off the grave clothes and let him go."[1] Faster now, I moved toward his voice and reentered the world of men.

❦

Jesus' disciples Peter, James, and John, as well as Samson and Patrick had rolled away the stone from the grave. They jumped back in terror as I groaned under the burden of a hundred pounds of burial spices.

Mary ran up the path as Peter and the others sprinted away. "He's alive!" Mary cried.

"Something is ..." Peter's voice trembled.

"Come help me!" Mary snatched Peter's fishing knife from his belt and, gathering her skirts, ran to me. "David! David!" She laughed and wept at the same time as she charged to the mouth of the tomb.

Others hung back, at once terrified and astonished by the sight of me standing in my shroud. I saw them motionless and wide-eyed below. All but Mary! My sister had no fear of what lay beneath the shroud.

"David! Alive! You are …"

She was breathless when she reached me. Wrapping her arms around my cocoon, she would not let me go.

"Mary," I cried! "Cut me loose!"

She laughed and babbled and set to work with Peter's blade. "Four days! Four days away from us, my dear brother!"

"Only four?" I marveled. "Four days?" I imagined centuries had passed in my absence. Time was nothing beyond this world.

Mary loosed my arms. "Oh, I thought my heart would break except the thought that you were with Eliza and the baby. Oh, David!" She filleted my spice-stiffened shroud like I was a giant fish. "You're back. You've come back to us!" The weight of spices in the grave clothes was soon cut away.

Her joy at our reunion was not something I shared. "I saw them, Mary," I told her quietly. "They're all there. Waiting for us to join them." I could not tell her the glory and beauty I had left behind. This world was a faded image of what I had experienced. "Eliza and my son. Only he's all grown. A perfect, beautiful young man!" I worked with her to free my legs. Now others in the fearful crowd walked cautiously toward us.

"David! Our hearts were broken! Broken! It seemed so … so unfair that you, of all, would perish."

"But Mary!" I stepped free. "I didn't perish. I was alive, more alive … oh, the colors! Music! Mountains higher and more majestic than you could ever … Our dear ones who have gone before … they came to meet me! And so many others! How can I ever explain?"

I spotted Jesus over Mary's shoulder. Sorrow for me filled his eyes. Of all those who witnessed my return from the vine-yards of heaven to fallen earth, only Jesus knew what joy and beauty I had left behind.

Chapter 31

Word of my return to life after being dead for four days spread about the country. I could not leave home without being surrounded by a mob. The crowds wanted to see Jesus, but they also wanted to see me.

I was bemused by the attention. After all, I was the recipient of healing, not the Healer. Still, I understood their awestruck wonder.

When I had witnessed my cousin's daughter's illness in Capernaum, I knew Deborah was very, very ill. Ravaged by fever, her body could not keep the spark of life within it.

I watched her sink toward the abyss of the grave.

I saw her just after her last breath fled. She was dead—not sleeping, as we know sleep, but gripped by the utter stillness that banishes hope.

When Jesus returned her life to her, I was utterly dumbfounded, never dreaming I would have the same experience myself.

Jairus's neighbors crowded around to see Deborah. Before long, Galileans from as far away as Nain journeyed to meet the young woman and hear the stories from her mother and father.

Soon afterward complete strangers, covering distances from Caesarea Maritima on the west to Caesarea Philippi in the north, converged on the tiny lakeside village.

Jesus himself had departed, but the fame of the healed ones continued.

And now I knew the truth of that for myself.

I was besieged. I had even hired some men to patrol my vineyards and orchards to keep the curious from trampling my vines or helping themselves to the early figs.

Soon enough, undeserved fame was the least of my worries.

Late one evening, after the crowds had finally given up hoping for another glimpse of me pruning my roses, there was a furtive knock at the garden gate.

My aged porter answered the summons. Nicodemus was wrapped in a cloak up to his eyes, with a hood over his head. The Pharisee was ushered into my office. When I offered him a seat, he accepted but closed the door behind him.

I suggested a cup of my best wine, but he declined.

"I don't want your sisters to worry," he said, "nor even to know about this until we decide what's to be done."

"Worry about what?" I demanded as I trimmed the smoking wick of an oil lamp. "Done about what?"

Flipping the hood back off his head, he put both elbows on his knees and leaned forward. "They are seeking your death!"

I was shocked. So far as I knew, I had no enemies worthy of the name. If I had gained some unmerited celebrity, surely envy could not rise to the level of murder. "Who? Who wants me dead … again?"

"The Temple authorities," Nicodemus declared. "I have very few friends on the Council, as you know, but there are still some with just enough remaining conscience to send me anonymous notes. The latest said that Lord Caiaphas wants to kill Jesus … and you!"

"But why? For bringing me back from the grave? This

is a reason for murdering both of us? Your source must be mistaken."

"Listen!" Nicodemus demanded, fixing me with a forceful gaze. "And believe it! Here's what happened in a secret meeting, to which I was not invited. You know how the scribes and certain Pharisees try to discredit Jesus?"

"Of course! They try to trap him with words, accuse him of Sabbath-breaking, of sorcery. Try to get him in trouble with the authorities over paying taxes. Remember, I saw what they attempted to do with my own sister."

Nicodemus nodded and stroked his beard. "They haven't stopped. After your ... restoration ..."

No one quite knew how to report that someone had been brought back to life. Raised? Revived?

Nicodemus continued, "There was a furor in the Council at the lack of success in destroying Jesus' reputation, and now about you! 'What are we accomplishing?' they said. 'If he goes on like this, everyone will believe in him, and the Romans will come and take away our leadership positions and our nation.'"

I snorted. "Right to the heart of the matter: their wealth, their importance, their ability to stay on good terms with Rome. It doesn't matter that Jesus teaches us to love our enemies."

"Or that he raises the dead. No, that makes him worse in their eyes. You can dismiss the teaching of a rabbi from the Galil, but you can't argue when the evidence of divine authority walks around the streets of Jerusalem. You again, you see?"

Suddenly I understood the threat I represented. Alive, I was a witness to Jesus' power. I was the ultimate testimony to the truth of his claims. As was Peniel, the once-blind man. "And how did Caiaphas respond?"

"He told them they were stupid and ignorant and easily

panicked. He told them ..." Nicodemus lowered his voice and motioned for me to bring my ear close to his lips. "He told them it was better for one man to die for the people than that the nation perish."

"He said that? The high priest?" Amid my words of protest I knew the truth of the report. Lord Caiaphas and all his cadre were perfectly capable of killing anyone they saw as a threat to their ability to remain in power. "And that plot includes me?"

Nicodemus nodded grimly. "You especially. Jesus must withdraw from Judea, and you must go with him. In time this may blow over ... or Caiaphas may die ... or something. But for now, you both must leave."

"Jesus certainly must go," I said. "But me? How can I say this? I'm not afraid of dying. Never will be, ever again."

My friend's gaze bored into my own. He saw there that I spoke the absolute truth. Still, he shook his head. "But others may be hurt trying to protect you. Think of Mary. Think of Martha. Carta and Patrick. If they tried to rescue you, they would die too."

I understood but still was not ready to agree. "Let me think and pray over this tonight. We'll talk again tomorrow."

Again, the good-hearted Pharisee disagreed. "No, nor can we meet again anytime soon. I'm certain the high priest's assassins will try to follow me to you or to Jesus. I'm glad you hired bodyguards, but it's not enough."

"They're not bodyguards," I protested. "Those men are here to protect the grapes, not me."

Nicodemus dismissed the difference. "Doesn't matter. They may be the only reason you haven't already been attacked. But you can't stay inside your fences forever. They will certainly try to kill you in Jerusalem and make it look like the act of a thief or a Zealot. Or they might bribe one of your guards to kill you himself." Nicodemus shuddered.

Bowing my head in thought, I said, "We need to know what's going on inside the Council. Who can we trust to bring the news?"

"Already allowed for. Our friend Peniel can easily travel among the beggars of Jerusalem. He can go and come without exciting notice."

"Isn't he also a target?"

"Not anymore. Not since you have given them a much bigger, more important one." He stood and replaced the hood, then grasped my hand. "You must believe me."

Solemnly I promised, "I'll pray it through tonight and send you word tomorrow. Thank you, my friend. You are also taking a risk by coming here."

Chapter 32

It was the dawn of a gorgeous, late winter day. A bright yellow sun rose over Bethany on the morning after Nicodemus's visit. The air was scented with the promise of spring. Passover was not far off, when a million pilgrims would converge on the Holy City.

The vines of Faithful Vineyard were budding. There was some small threat that a late season frost would damage the new growth, but I did not expect it.

In fact, the morning was so perfect I had difficulty taking Nicodemus's warning seriously. Surely he was exaggerating the danger. Lord Caiaphas and his minions postured and threatened, and they were bullies and cowards, but would they attempt assassination? Looking at the orange, red, and yellow poppies springing up between the vine rows, and at the pastel-blue-tinted sky, I could not believe it possible.

The contrast between night and day left me torn in my spirit over what I should do.

Before the nocturnal visit from the good Pharisee I had planned to visit the Temple this morning. I had the tithe from a recent sale of wine, and I was eager to offer it to God.

Grabbing a hasty breakfast, I almost managed to get away

from my home unchallenged, but not quite. "Brother," Martha said, catching me by the sleeve, "Porter says Master Nicodemus was here late last night. Is that true?"

"Yes, very late," I admitted.

"And he was in disguise?"

"Not exactly a disguise," I argued. "You know how the curious want to question me and everyone who knows me. He just wanted to avoid any delay."

Despite my attempt to make light of the circumstances of Nicodemus's visit, my sister was not convinced. "But what did he want that made him come so late? Why couldn't it wait until today?"

"He is concerned about Jesus' safety," I confessed. "He heard of a plot and thinks Jesus should avoid Jerusalem for a time."

I was never able to hide anything from my sister. "And the plot names you as well, doesn't it? He could have gone straight to Jesus' encampment in the fig grove, but he came to you."

"You're right," I admitted, then hurriedly added, "but I'm sure he's wrong."

"Brother," Martha said sternly, with the voice of sisterly authority I had disliked for decades, "he's right. You have no idea how much darkness hates the light and will do anything to quench it. You and Jesus must both leave today. At once!"

Gently chiding her, I said, "Martha, I am going to the Temple. I will pray and reflect on what you say, but look ..." Spreading my hands wide, I motioned toward the breathtaking view of the mist hanging in the vale below Faithful Vineyard and the dark green mass of our fig trees.

Martha was unmoved. "You must go with him."

I nodded. "I will tell you something. I don't ever want to be away from him. Wherever he goes is where I also want to be.

Not just today, but forever. That's what I'm going to pray about. How can I leave my responsibilities here? Yet if he is leaving, how can I remain behind?" Leaning forward, I kissed the worry lines of her forehead. "I'll be back soon."

At Martha's insistence I had two of my sentries accompany me into Jerusalem. I admit I chose men well known to me and trustworthy. Having been up most of the night patrolling the orchards, they yawned and grumbled. They were in no mood for conversation on the brief hike over the Mount of Olives.

I deposited my tithe in the trumpet-shaped mouth of the offering box, then went into the inner court to pray. Some worshipers recognized me and crowded near. Their expressions suggested that rubbing elbows with me would improve the answers to their prayers.

I tried not to study every man with suspicion. Was there evil in that one's eyes? Was another's movement furtive? Did I see the outline of a dagger beneath another's robe?

It was outside Nicanor Gate that Peniel found me. "The Master sent me to you," he said. "He's traveling today and wants you to come with him."

I experienced such a rush of joy and relief. The decision had been made for me. There was no question now about going or staying behind. If Jesus called me, I would answer.

Even that brief thought resonated like the trumpet blast of a shofar. From across a great gulf I remembered Jesus calling me by name: "Lazarus! Come forth!"

Descending the steps by the Sheep Gate, the way was crowded with worshipers going up as we four tried to descend. At a particularly narrow turning, three men abreast left almost no room for us to pass. All were husky-built, broad-shouldered chaps. They were dressed alike, wearing nondescript brown robes topped by dark blue hoods. It was almost like a uniform, though I gave little thought to it then.

Unaccountably, Peniel stumbled on the hem of his robe. His lunge knocked me sideways past the oncoming trio. There was a chorus of complaints and a strange, momentary hissing that did not register with me at the time. My two sentries helped get the tangle sorted out, and then we continued downward.

"Sorry, sorry!" Peniel said, smiling. "Sometimes I think I'm still not used to walking by sight, instead of by faith alone. It has taken some getting used to."

It was not until we reached the outskirts of Jerusalem that one of my guards called my attention to a tear in the fabric of my robe. My thoughts flashed back to the encounter on the stairs. Now I understood. The sound I had heard like steam escaping from a kettle was of an extremely sharp blade slitting cloth. My garment was sliced from chest to waist, without touching my skin.

If Peniel's fall had not pushed me out of harm's way, would the dagger have lodged in my heart?

I had no way to know.

The village of Ephraim was where Jesus chose to lead his band of followers on his self-imposed exile from Jerusalem. It was about ten miles north of the Holy City. The tiny hamlet lay very near the border between Judea and Samaria and was even smaller than his home in Nazareth.

As far as I could judge, Ephraim possessed only two claims to fame. Situated on the highest hill along the spiny ridge stretching from David's City to the Galil, it had a magnificent view in every direction. From its summit I saw the sink of the

Dead Sea, a great swath of the Jordan Valley, and the summit of Mount Hermon far to the north.

I watched a curling, black smudge on the southern horizon where the smoke of the Temple offerings rose to the Almighty. I studied the Temple itself, standing like a snow-capped peak above the buff-colored sandstone walls.

I thought about what went on within its courts: prayers and tears, repentance and supplication, joy and thanksgiving ... envy and plots.

Two of Jesus' closest followers stood beside me. Phillip remarked, "If they send a troop of soldiers after us, we can see them coming for miles."

"And then what?" Thomas returned drily. "Throw rocks?"

Ephraim's other significance was that it lay above one of the pilgrim routes to the sacred feasts. When Passover arrived, as it would in a short while, hundreds of families from Galilee would pass almost beneath our noses.

"You know he still intends to go back there for Passover," John, one of the Zebedee brothers, remarked. "We're only staying here until he can return to Jerusalem with friends from home."

"Perhaps I can talk him out of it," mused Peter, the one they called "Rock" or "the big fisherman."

"You've had no great success with that before," Andrew, Peter's brother, observed. "Not once."

"And he must go," Judas Iscariot said sharply. "It's time for him to reveal himself. If he misses this feast, everyone will say he's afraid. He's already losing popularity by disappearing, like he has now. He must assert himself, and then they'll all rally to him."

While the disciples continued squabbling among themselves, I thought more about Judas. He was a curiosity among the inner circle of the rabbi from Nazareth, since he was the only one not from Galilee. He was an educated, well-spoken man and had a head for business. He was trusted by the group to manage their meager finances, doling out coins from the money bag to buy bread or dried fish, but always grudgingly.

Peter said this stingy quality made him a good steward.

I thought it merely made him unlikable, but it was not my place to say anything.

The sun set and the light faded. Brilliant blue-white stars twinkled overhead. Facing south, I picked out moving orange dots that marked where Roman soldiers marched or Jerusalem Sparrows lit the way for travelers to cross the great city in safety.

The argument among the disciples moved on to which of them would be greatest in the Jesus' kingdom. Peter expected to be made the chief steward. Judas argued that as royal treasurer, his was a higher rank than Peter's. James and John claimed the preeminence was theirs, as they were his closest advisers and his cousins.

The quickest way to divert a discussion among the followers of Jesus was to pose the question, "What is the Kingdom of Heaven like?" No matter how many times Jesus tried to explain it or gave another example, there were always additional questions.

That was part of the skill of a master teacher, which Jesus certainly was. Early on, when he was training his disciples, they thought they knew everything there was to know.

Jesus had spent three years with them, proving how wrong they were. He also used each additional opportunity to help them dig a little deeper, explore a little further. He wanted them to wrestle with questions of faith.

Since I had been in *olam haba*, the world to come, I had been asked many questions about what I saw there. I tried to answer each to the best of my ability.

But heaven was not the kingdom to which the inquiry referred.

The question really referred to the citizens of the kingdom, not its location.

The disciples, including me, believed that the Kingdom of Heaven would be wherever Jesus reigned, inaugurated whenever and wherever he chose to rule. So, what were the attitudes that defined the members of his kingdom?

A bulging, waxing moon climbed up the eastern bowl of the sky. Its brilliance washed out many of the stars, but not Regulus, the Little King. That brilliant, blue-white star marked the front quarter of the image of the Lion of the Tribe of Judah. The Holy Spirit swam into view just behind the king's own constellation.

When Jesus joined the circle around the campfire, it was Peter who inaugurated the dialogue with the old familiar phrase, "Tell us more about the Kingdom."

Instead of immediately replying, Jesus looked at me. "David, when you fought and overcame the plague of locusts, did you have help?"

"Of course, Master," I said, mentally reviewing the army of men I had hired on that occasion. "I think I sent for four groups of workers."

"And so some worked longer than others?"

"Certainly," I agreed. "I called more and more as the situation grew more desperate."

"Now listen," Jesus encouraged, though all of us already hung on his every word. "The Kingdom of Heaven is like a landowner who went out early in the morning to hire men to work in his vineyard, yes?"

This was good, familiar territory. When the Sea of Galilee was too rough or the fishing too poor, many of the listeners hired themselves out as day laborers to crush grapes or winnow wheat or pluck olives.

Jesus continued, "The landowner agreed to pay them a denarius for the day and sent them into his vineyard. About the third hour, around the middle of the morning, he returned to the marketplace and hired more workers, telling them he would pay them what was fair.

"At noon he went again, hired more, and said the same."

A cock quail called from a heap of rocks on the slope below where we camped. Immediately afterward, another replied to the challenge from the opposite side of the hill. The boisterous exchange made me recall the miracle of the quail cleaning up the remainder of the plague.

"Again, in the middle of the afternoon, when the first group had been working for nine hours already, he hired still more laborers. Finally, at the end of the day, he found still more and asked them why they were just standing around. They answered, because no one had hired them. And he sent them to the vineyard to work also, even though there was only an hour of daylight left."

There was a stir among the listeners. Where was this story going? A breeze swirling up from the valley below mingled two scents: roasting meat vied with the sharp, spicy aroma of juniper brush.

Jesus resumed: "At the close of the day, the landowner told his steward to pay the men, beginning with the last ones hired, then counting backward to the first. The last men hired received a denarius ... a day's wages. When those who had worked all day saw this they thought, *If these fellows who worked just an hour get a whole day's pay, how much more will we get?* But when their turn came to receive their wages, they got … what did they get, David?"

Jesus' sudden pivot toward me caught me off guard.

I blurted out, "I paid every man a denarius, last or first, all the same."

"And what did the earliest hired think of that?"

"There was some grumbling," I admitted.

"And how did you answer them?

"I told them they were each receiving what had been promised. I said it was my money to do with as I pleased, wasn't it?"

Jesus nodded: "Just so. You were not being unfair to the first by being more generous to the last. And it was, as you say, your money to expend as you saw fit."

Then Jesus brought home the point: "And so it will be in the Kingdom of Heaven. The last will be first and the first last.[1] Remember this the next time you argue about who will be the greatest."

Leaning toward me, Andrew said with a sheepish grin, "I didn't know he heard us this time."

As we headed toward our bedrolls, Peter gazed up at the sky and idly remarked of the moon, "Nearly full. The next full moon we see will be the Passover moon. Wonder where we will be when we see it."

❦

The trickle of pilgrims passing below Ephraim increased to a steady stream. Passover was still more than a week away, but many travelers from Galilee arrived early to secure lodging and see the sights.

This morning a band of at least a hundred had stopped to

drink from Ephraim's well. John bar Zebedee and I watched their leader set them in motion again with a booming voice: "Let's get going! Half a day more and we're there. Come on! Sing with me!"

"I lift up my eyes to the mountains—
    where does my help come from?"

When the rest of the weary travelers did not immediately share the enthusiasm, the leader exhorted them still further: "Come on, sing with me, brothers!"

The shouted directive bounded among the rocks of the knoll. "Sing with me ... with me ... with me ... with me!"

Now more throats, some quaking with age, some brash and eager, some piping and youthful, joined in:

"My help comes from the LORD,
    the Maker of heaven and earth.
He will not let your foot slip—
    he who watches over you will not slumber;
indeed, he who watches over Israel
    will neither slumber nor sleep."[2]

Suddenly Jesus stood beside us, watching the procession. "It's time," he said.

John and I looked at each other. Both of us knew what he meant: the time for us to return to Jerusalem had come.

Jesus gathered his closest companions around him. I stood alongside Peniel, outside the circle of the twelve, but still close enough to hear what he told them.

"We are going up to Jerusalem," he said. "And everything written by the prophets about the Son of Man will be fulfilled."

Philip and James exchanged a worried glance. Thomas frowned.

Twice before John had shared with me that Jesus, while ministering in Galilee, had spoken to them in these terms. John freely admitted that neither he nor any of the others understood what their leader meant. Would he be more specific this time?

"The Son of Man," Jesus continued, "will be betrayed."

Peter scowled and clapped his hand to the hilt of the fisherman's knife he wore in his belt.

Judas stared in the direction of the Temple.

"The chief priests and teachers of the law will condemn him to death and hand him over to the Gentiles to be mocked," Jesus said.

Peter mouthed the words: "Over my dead body," but no one interrupted.

"They will mock him, spit on him, flog him, and crucify him."

This was now suddenly very specific — much too specific for some of the disciples, who turned their heads away.

Matthew narrowed his eyes and stared at his sandals.

On my left Nathanael whispered, "Then why are we going?"

"On the third day he will rise again."[3]

For a moment there was dead silence throughout the group as all struggled to grasp what Jesus meant. Our minds were still reeling from the horrors He had prophesied betrayal, trial, torture, and death.

From the expressions all around me, none of us were able to cross from the picture raised by the sensation of dread to what "rise again" foretold.

"What does that mean?" Thomas hissed.

"Gather your things. Let's be going," Jesus concluded. He spoke in a matter-of-fact tone, as if the portrait of terror he had just painted had to be accepted without question.

A scrub jay scolded us from the brush as we formed a line and started down the path.

John walked beside me. "You, of any of us, may understand what he's saying," John murmured. "You who have been across the gulf and come back."

"Been called back," I corrected. "It was Jesus' voice who summoned me. If he is dead—as dead as they tell me I was—who will call him to rise again? Can I? Can you? Can any of us? No, John, I don't understand it either. Sometimes I think I catch a glimmer of what he's saying, like the glimmer of light around a corner in a dark hallway. But when I reach the corner, the lamp is still not there. It's still shining ahead somewhere, but not yet fully seen."

John cleared his throat. "He loves you very much. And me as well, I think. Perhaps we can get him to explain further?"

I shrugged. "It's not a failure of his love or of his willingness to speak plainly. How much more plain can he be than to use the word *crucify*? As for the rest, it's a failure on our ability to comprehend, that's all. If I was again in *olam haba*, someone there would teach me ... but not here. We must muddle through as best we're able. We must trust him to bring us full understanding when it's time."

Halfheartedly we sang:

"The LORD watches over you—
the LORD is your shade at your right hand;
the sun will not harm you by day,
nor the moon by night.

The LORD will keep you from all harm—
he will watch over your life;

the LORD will watch over your coming and going
both now and forevermore."[4]

Two phrases reverberated in my thoughts: *"All the prophets
wrote about the Son of Man"* and *"Rise again."* I could not begin to
define or even comprehend what all that meant. With each step
nearer to Jerusalem, I was certain we would very soon find out.

Chapter 33

We descended the hill of Ephraim and set out toward Jerusalem. Instantly we were surrounded by old friends. The first family I met was that of my cousin Jairus, the cantor from the Capernaum synagogue. With him was his daughter, Deborah, whom Jesus raised from the dead.

The girl spotted Jesus while they were still some distance apart. She ran to him and, casting aside any reserve, threw her arms around him. He hugged her in return, the embrace growing in intensity and participants as Deborah's father and mother also sealed the reunion.

The gloom that had settled on the disciples over Jesus' talk of his death was instantly dispelled. Instead, we felt the radiant joy of life restored and families reunited. Just as morning sun over Faithful Vineyard drives away mist, so joy made our anxiety vanish.

The two pilgrim groups mingled. Deborah walked beside me, impulsively seizing my hand. "Dear cousin, how glad I am to see you again," she gushed. "And I hear we share something few others can speak of." She confided in me: "I know my death caused great sorrow for my family. But when I am again in *olam haba*, if it's up to me, I won't come back here again."

My heart was carried back to my precious wife and son. "I

know," I agreed. "What makes it possible for me to remain here now with any happiness is—"

"The presence of Jesus," she concluded for me.

"Exactly."

We walked along together. Different knots of old friends met and coalesced like raindrops splashing into puddles and the puddles in turn overflowing to form rivulets.

Jairus brought me to another man whose life had also been transformed by Jesus. "You know Simon. He's a Pharisee, but he has a good heart!"

Simon owned two estates—one in Galilee and another not far from my own in Bethany—but we had never been close friends.

"My sister Mary told me more of you," I said, shaking his hand. "It was at your home she anointed Jesus' feet after he saved her life and set her on a new path."

A twinge of anguish crossed Simon's face. "I was still a self-righteous fool in those days."

"Me too," I said, breaking into a big grin.

"Then I was known as Simon the Pious; Simon the Pharisee. That was before I became known as Simon the Leper. Jesus took away both my diseases—my skin ailment and my heart trouble! And do you know what meant more to me than anything else?"

"Tell me!"

"His embrace," Simon said. "I tried to hide my leprosy. I tried every medicine you can imagine, even sorcery." He shuddered at the recollection. "When my secret came out, everyone abandoned me. My friends turned against me. Not really their fault," he admitted. "I would have done the same to them. Forced to live away from everyone, to cry, 'Unclean!' wherever

I went. When I went to Jesus, I was afraid he would not want to heal me, knowing who and what I had been, how I had treated others. I said to him, 'Lord, I know you can heal me … if you want to.' And he replied, 'I want to,' then hugged me. Me! A leper! He could have stood far off and healed me without coming close. I believe it! But he did the opposite. His touch meant more to me than anything in the world, if you understand me."

"I do!" I fervently agreed. "With me it's his voice, calling my name: 'Lazarus, come forth!' "

Halfway between Ephraim and Jerusalem a Roman centurion galloped up on a black horse. The file of pilgrims moved off the road to let him pass. Some spat on his shadow as he went by.

But when he reached me, he reined up and got down to walk beside me. "*Shalom*, David ben Lazarus," Marcus Longinus greeted me. Then he added, "So you could not persuade him not to come."

"I didn't even try," I said. "Jesus made it clear he knows the danger but is determined to go anyway."

Marcus nodded. "He *is* in danger, you know. Every mile nearer the city increases the risk. Your chief priests would like to arrest him openly and charge him with heresy or sorcery or leading others astray." The Roman looked around. "They won't do it, though. Not while he's in the middle of a crowd. Whatever they do, they will do secretly. If they can, they'll kill him and blame someone else."

"I know," I said, recounting the tale of my own encounter with a would-be assassin on the Temple Mount. "So we keep to big crowds … not a problem during Passover week, eh? But what of Rome, Marcus?"

The centurion considered. "Pilate has made too many missteps already. He will take action only if he thinks it'll be seen favorably by the emperor. Pilate came to Judea headstrong and sure of himself and sure of his support in Rome. Now he's lost both his backer and his backbone. That's both good and bad, I suppose. As long as Jesus does not raise a riot or preach treason, Pilate won't act unless pushed to do so. And he can't be pushed unless he's threatened with another bad report to Rome that's undeniable. Is that clear?"

I shook my head and laughed without mirth. "About as clear as all the rest of the political intrigue in Judea. I know Rome doesn't care about Jewish religion. You know that Jesus teaches meekness. What about him is any threat to Rome?"

A pair of mockingbirds flitted in and out of the brush ahead, keeping pace with the cavalcade. "I did not see you there, but I hear you witnessed it when he miraculously fed the thousands on the hillside?"

I agreed that I had been present to see that astonishing event.

"Here's what Rome saw: he had the crowd sit in groups of fifty and one hundred—just as Roman soldiers are fed—only Jesus doesn't need a quartermaster or a commissary or a supply train. If a Roman soldier is wounded, he must be cared for, and he is a drain on the army's resources. But one of Jesus' soldiers can be healed by him. And if one of them should be killed ..." He met my gaze directly. "You know, the last time I rode out of Jerusalem to Jesus' camp it was to carry the news that you were sick enough to die ... and then, you did die. Yet here you are, marching again beside him."

"Oh," I said. The kind of threat Jesus represented to Roman rule was suddenly very clear. "But he preaches no sedition. Never has."

"I know," Marcus said. "That's why Rome makes no move

against him." He stopped me with a hand on my arm. "I have to ride back now. It's not good for either of us, or for Jesus, for me to be seen entering the city with you. I probably won't be able to visit you again until Passover is done, but you can send Peniel to me if you need me. You know I'll do whatever I can." With that the centurion remounted the war stallion.

"*Shalom*, Marcus," I said.

"*Shalom*," he returned. "Keep a crowd around him at all times. No lonely places. No small groups. Understand?"

"I understand. We're going first to my home in Bethany. After that … we'll see."

My home in Bethany was too small to accommodate all those who wanted to see Jesus. I reminded Mary of the healing of a crippled man in Galilee. His friends took apart the roof slates so the paralyzed man could be lowered into the presence of the Lord.

It was not practical to take off our roof, so we accepted an invitation from Simon the Leper to use his home for the feast. Even Simon's sprawling estate overflowed with guests. My sister Martha was in her element, bustling about. Simon's wife graciously moved aside to let Martha take charge, assisted by Jesus' mother.

Martha ebbed and flowed like the ceaseless tides, ordering tables and chairs to be rearranged. She dashed off to the kitchen to supervise Delilah's cooking, then sent Samson back to our storage shed for beeswax candles. She ordered Carta, Tavita, Patrick, and Adrianna about as if dispatching reserve troops into battle. She was in constant motion but remained entirely unflurried.

Mary and I kept out of her way. Since Jesus was the guest of honor, we stood beside him, welcoming all the rest.

It occurred to me that we two were good representatives of his ministry.

Jesus had said of himself: "I have come that you might have life and have it abundantly."

In my case he had restored my physical life. After four days in the tomb I was dead, dead, dead. No one argued about that. Many had seen me dead, seen me entombed, and then seen me not only alive again but healed and restored to perfect life.

With Mary I recognized the other side of Jesus' touch: healing the soul. Mary's soul had been blighted, like a vine so diseased that it would never produce good fruit. Normally it would be ripped out of the ground and burned before it infected others.

But just as seemingly lifeless vines in the dead of winter await the touch of the sun, so it was with my sister. The touch of the Son had brought her new life and given it to her abundantly. She had always been beautiful; now she was radiant. She was gracious, kind, compassionate. If she had been self-centered before, all those useless canes had been cut away. Now she was entirely other-centered and most gentle to hurting souls.

I noticed a large stone flask protruding from the pocket of Mary's apron. When I asked her about it, she waved away the query. She turned to greet another arrival, brought forward by Simon to greet the Lord. The house was packed with souls that had been hurt. Many were crushed by life's winepress until Jesus turned their injuries into a fragrant vintage of hope restored.

Zadok, the muscular former chief shepherd of Israel who had been present in Bethlehem at Jesus' birth, was also there. With Zadok were his three adopted sons, Avel, Ha-or Tov, and Emet, who had once been one of the Jerusalem Sparrows.

Zacchaeus the tax collector was there, the much-maligned businessman from Jericho. He was part of the newest vintage from the Lord's winery since he had only met Jesus two days earlier.

At the Lord's elbow stood Peniel, beaming at everyone, recording names on a wax tablet and listening attentively to every remembrance. His bright, shining eyes reminded me of one who was missing at this gathering: Centurion Marcus Longinus. The Roman had warned me that he could not seem to be too friendly with Jesus. "If I can serve the Lord and remain a soldier, it's better if I keep some distance," he had said. "The Lord knows I love and honor him. He will understand my absence."

Martha summoned us all to the meal.

As was the custom, the men reclined around a large, horse-shoe-shaped table. We lay on our sides on couches, with our heads toward the center and our feet toward the walls. The women and children ate in a separate room, but they moved among us, pouring wine and handing around the serving trays.

I had brought all that remained of an oak-barreled vintage from Faithful Vineyard. As I had noticed on other occasions, some imbibers stopped to savor and sense the nuances of the wine. Others drank, raised their glasses, and called for more. Judas Iscariot was one who acted in that way.

The Lord was very complimentary of my work.

"Thank you, Lord," I replied. "Coming from you, a master winemaker yourself, that's high praise."

Because not all who were at this dinner had witnessed the miracle at the wedding in Cana, those of us who saw it happen recounted the event.

There was some confusion at the meaning of the miracle.

Even those who had absorbed the Lord's teaching for years were still puzzled. It was not a miracle of healing a cripple or curing the blind or raising the dead. The closest link was to the times when Jesus miraculously fed multitudes from a handful of provisions. Even those comparisons failed to explain the significance of turning water into wine.

I said, "I think it's far more than just a kindness to keep a family from embarrassment. Part of the importance is because of the words that were spoken. Remember the *b'rakhah* at a wedding? 'Blessed art Thou, O Lord God, King of the universe, who gives us the fruit of the vine?' There was a message there, but we didn't understand it until later. Am I right, Lord?"

Jesus did not reply but motioned for me to continue.

Now that supper was ending the women came to retrieve the platters. Not wanting to interrupt the discussion, they stood around the sides of the room, listening. Mary stood near the Lord's feet.

Apart from Judas, who whispered to the man on his right, the rest of the room listened as I said, "As a winemaker myself, I've thought about how much greater that sign was, even if I didn't comprehend it at the time. Each winter I prune the dead canes. Each spring I wait to see that a new birth will occur. I water between the rows, to make the roots stretch for the liquid and so grow stronger. I thin the leaves and the bunches so that all the energy of the sun and the vine will concentrate in making the finest fruit."

Nodding toward Patrick and Samson, I said, "Sometimes I fight pests that would devour the crop. If I succeed in keeping the grapes safe until harvest, they must be gathered at the peak of ripeness ... not too green, nor too sweet ... and then they must be crushed to release their juice. Think about that! We tend the vines all year long, defend them, fight for them, so that we can take their fruit and utterly crush the lifeblood out of it! Even then, it is a combination of skill," I pointed out Patrick and Samson again, "and faith that what emerges from the barrels in another year's time will be drinkable and not vinegar!"

The audience laughed.

"So here's what I know about Jesus of Nazareth, winemaker: He is able to take the water that comes from heaven as rain or from the springs as a gift of almighty God and bypass all those steps! He alone is able to go from water to the finest wine that ever was!"

Suddenly I was embarrassed that I had been lecturing, and everyone was hanging on my words.

It was my sister Mary who redirected the attention of the group.

Drawing an alabaster bottle from her pocket she uncorked it and poured the contents over Jesus' outstretched feet. It was the same gesture she had performed at Simon's house in the Galil some years before. I had not been there on that occasion, but I knew that after Jesus had saved her life, telling her to "go and sin no more," she had been transformed. In gratitude she anointed his feet with expensive perfumed lotion.

She did the same again now.

The powerful aroma of costly spikenard filled the chamber, easily overpowering the remaining scents of the dinner. The air was charged with inexpressible sweetness.

Mary allowed her hair to fall across his feet, and I saw her embrace them, scrubbing Jesus' feet with her reddish locks and mingling her tears with the ointment.

I heard Judas mutter, "Such a waste. Terrible expense!"

When Jesus sat up to thank Mary for her kindness, she

wanted to anoint his head as well, but the remaining spike-nard would not come out of the flask. Without hesitation, Mary shattered the vial on the flagstones. Scooping the remaining lotion up with her hands she applied it to Jesus' hair.

Judas raised his chin and said with utter contempt, "Why wasn't this perfume sold and the money given to the poor? Why has this woman been keeping this back from us? It's worth a year's wages!"

Jesus addressed Judas, but he kept his gaze fixed on Mary. When he gestured, she raised her downturned face, and he looked into her eyes. "Leave her alone. It was intended she should save this perfume for the day of my burial. You will always have the poor among you, but you will not always have me."[1]

I couldn't keep my thoughts from returning then to my vineyard. The grapes, so carefully tended, had to be crushed before they became wine. Even then the juice had to undergo a transformation before being released from the tomb of the barrels.

What in Jesus' words put all that in my mind?

What did it all mean, and when would I fully understand?

Chapter 34

*L*ike the spokes of a celestial wheel, radiant beams jutted up from the far eastern horizon before the coming of the sun. Pink and orange banners streaked the sky. The first day of the week that ushered in Passover began with a coronet of golden light, as if heralding the advent of a king.

Somehow the word had gone out overnight that Jesus of Nazareth had returned to my home in Bethany. When I awoke early on that morning, entire villages of pilgrims were camped all around my property. Orchards and vineyards were planted thick with thousands of travelers. My fields offered a rich harvest of eager souls awaiting the touch of the Master Vinedresser.

The question on everyone's lips was whether Jesus would enter the city or not. Everyone knew there were threats on his life. He had come this far, returning from exile in Ephraim, but would he challenge the authorities and go to the Temple?

What would the Romans do? If they suspected the least chance of a riot, they might disperse the assembly with clubs.

Jesus did not leave the crowds waiting in suspense for long. Gathering his disciples around him, he summoned me to his side. "Take Peniel with you," he said. "Go into the village up ahead. There you will find a donkey tied, together with its colt, which has never been ridden. Bring them to me. And if anyone asks you why you're untying them, tell them, 'The Master has need of them.' "[1]

As we approached Bethphage, I saw a curl of smoke drifting up from the chimney of Patrick's cottage. When we rounded the hillside, Patrick's vineyard came into view. Derelict the year before, now the black and twisted ancient trunks were bursting with new life. Covered in leafy green canopies, the rows saluted the morning.

Tied to the thickest, oldest trunk of the ancestor vine, like a brace of giant ripe grapes, were a pair of dark, wine-red donkeys. "Happiness and her colt Joyful," I remarked to Peniel. "I should have known."

As Peniel and I began to untie the mare and her colt, Patrick emerged from his home. Shielding his eyes against the glare of the morning sun, he demanded, "What are you doing there?"

"Ho, Patrick," I returned. "The Master has need of them."

The words Jacob prophesied over his son Judah more than two thousand years earlier struck me like a thunderbolt:

> The scepter will not depart from Judah,
>> nor the ruler's staff from between his feet,
> until he to whom it belongs shall come
>> and the obedience of the nations shall be his.
> He will tether his donkey to a vine,
>> his colt to the choicest branch;
> he will wash his garments in wine,
>> his robes in the blood of grapes.[2]

Jacob's words were about Jesus! About this very moment! Jesus was the heir of Judah, the king predicted centuries before! The prophetic fulfillment was his; the time was now!

"Lazarus?" Patrick said, puzzled by my reverie.

"Sorry! What?"

"Jesus is going into the city, then?"

I shook my head to clear it. "On his way even now. Peniel and I will meet him on the road."

"And we will join you," Patrick returned. "Adrianna and I wouldn't miss this!"

By the time we led the pair of donkeys halfway back to Bethany, a swirling cyclone of worshipers reached and engulfed us. At the center of the storm was Jesus. With him were my sisters and his disciples and his mother.

Sweeping my cloak from around my shoulders, I flung it across Joyful's back. Peniel did the same. Peter and Andrew tied these makeshift saddles in place with knots known more to ships and sailors than to beasts of burden, yet they served the purpose.

The crowd began to chant a hymn of ascent:

"Those who trust in the LORD are like Mount Zion,
    which cannot be shaken but endures forever.
As the mountains surround Jerusalem,
    so the Lord surrounds his people
    both now and forevermore."[3]

Nicodemus, out of breath from running all the way from the city, hurried up to me. "He won't be persuaded to stay away?"

I waved my hand toward the singing multitude. "Do you think anyone would attempt to harm him in the middle of this? Those who tried would be torn limb from limb. The crowd would turn on Caiaphas himself afterward."

"The scepter of the wicked will not remain
    over the land allotted to the righteous."[4]

We sang with gusto, recognizing the power of the moment. "He has never let the people proclaim him king before," Nicodemus murmured.

"We are being swept along on a tide that cannot be resisted," I said. "Listen."

"LORD, do good to those who are good,
　　to those who are upright in heart.
But those who turn to crooked ways
　　the LORD will banish with the evildoers."[5]

"Have you ever heard such joyful anticipation?" I added. "I think half of Galilee is here. They are bringing their king to Jerusalem."

"It's more than that." Nicodemus eyed the donkey. "It's a prophecy fulfilled. The prophet Zechariah wrote:

"'Rejoice greatly, O Daughter of Zion!
　　Shout, Daughter of Jerusalem!
See, your king comes to you,
　　righteous and having salvation,
gentle and riding on a donkey,
　　on a colt, the foal of a donkey.'"[6]

"Do you think Jesus is deliberately acting out the prophecy?" I queried.

"No!" Nicodemus said sharply. "I think Zechariah looked across more than five hundred years and saw this very day!"

The day was warm and the road dirty. To keep the celebration from disappearing behind a veil of dust, the crowd began to strip off their cloaks. Running ahead of the procession, they lay their garments on the road in front of Jesus for him to pass over. The tramping of thousands of feet on a heap of red and brown robes was like the winepress of all the ages, crushing out everything that had gone before.

The vintage created from this year's pressing would be the most magnificent of all time, I thought.

Not to be outdone, others seized on the trees that had been planted by the old Butcher King. Fronds, wrenched from these palms, were also strewn in the way until the highway was thickly carpeted with green.

As the multitude swarmed up the slope of the Mount of Olives, I was reminded of the great crowd Jesus fed from five loaves and two fish. I wondered how many of today's enthusiastic supporters were present because they expected something similar this time. It was easy to applaud one who fed you for free.

At the crest of the hill an oncoming horde of people met us. Racing excitedly out of Jerusalem was a host equally as large as the one I was in. The word that Jesus was arriving had reached the Holy City, and its citizens emerged to greet him.

"Hosanna!" they cried. "Lord, save us!" Snatching up more palm branches, the newcomers waved them in acclamation.

The two surging tides of people met, clashing together like competing ocean waves.

Nicodemus shouted over the chants, "This could be dangerous! This is the welcome a nation gives a returning hero. This is the way Rome receives a victorious general or the victor at the end of a war of succession. This is the way they usher in a new king!"

> "Blessed is he who comes in the name of the Lord!
>   Hosanna to the Son of David!
> Blessed is the king who comes in the name of the Lord!
>   Hosanna in the highest!"[7]

There! It was out in the open. It was no longer possible for Jesus to discourage the common people from proclaiming him king. This time he did not disappear. This time he did not forbid them.

Jerusalem's population doubled every Passover with arrivals from other provinces and foreign lands. What would happen if Jews from places like Cyprus and Cyraenea, Italy, and Ephesus joined with those from tiny Nazareth and boastful Jericho? What if the Roman garrison felt threatened by the calls for independence?

What would the high priest do?

What would Governor Pilate do?

"Blessed is he who comes in the name of the Lord," the Galileans east of the city chanted.

"From the house of the Lord we bless you," returned the worshipers from Jerusalem at the west.

Beside me I saw Nicodemus look up sharply, then shiver despite the warm sunshine of the morning.

"What is it?" I demanded.

He tried to wave away my inquiry, but I would not be dissuaded. "What?" I said again.

"Don't you know the rest of this psalm? It's the one recited when the ram or bull is being prepared for slaughter. The next verse says, "With boughs in hand, bind the sacrifice to the horns of the altar."[8]

Then I also shuddered as I watched the thousands of people waving their boughs. Jesus, sitting on the donkey named Joyful, was led along the path leading toward Mount Moriah and the place of sacrifice. We were heading toward the spot where Abraham had prepared to offer up Isaac. Where David had brought the ark of the covenant to stop a plague that was decimating

Israel. Where untold thousands of sacrificial animals had spilled their blood over the last thousand years. Where almighty God had said that he would provide himself, the sacrifice.

But where would it all end?

It was a place steeped in blood yet still was not quenched. Would there ever be enough sacrifices ... or one sacrifice great enough ... to cause the need for sacrifice to cease?

Some of Nicodemus's brother Pharisees arrived then, bustling with self-importance. Thrusting themselves through the assembly, they stood in front of Joyful and demanded, "Rabbi! Make them stop!"

"Rebuke your followers! Don't let them cry, 'Hosanna!' to you!"

Jesus looked at them and then at me before pointing at the stones of the roadbed. "Even if they stopped," he said, "then the very stones themselves would cry out. The rocks would prophesy."[9]

The stones of Jerusalem had witnessed kings and prophets, celebration and tragedy, David and Solomon and Isaiah and Abraham and now Jesus of Nazareth. Was that a buzzing, a low humming underfoot? Were these stones of witness also crying out, "Hosanna"?

The Pharisees were shocked and their expressions showed it. In our language *stone* spelled backward is *prophesy*. Inside out, upside down, backward, or forward, there was no preventing what was happening. Jesus was proclaimed the King of the Jews that day.

He would sweep all before him! After that day even the religious leaders would see the validity of his claim. Caiaphas and the rest would have to move aside for him. Rome would bargain with him. Perhaps they would replace the foul wretch Antipas with Jesus.

"Hosanna!" I shouted. "Blessed is the coming kingdom of our father David! Hosanna to the Son of David!"

The cavalcade paused at the crest of the hill, with all Jerusalem sprawled out before it. Leaving Jesus surrounded by his closest followers, the rest of the multitude spilled over the slope. Waving their cloaks and brandishing branches, they gushed like a flood toward the city gates. Soon there would be no one in the Holy City who had not heard that Jesus had arrived! The new king had been proclaimed!

But I stood nearby, my gaze fixed on Jesus' face. As I watched, despite being surrounded by ten thousand admirers, sadness plucked at his eyes and mouth. Quietly ... so quietly that only a handful of us nearest to him could catch it, we heard him say, "If you, Jerusalem, had only known on this day what would bring you peace—but now it is hidden from your eyes. The days will come when your enemies will not leave one stone on another ... because you did not recognize the day of God's coming to you."[10]

If only they knew, I thought. *If only they believed! All the suffering of all the ages could have ended on that very day ...*

And Jesus wept.

Notes

Chapter 3
1. Luke 3:7–8
2. Luke 3:8
3. John 1:19–22
4. John 1:23–26
5. Psalm 2:1–2, adapted from NKJV
6. Psalm 2:3–9, adapted from KJV
7. Psalm 2:10-12, adapted from KJV

Chapter 4
1. John 1:29 ESV
2. John 1:30
3. Mark 1:11 ESV
4. John 1:32–34

Chapter 5
1. Psalm 132:10–12, adapted from KJV
2. Psalm 132:13–16, adapted from KJV
3. Psalm 133:1–2, adapted from KJV

Chapter 9
1. Song of Songs 2:14–15
2. Song of Songs 4:9–10, adapted.
3. Read the story in John 2:1–10. Quote from verse 10.
4. Psalm 104:14–15, with first phrase added by authors
5. Psalm 80:14–15

Chapter 10
1. Psalm 136:1, adapted; Hebrew and last line are from the actual Hebrew translation
2. Psalm 105:1–2
3. 1 Chronicles 16:35

Chapter 11

1. John 8:1–11, adapted

Chapter 13

1. Matthew 21:28–31, adapted
2. Matthew 21:32, adapted
3. John 15:1–8, adapted
4. Luke 14:16–24, adapted

Chapter 14

1. John 6:25–70, adapted

Chapter 15

1. John 8:31–59, adapted

Chapter 16

1. John 9:1–7, adapted
2. John 9:13–34, adapted

Chapter 18

1. Psalm 80:3, 8–9 NKJV adapted
2. Psalm 80:10-12, 14 NKJV adapted
3. Psalm 80:14-15, 17–19 NKJV
4. Joel 2:25 ESV, adapted

Chapter 22

1. Exodus 15:1, 4 adapted from NKJV
2. Song of Songs 6:2–3, adapted
3. Song of Songs 6:9, adapted

Chapter 23

1. John 5:1–9, adapted from NKJV
2. John 5:10–13, adapted from NKJV
3. John 5:14–15, adapted from NKJV
4. John 5:19–29, adapted from NKJV
5. John 5:41–47, adapted from NKJV

Chapter 24

1. Psalm 118:15–16
2. Matthew 6:24 ESV
3. Psalm 118:19–21 (1984 NIV)
4. John 10:24–30, adapted from ESV
5. Psalm 118:26
6. John 10:31–38, adapted from ESV
7. Psalm 118:22–23
8. Psalm 118:28–29

Chapter 25
1. Exodus 15:21 adapted

Chapter 29
1. Read the whole story in Genesis, chapters 37, 39–46.

Chapter 30
1. For the entire story of Lazarus, read John 11:1–44.

Chapter 32
1. For the entire story, read Matthew 20:1–16.
2. Psalm 121:1–4
3. Matthew 20:17–19, adapted
4. Psalm 121:5–8

Chapter 33
1. Read the story in John 12:1–8.

Chapter 34
1. Matthew 21:1–3, adapted
2. Genesis 49:10–11
3. Psalm 125:1–2
4. Psalm 125:3
5. Psalm 125:4–5
6. Zechariah 9:9, adapted
7. Adapted from Matthew 21:9; Mark 11:9
8. Psalm 118:27, adapted from NKJV and NIV
9. Luke 19:39–40, adapted from NIV and ESV
10. Luke 19:41–44, adapted

About the Authors

Bodie and Brock Thoene (pronounced *TAY-nee)* have written over sixty-five works of historical fiction. That these bestsellers have sold more than thirty-five million copies and won eight ECPA Gold Medallion Awards affirms what millions of readers have already discovered—that the Thoenes are not only master stylists but experts at capturing readers' minds and hearts.

In their timeless classic series about Israel (The Zion Chronicles, The Zion Covenant, The Zion Legacy, The Zion Diaries), the Thoenes' love for both story and research shines. With The Shiloh Legacy and *Shiloh Autumn* (poignant portrayals of the American Depression), The Galway Chronicles (dramatic stories of the 1840s famine in Ireland), and Legends of the West (gripping tales of adventure and danger in a land without law), the Thoenes have made their mark in modern history. In the A.D. Chronicles they stepped seamlessly into the world of Jerusalem and Rome in the days when Yeshua walked the earth.

Bodie, who has degrees in journalism and communications, began her writing career as a teen journalist for her local newspaper. Eventually her byline appeared in prestigious periodicals such as *U.S. News and World Report*, *The American West*, and *The Saturday Evening Post*. She also worked for John Wayne's Batjac Productions and ABC Circle Films as a writer and researcher.

John Wayne described her as "a writer with talent that captures the people and the times!"

Brock has often been described by Bodie as "an essential half of this writing team." With degrees in both history and education, Brock has, in his role of researcher and story-line consultant, added the vital dimension of historical accuracy. Due to such careful research, The Zion Covenant and The Zion Chronicles series are recognized by the American Library Association, as well as Zionist libraries around the world, as classic historical novels and are used to teach history in college classrooms.

Bodie and Brock have four grown children—Rachel, Jake, Luke, and Ellie—and eight grandchildren. Their children are carrying on the Thoene family talent as the next generation of writers, and Luke produces the Thoene audio books. Bodie and Brock divide their time between Hawaii, London, and Nevada.

www.thoenebooks.com
www.familyaudiolibrary.com

Thoene Family Classics™

THOENE FAMILY CLASSIC HISTORICALS
By Bodie and Brock Thoene

Gold Medallion Winners*

The Zion Covenant
*Vienna Prelude**
Prague Counterpoint
Munich Signature
Jerusalem Interlude
Danzig Passage
*Warsaw Requiem**
London Refrain
Paris Encore
Dunkirk Crescendo

The Zion Chronicles
*The Gates of Zion**
A Daughter of Zion
The Return to Zion
A Light in Zion
*The Key to Zion**

The Shiloh Legacy
*In My Father's House**
A Thousand Shall Fall
Say to This Mountain
Shiloh Autumn

The Galway Chronicles
*Only the River Runs Free**
Of Men and of Angels
*Ashes of Remembrance**
All Rivers to the Sea

The Zion Legacy
Jerusalem Vigil
Thunder from Jerusalem

Jerusalem's Heart
The Jerusalem Scrolls
Stones of Jerusalem
Jerusalem's Hope

A.D. Chronicles
First Light
Second Touch
Third Watch
Fourth Dawn
Fifth Seal
Sixth Covenant
Seventh Day
Eighth Shepherd
Ninth Witness
Tenth Stone
Eleventh Guest
Twelfth Prophecy

Zion Diaries
The Gathering Storm
Against the Wind

Jerusalem Chronicles
When Jesus Wept

THOENE FAMILY CLASSIC ROMANCE
By Bodie Thoene

Love Finds You in Lahaina, Hawaii

THOENE FAMILY CLASSIC AMERICAN LEGENDS
Legends of the West
By Brock and Bodie Thoene

Legends of the West
Volume One
Sequoia Scout
The Year of the Grizzly
Shooting Star

Legends of the West
Volume Two
Gold Rush Prodigal

Delta Passage
Hangtown Lawman

Legends of the West
Volume Three
Hope Valley War
The Legend of Storey County
Cumberland Crossing

Legends of the West
Volume Four
The Man from Shadow Ridge
Cannons of the Comstock
Riders of the Silver Rim

Legends of Valor
By Jake Thoene and Luke Thoene

Sons of Valor
Brothers of Valor
Fathers of Valor

THOENE FAMILY CLASSIC CONTEMPORARY
By Bodie and Brock Thoene

Icon

THOENE CLASSIC NONFICTION
By Bodie and Brock Thoene

The Little Books of Why
Why a Manger?
Why a Shepherd?
Why a Star?
Why a Crown?
Writer to Writer

THOENE FAMILY CLASSIC SUSPENSE
by Jake Thoene

Chapter 16 Series
Shaiton's Fire
Firefly Blue
Fuel the Fire

THOENE FAMILY CLASSICS FOR KIDS
SHERLOCK HOLMES &
THE BAKER STREET DETECTIVES
By Jake Thoene and Luke Thoene

The Mystery of the Yellow Hands
The Giant Rat of Sumatra
The Jeweled Peacock of Persia
The Thundering Underground

The Last Chance Detectives
By Jake Thoene and Luke Thoene

Mystery Lights of Navajo Mesa
Legend of the Desert Bigfoot

By Rachel Thoene
The Vase of Many Colors

THOENE FAMILY CLASSIC AUDIOBOOKS

Available from

www.thoenebooks.com
or
www.familyaudiolibrary.com

Beyond the Farthest Star

A Novel

Bodie and Brock Thoene

When a nativity display on public property is torched by a former US Senator, the media spotlight falls on the forgotten small town of Leonard, Texas, and on the new pastor of its only church—Adam Wells. Emboldened by the prospect of leading his tiny congregation in a nationally televised First Amendment debate, which he considers to be a "fight for the heart and soul of America," Pastor Wells determines not to let anything or anyone, including his wife and rebellious sixteen-year old daughter, stand in his way. But when an old high school friend shows up unexpectedly and a past secret is revealed, Pastor Wells's constitutional crusade collides with an even greater fight—the fight for the heart and soul of his marriage, his daughter, and, even his own life. In this modern-day story of betrayal, forgiveness, and redemption, Adam Wells discovers, for the first time, the meaning of the story he's been preaching all his life ... and his desperate daughter understands what really is beyond the farthest star. Award-winning authors Bodie and Brock Thoene have written an emotional and authentic drama based on Andrew Librizzi's screenplay, which is now a major motion picture.

Available in stores and online!

Share Your Thoughts

With the Author: Your comments will be forwarded to
the author when you send them to *zauthor@zondervan.com*.

With Zondervan: Submit your review of this book
by writing to *zreview@zondervan.com*.

Free Online Resources at
www.zondervan.com

Zondervan AuthorTracker: Be notified whenever your favorite
authors publish new books, go on tour, or post an update
about what's happening in their lives at www.zondervan.com/
authortracker.

Daily Bible Verses and Devotions: Enrich your life with daily
Bible verses or devotions that help you start every morning
focused on God. Visit www.zondervan.com/newsletters.

Free Email Publications: Sign up for newsletters on Christian
living, academic resources, church ministry, fiction, children's
resources, and more. Visit www.zondervan.com/newsletters.

Zondervan Bible Search: Find and compare Bible passages in
a variety of translations at www.zondervanbiblesearch.com.

Other Benefits: Register to receive online benefits like
coupons and special offers, or to participate in research.

ZONDERVAN.com/
AUTHORTRACKER
follow your favorite authors